# THE RUM RUNNER

Arctic Fire Press
PO Box 1445
Jacksonville, OR 97530

Edited by: Sue Kenney

Illustrations by: Mad Scientist

Cover Design by: Books Covered

Cover photographs © Shutterstock

Interior Formatting: Streetlight Graphics

ISBN 0-692-71867-2

10 9 8 7 6 5 4 3 2 1                                           16 17 18 19 20 21

First Edition

For Jenny, Allison, and Westley.

# PROLOGUE

**M**AXWELL CRAIG CONSIDERED THE DAY he had bought the gun: he had purchased the steel-framed 9mm pistol at a seedy pawnshop off Biscayne Boulevard in Miami. He had wanted the gun to put a bullet into his own head.

He remembered the careful selection process he had gone through in choosing just the right pistol. First, it had to be a 9mm. No other caliber would do. And he needed to find one that would be comfortable in his mouth should he decide to "eat" the gun rather than simply placing the muzzle to his temple. Max had ultimately chosen the Smith & Wesson 6906. Before finding a holster for the gun, he had carefully removed the sharp-edged front sight from the firearm, leaving a nice smooth surface around the muzzle.

Presently, the pistol hung limply by his right side. The last swill of straw-colored liquid swirled around inside the bottle he held in his left hand; a smoky black glass bottle adorned with the simple image of a black fleur de lis.

Max's feet stepped close to the edge. The drop from the rocky shore of the *ilet* would only be about ten feet, and he would land in the nearly still Caribbean water of Le Robert Bay. He wondered: Should he fall in, would he even try to swim? Perhaps he would forget how. It was such a peaceful place. He wouldn't find an easier end to his life's story, tragically as it seemed to have ended.

Dirt crumbled below Max's feet as his toes draped over the

1

edge. The lightweight pistol felt good in his hand; his finger curled around the stainless steel trigger.

Max drained the bottle, holding it upright for a long time, not wanting to waste a drop. Best stuff in the Caribbean, they say. He dropped the bottle. Glass shattered over a partially-submerged rock below. The jagged shards washed away slowly, taken by the gentle ripple of the tide.

Max released the magazine from the gun and examined its ammunition. There were only three rounds inside—Federal Hi-Shok with 147 grain bullets. He slammed the mag back into the pistol and racked the slide.

Max leaned forward. Whether he was controlling himself or not, the pistol in his hand began to rise up, his arm crooked.

A force, like a strong hand, gripped the back of Max's shirt. It pulled him back away from the ragged edge of the ilet's shore. Next thing he knew, Max was laying flat on his back. Stars swirled overhead like water draining from a tub.

And then, the world went black, and Max knew nothing.

# CHAPTER 1

B LACK WATER SKIMMED UNDER THE bow of *The Cash Settlement* as Max eased both throttle levers forward. In response, all four of the eight-cylinder outboards by Seven Marine growled deeper, and the boat raced on even faster than before.

"How much horsepower you think she's got?" Max asked Josue, who stood nearby, clinging to the port side handrail beside the console.

"A lot."

Max nodded. "How much you think it cost?"

"A lot."

"No, I mean really, how much you think? Two hundred grand? Half a million?"

"Probably closer to a million—U.S.," Josue said, his words infused with the French Creole influence of Haitian-accented English. "It's custom, made by Hydra-Sports. Very expensive."

The water grew choppier as the boat gained distance from the island. Max tinkered with the trim switches of the outboards to keep the bow from bobbing up and down in that nauseating and inefficient rhythm of a poorly trimmed boat. The powerful center console fishing boat responded almost effortlessly, and skipped across the swells as if skating on a sea of glass.

Max looked at Josue, the young Haitian, who stood as still as a statue. His tight black Under Armor shirt stretched over long sinewy muscles; baggy black cargo shorts hung over angular calves; and black leather gloves made by Oakley wrapped his powerful fingers. A dark gray UV buff covered all of Josue's face, except for his dark eyes, which squinted against the wind as the stolen sport boat cut through the warm Caribbean evening.

Josue reminded Max of a puma. Maybe it was the way he stood so still; so patient; so quiet—so dangerous. Josue turned on the balls of his feet and faced the stern. He peered sharply through a pair of Nikon binoculars, delicately twisting the optic's focus ring.

"What is it?" Max asked.

"Somebody follows," Josue said, letting the binoculars hang by their strap around his long neck.

"It's not one of those geofence things, is it?" Max said, tapping the bright seventeen-inch LED screens, toggling through to find some evidence of a tracking app. "You *did* disable the Nav-Tracker?"

Josue nodded.

Red and blue lights flashed at the stern, contrasting their bright hues against the foamy white water of *The Cash Settlement's* generous wake. The vivid colors bounced off the shiny white fiberglass of the sport fishing boat's console roof, unnerving Max as he craned his neck for a glimpse of his pursuers.

"Cops?" Max said, incredulous. "Where did you get this boat?"

"Marina," Josue said, not seeming overly concerned by the pursuing police boat.

"I guess somebody was watching the marina," Max said. He felt a childlike grin spreading over his face, underneath his own UV buff that concealed his identity. "Probably because there was a million dollar sport fishing boat tied up there."

Josue nodded. "Probably why."

Max patted his friend on the back.

"Sorry, Boss."

The pursuing craft was a Zodiac Hurricane: a small fiberglass boat rimmed by an inflatable collar, and powered by twin two-hundred-horsepower outboard motors. The small boat featured a stand-up console for the pilot, and not much else. It was the type of vessel designed to cut quickly through swells, delivering armed law enforcement officers to your boat's gunwale before you even knew you were being pursued.

"Gendarmerie Nationale," Josue said.

"Hand me those binocs and take the wheel, would you?" Max asked, grabbing the powder-coated tubing that supported the hard top above the console and turning to face astern. He took the optics from the other man.

"There's only two on the boat," Max said, making sure his face was fully covered. "One pilot, one guy with a bullhorn and a shotgun."

Josue's hand covered the throttle levers. "You want me to go?"

"No, my young Haitian friend. Not quite yet."

"*Arrêter le bateau!*" the man with the megaphone shouted, his voice high-pitched, and sounding a touch berserk, as he was clearly very much on edge.

Max checked *The Cash Settlement's* Garmin touchscreens. "We're barely doing thirty knots. How fast do you think that raft can go?"

Josue shrugged.

Max opened a big black duffel bag which lay on deck at the stern, just in front of the purloined vessel's quad outboards. He slipped out a Ruger Mini 30 and locked in a fresh twenty-round magazine. Max yanked back the slide handle and released it, slipping a full metal jacket round into the rifle's chamber, and then he slipped off the safety.

He aimed the rifle carefully, targeting the water ahead of the pursuing police boat; he wanted to send a message, not kill anyone. Max squeezed the trigger over and over in rapid succession, sending dozens of .30 caliber bullets hurtling into his own wake. The muzzle flash was bright and startling, even against the brilliant flashing of the pursuing police boat's lights.

The Zodiac continued to pursue, undaunted.

Max tapped Josue on the shoulder, and the young man slid over to the port side seat. Max took over the helm, settling into the comfortable captain's chair which was wrapped in some sort of marine-grade white leather-like material.

Gunfire erupted from the police boat. Mr. Megaphone was firing rounds, likely buckshot, from his shouldered tactical shotgun.

"I'm impressed," Max said, as a scatter of shot zinged past his head, shattering a pizza-sized hole in the boat's hard top, "I really thought they'd bug out when I started firing the Mini."

Josue nodded.

"Did you secure the load? I mean secure it good?"

Another nod from the reserved Haitian.

Max turned the wheel to starboard and pushed both throttle levers even further forward. The boat pulled away from the police Zodiac in a wide arc, leaving them in a wake so wide it might have been made by an ocean liner. Max held the sport fishing boat in a wide, disorienting circle; a course the determined pilot of the police boat worked hard to maintain.

"What are you doing?" Josue asked. He looked at Max with big eyes and a furrowed forehead.

"Confusing them. If you were chasing a guy and he started going around in circles like this, you'd be confused, right?"

Josue nodded. "Yes. Very confusing."

"Hang on. Watch this," Max said with a concealed half-smirk. He whipped the wheel hard to port, while continuing to give the stolen Hydra-Sports boat a generous amount of throttle.

The Zodiac turned hard to port, the pilot obviously determined not to give up the chase.

Max threw the throttles all the way forward and whipped the wheel hard back to starboard. The four outboards roared ferociously, and the boat lurched to the right, almost effortlessly.

The Hydra-Sports boat pulled away from the pursuing craft like a fighter jet taking off.

The police boat's pilot yanked the Zodiac's wheel hard from port to starboard, desperate to keep up with the stolen boat. The small craft rolled hard to port just as it hit the massive wake caused by *The Cash Settlement's* ferocious acceleration.

The Zodiac launched off the wake like a ski jump. The small craft capsized. The resulting crash hurtled Mr. Megaphone into the sea like a rag doll.

Max backed off the throttle just long enough to survey the damage. The overturned police boat's hull bobbed on the choppy surface of the Caribbean Sea, its red and blue lights casting a bright, eerie glow beneath the surface of the otherwise dark ocean water.

The pilot bobbed in the water, clinging to the hull like a leech. Miraculously, the megaphone guy still clung to his instrument, shouting, "*arrêter le bateau*," or "stop the boat."

Max shoved the throttles forward and trimmed the engines again. In seconds they skimmed across the open sea at close to seventy knots, leaving the carnage behind inside their massive, frothy wake.

About ten minutes later, Max corrected course, turning the boat almost a hundred and eighty degrees southwest. He wanted to be certain the police had no idea which way he was heading. His rendezvous point would be nearly fifty miles from Martinique, in the open water of the Caribbean Sea.

"You have the coordinates?" Max asked.

Josue produced a slip of paper from his pocket. The paper flapped in the wind.

"Don't lose that," Max said. "I'd hate to have to go back looking for it."

The younger man compared the numbers on the paper to the

navigational chart on one of the vast Garmin displays. "Nearly there. Two miles or so."

Max fiddled with one of the other displays. The expensive boat was equipped with open array radar, and he tapped buttons on the touchscreen until he observed a two-mile radius of radar data.

"What's all this?" Josue asked, stabbing a finger at a cluster of small objects that appeared bright red on the radar display.

"Probably those ominous clouds," Max said, nodding through the gaping hole in the boat's hardtop. Even through the dark night sky, the menacing clouds were visible. Max adjusted the wheel, ensuring he was on course toward the preplanned rendezvous point.

Within two minutes another distinctive shape crept inside the outer ring of the radar's display. "That's definitely another boat," Max said. "Stay sharp."

Another minute and they had visual contact with another vessel, this one a fifty-five-foot sport yacht made by Viking. The vessel's light blue hull bobbed in the distance, the boat's tall tuna tower looking skeletal as it swayed in the murky moonlight.

"Get the fenders ready, Josue," Max said, feeling his heart race as he neared the other boat's port side.

Max throttled down, approaching the other vessel with extreme caution.

As *The Cash Settlement* slowed, the ocean swells grew more pronounced, and the boat began to rock.

"Ahoy, Captain Craig," a voice shouted from the stern of the Viking, where a man with long curly graying blond hair stood bathed in the bright blue glow of the yacht's LED deck lights. The man wore a Jimmy Buffet t-shirt that depicted a parrot dressed as a pirate, bright turquoise shorts, and flip flops. A UV buff with a skull face wrapped the red-tanned skin of the man's throat. "I was startin' to wonder if you'd make it out tonight." The man brought the neck of a Landshark lager bottle to his lips and took a long swig.

"Jacques, my man!" Max shouted. "Fancy meeting you way out here."

Jacques threw his own rubber boat fenders over the side of the Viking, which bore the bright red lettering *Plan B* on the back. The laidback mariner also threw across a braided nylon line tied off to his own vessel's stern. Josue caught the line and hauled it, bringing the two boats together.

A woman wearing a pink camouflage bikini and a black bandanna tied over her braided blonde hair tossed a bow line from the front of the boat. Despite the moderate swells, the two boats were joined securely back to front in no time, and bobbed on the waves as one.

"Permission to come aboard?" Max asked.

"Permission granted," Jacques said, showing a broad, toothy, almost goofy grin, "but only if you've got rum."

Max nodded to Josue, who began to untie a cargo net that covered the twenty or so cardboard boxes stacked and secured to the bow of *The Cash Settlement*.

Max grabbed a case of rum and handed it over the rail to Jacques before stepping over the rails of both boats and embracing Jacques with a rather masculine hug, the kind that involves lots of back slapping and a minimal amount of chest touching. Within fifteen minutes, the three men had transferred the entire load of boxes onto the yacht's rear deck. Max grabbed a case and stepped into the elegant dimly-lit salon area of the *Plan B*. The décor consisted of lots of maple paneling and flooring, and featured leather sofas and cushioned barstools.

"Hey, stranger," the bikini-clad woman said, embracing Max and kissing his cheek. She wore no makeup, which unabashedly revealed the crow's feet beside her eyes and the slight wrinkles on her cheeks and forehead. To Max, she looked exactly like what a woman in her mid-forties should look like: not polished or perfect, just healthy, natural, and real.

"Hi, Suze," Max said. "Nice place you've got here."

"This old thing?" She smiled and put her hand on her hip, turning around to look at the luxurious salon area of the yacht. "Jacques and I like to rough it when we go island hopping."

"Retirement suits you," Max said.

"Selling the firm really *was* the best thing Jacques and me ever did. I almost feel stupid for not having done it sooner."

"Hold on, Susan. You gotta meet *this* guy," Max said, waving over Josue, who stood near the fighting chair on the rear deck, watching the pleasantries exchanged with some degree of caution. The tall Haitian entered the Viking's galley, standing like a child waiting to be introduced to the grown-ups.

"This is Josue Remy," Max said with a great deal of pride. "He's my right-hand man. I could not do what I do without him. Formerly of Port au Prince—and Miami—and now a resident of Ilet d'Ombres, Martinique. Without this guy I would likely be lying facedown in a gutter somewhere."

"That's an interesting name," Susan said. "How do you spell that, Haw-soo-eh?" she asked, sounding out the name, as if trying to dismantle it and examine all the parts.

Max spelled it for her.

"I love it," Susan said with a big smile. She hugged Josue tightly around the neck.

Josue smiled in his shy, boyish way; he looked as though he didn't know what to do with his hands.

Then Josue shook hands with Jacques, who was just returning from the forward stateroom, where they had stowed all of the rum, a bottle in his hand. The black smoky glass bottle featured the image of a fleur de lis, and the words *rhum élevé sous bois.* "May I?" Jacques asked.

"Of course," Max said. "They're yours."

Jacques peeled off the plastic seal and removed the corked wooden lid. He inhaled the fragrance of the rum with an expression of euphoria on his face. "Mmmm," he moaned, before taking a long swig from the bottle.

"Oh, my." Jacques clutched his chest as if he were in pain. "That is... so... good." He passed the bottle around the group and everyone had a drink. Then Jacques produced a thick roll of one-hundred-Euro notes bound by a rubber band. He grinned and handed it to Max. "Two hundred a bottle okay?"

"I said one-fifty," Max protested.

"You know, even back at Florida State, you always sucked at negotiation," Susan said with a smirk. "Remember every time you wanted to eat lunch at San's Wok, but me an' Jacques would say 'no, let's get pizza,' and you'd say 'okay, whatever.' You're supposed to ask for more, not lowball *us*."

"Yeah," Jacques said, after taking another long sip from the bottle. "How're you ever gonna succeed as a businessman? If you knew how much I was gettin' for this stuff on Grand Cayman you wouldn't feel bad about taking two hundred. Word is getting out, man. I'll drop off cases at a dozen beach bars between here and the Bahamas before we head home, and each one of them is paying top dollar for your product. Customers are coming in to our place and asking for the rum with the fleur de lis on the bottle. They're slapping fifties down on the bar—and that's for one shot."

"Word is out, Max," Susan said. "You're the next big thing in the Caribbean. You are big business."

"Speaking of which, business must be good by the looks of that boat," Jacques said, taking a glance through the port side window at *The Cash Settlement*, "if you can afford the likes of that."

"It's... borrowed," Max said awkwardly. "From a friend."

"Does your friend know that you have his boat? And have you

ever made your friend's acquaintance?" Jacques asked with the stern altruism of an older brother.

"Not exactly."

"You know, and I say this as one of your oldest friends, Max, running unregulated rum to a few beach bars isn't the crime of the century. I imagine if you got caught you'd probably be facing a bunch of fines. But stealing a boat like that is gonna get you noticed. Sooner or later."

"Finished?" Max asked.

"Just be careful. All right?" Jacques looked Max squarely in the eye, and shook his hand.

Max nodded.

"How *is* your place on Grand Cayman?" Max asked. "Suzy's Hurricane Hideout, you said it was called?"

"The place is off the chain, Max," Jacques said, passing the open bottle of Fleur de Lis to Susan. "Packed every night: tourists, locals, you name it. It is literally a party every day. I don't even like being away from it to cruise the islands. I'd rather be there."

"I'm glad you guys are happy. You deserve it. You've both busted your humps since college, and you've earned everything you've got."

"Hey, before I forget, when we were down in Saint Lucia last week we ran into some dude in this dive bar. The place sold these crazy shrimp fritters with this sweet-hot dipping sauce. Oh, man."

"Stick to the story, man," Susan said, faking a stern look at Jacques.

"Anyway, this guy looked totally out of place, and he was asking about you," Jacques continued.

"What do you mean... out of place?" Max asked, feeling a slight twisting inside his gut, though he wasn't sure why.

"Everyone in the place was dressed like us," Jacques said, tugging at his t-shirt and tipping his head toward his bikini-clad wife, "but this fellow wore a shark-skin suit and thousand-dollar shoes. Said he wanted to buy some Fleur de Lis rum. He actually bought all three bottles they had behind the bar. Didn't even care how much, just flicked down hundreds 'til they said it was good."

"Hmmm," Max said.

"You're famous," Susan said, sounding bubbly.

"Was anybody with him?" Max asked. "With the guy with the suit?"

"Yeah," Jacques said, looking off toward the sliver of moon that peeked between the just-parted stormy clouds, as if trying to recall the details. "Cuban, maybe. Bad-looking guy, tatted-up arms. I remember his hair was weird: well-oiled and black, with white streaks on both sides. Creepy guy actually, now that I think about it. Dude's wearing shorts and flip flops, and this long olive drab coat with the sleeves rolled up, like he was some kind of Sandinista or some damn thing. Who does that?"

"That's good," Max said.

"Good?" Jacques said, sounding perplexed.

"Yeah," Max said. "It's perfect, in fact."

# CHAPTER 2

MAX LIKED MAISIE'S BEACH CAFÉ: it was quiet, out of the way, and had the best Ti' Punch on Martinique. The place wasn't much, mainly a framework of wooden roof trusses and four-by-four beams which made up almost the entire structure. Bright red, blue, yellow and green paint covered the framework, seeming to leave each board a different color. The roof consisted of a dozen or so panels of weather-beaten corrugated metal sheets, which offered a welcome respite from the oftentimes oppressive afternoon sun. The place had a long red bar well-stocked with the usual Caribbean beers, spirits for blending the popular tourist-loved drinks, and all of the local island rums. Behind the bar, through a small square opening in a red plywood wall, one could catch just a glimpse of Maisie in the kitchen, grilling, frying, and sautéing up a whirlwind.

Max took his usual table in the corner. He chose it because there were no gaps in the metal roof panels directly overhead. This cast his particular table into murky shadow beside those which sat in the dappled sunlight peeking through gaps in some other parts of the roof.

The only other patrons in the place were two locals: an elderly couple, expatriates, likely from the French mainland, who occupied a table closest to the beach. All of the six tables on the beach, unsheltered from the full sun, sat empty.

Max picked up a salt shaker, really just a Bière Lorraine bottle with a perforated cap, and absent-mindedly rolled its bottom around in circles on the bright yellow tabletop.

"Salut, Max," the waitress said, placing a napkin down on his table and placing a short glass on top. Three ice cubes and a wedge of lime swirled in the clear liquid of the glass.

"Salut, Angelique," Max replied, placing the salt shaker back down on the table. "How are you? Pretty dead in here, isn't it? For lunchtime, I mean."

"Oui," the waitress said, placing her palms on Max's table. She was a pretty local girl of maybe twenty with toasted marshmallow-colored skin and long curly black hair, which she kept tied up in a ribbon. "Busy last night, full moon. Suppose folks are still sleeping it off."

"And to think, I was in bed by eight," Max fibbed. He and Josue hadn't made it back until three a.m. the night before. "Suppose that's what happens when you get to a certain age."

Angelique giggled. "*Chatrou fricasse* on special today," she teased. "Diver brought in a whole bunch of 'em this morning, you shoulda seen all of 'em."

"Ooh, tentacles. No thanks," Max said, showing his lower teeth in a half-grin. "How about accras with that scotch bonnet dipping sauce and whatever fresh fruit you've got?"

"Sounds good," Angelique said, walking over to the little square window to deliver Max's order to Maisie.

Max sipped his Ti' Punch. It was a mixture of local rum from the Depaz distillery up in Saint-Pierre, lime juice, and a bit of raw sugar. Max liked it when the ice cubes melted a little; the cool water opened up the rum, unlocking more of the spirit's unique character.

He kicked off his shoes and kneaded his toes into the beach sand that made up the floor of the café. It felt good.

A deeply sunburned blonde woman wandered into the shade, stumbling in off the beach. At first, Max wondered if she was in distress. Maybe in her late twenties, the girl looked a bit like a refugee from somewhere else, having just washed up on shore in a modest coral-colored one-piece, wrinkled white sarong, and a massive straw hat, which seemed to have done nothing to protect her from the barrage of UV rays offered by the brilliance of the early afternoon sun.

Stepping into the shelter of Maisie's metal roof, the well-toasted woman plunked down a massive shoulder bag that must have contained everything she owned in the world, except sun block.

The young woman heaved a great sigh as she sat down at the table and took off her hat, placing it down on the chair beside her. Max noticed that her blonde bob haircut was windblown and rather wild looking.

His skin *hurt* just looking at the redness of this girl's cheeks. *She's cute*, Max thought. *Probably on vacation by herself, finding out that the Caribbean isn't everything she thought it'd be.*

"Bonjour," Angelique said to the woman.

"Oh, hello," the lobster-skinned woman said, "do you speak English? Please tell me you do."

It only took two words for Max to make out that the blonde's soft voice was graced by a sweet, lilting Scottish accent. *She's really cute.*

"Oui," Angelique said with a wink. "What would you like?"

"Get me one of those big, fruity rum drinks that's bright red, or blue, or pink and comes served in a hollowed-out pineapple, or a fishbowl, or something."

"I'm sorry, Miss. I can't let you order that," Max said, standing up, drink in hand, and shuffling across the sand to the Scottish girl's table, just two tables away from the elderly French couple.

"And just what are *you*, the island's beverage police?" the Scottish girl said. Her tone made Max wonder if she was being playful, or hostile.

"Yes, I am with the Martinique beverage police, and we're cracking down on tourists ordering crappy drinks."

She laughed with a loud, vibrant cackle. Max wondered if she'd already had a few drinks. But man, it was a great smile.

"I'm Isobel. Isobel Greer," she said, using her foot to push back the chair opposite her, sliding it backwards in the sand, offering it to Max.

Max placed his Ti' Punch on the table and sat. "Craig. Maxwell Craig."

"Ooh, the James Bond type," Isobel sneered. "I suppose that's your bit, then, in't it? You wait until the single touristy ladies order a fishbowl drink, and then you step in with your smile, your charm, and your dashing black hair. Does it work out for you much?"

"You're the first person I've ever seen him talk to in here," Angelique said, as she placed a plate of croissants on the French couple's table. "'Sides me or Maisie. An' he comes in every day."

"Thanks a lot, Angelique," Max said. "No tip."

Angelique stepped over and punched Max on the arm good-naturedly. "Yeah, right."

Max flashed the waitress a grin that said, "How could I possibly be mad at you."

"What are you, a hermit or something?" Isobel asked.

Isobel's lack of couth made something in Max's gut flutter. He liked this girl.

"I guess I would say that I prefer to be alone," Max said.

"So what about the drink then?" Isobel asked, taking off her oversized sunglasses and placing them down on the table, revealing the crisply-defined tan lines her shades had left around her eyes. Max thought her large blue-green eyes were sparkling and amazing. "You going to suggest something or just let me die of thirst? Look at what this Caribbean sun has done to my fair Scottish skin. I feel like I'm as dehydrated as a camel."

"Are camels dehydrated?" Max asked, trying hard not to laugh, lest she think it was at her expense. "I thought they were known for not needing water for a really long time."

"They must be as dried out as toast," Isobel said seriously. "They've gone so long without a drink."

"Look, I'm sorry, but I just couldn't sit there and watch you order some pedestrian tourist drink full of too much fruit juice and syrupy, mass-produced, saccharine-sweet rum. You are on Martinique—this is possibly the most magical place in the world to order a glass of rum."

Angelique set Max's accras down on the table that he now shared with Isobel Greer. "Have you decided what you'd like to eat, Miss?" the cheerful waitress asked, standing poised with a pad and pen.

Isobel took a quick look at the menu, which was printed on bright green copy paper; the menu changed every day based on whatever types of seafood the divers and local fishermen brought in each morning. "Oh, how about the *dorade grillée des îles*," Isobel said, sounding the words out carefully, trying to say it just right. It brought a grin to Max's face.

"Excellent choice," Max added, before dipping an accra in the spicy dipping sauce and taking a bite. "It's always fresh here."

"And can you bring us the full range of La Mauny?" Max asked Angelique. "What the French would call a *dégustation*."

The waitress nodded and headed toward the window to place Isobel's food order before going behind the bar to set up Max's drinks.

"Try an accra," Max said to Isobel. "Popular Caribbean cuisine; fritters made from salt cod that's been rinsed in cool water for a couple of days. Here at Maisie's they mix in some fresh chopped shrimp as well. The dipping sauce is a little spicy, so tread lightly."

Isobel dipped one of the fritters and took a bite. A look of grave concern overwhelmed her face. Beads of sweat appeared on her forehead, and tears welled up in her eyes.

"Angelique?" Max shouted. "A glass of milk, please."

The waitress brought a tall glass of ice cold milk, and Isobel did her best to put out the fire in her mouth, as Max continued to dip and munch his accras.

"What are you doing in Martinique," Max asked. "Just on a vacation by yourself?"

"Um, I was going to come here with a friend, but she got delayed," Isobel said. "I'll catch up with her in a few days. Until she arrives I'm staying at a tiny hotel down the road here called L'auberge Mignon. Hope I said that right."

Max smiled and nodded. "Sounded good to me. Where you from?"

"Sort of all over," Isobel said, "It all started in Perth, Scotland; then Kent, England; Cork, Ireland; Boston; Chicago; Miami. But I'm here now, and I'm starting to wonder if I ever want to leave."

"You've bounced around a lot," Max said, then he threw back the second half of his Ti' Punch, draining it.

"I'm a substitute kindergarten teacher. It lets me move around when I feel like it. Suppose I just haven't found home just yet," Isobel said, locking eyes with him and curling her lips into an adorable smile that melted Max, right in his middle.

Angelique returned with a large silver tray, upon which rested six bottles of rum, all of which bore a bright red and yellow label depicting a sultry Martinican woman standing amongst sugarcane stalks. Two tasting glasses with tapered mouths and wide bowls sat on the tray next to the bottles.

"We have these glasses in Scotland," Isobel said. "Whisky's kind of big there. They use these in the tasting rooms."

"First things first," Max said, handing Isobel a glass and pouring out the clearest of the rums. "This is not rum as you probably know it. This is *rhum agricole*. It has a distinct difference from the Bacardi or Captain Morgan or what have you. Typical mass-produced rum, the French call *rhum industriel.* It's made from molasses, which is what's left over from the cane juice after sugar has been refined off. The molasses is fermented, and distilled into rum. Then it's either bottled clear or placed in oak barrels to age, which is what gives it the darker amber color—of course some rums add caramel coloring to theirs, but I'm not going to get into that.

"Here, on Martinique, the rhum agricole is fermented and distilled from freshly cut and crushed sugarcane juice. The first thing you'll notice when you smell it is an aroma sort of like—"

"Like grass," Isobel said, scrunching up her face in a surprised expression as she looked up from her tasting glass.

"Exactly," Max said, "since sugarcane is in the same horticultural family as grass. This particular bottle is La Mauny 40° White, which is forty percent alcohol and has not been barrel-aged."

Isobel sniffed her glass again. "It's really nice, though. I can smell all kinds of things. It's very spicy."

"This one is known for its finish of black pepper and lime," Max said, sniffing his own glass. "Now, touch your tongue to the rum to get your mouth used to the 'burn' and then take a sip."

Isobel took a sip and scrunched up her face again, then shook her head. "Whew!"

"It takes a bit to get used to the alcohol when it's not mixed in a daiquiri or punch—although those aren't bad things, they just need to be done right. This rum is actually great for mixing, Ti' Punches, mojitos, daiquiris, and so forth."

After they had sipped their first rum, Max poured a dram into each glass from the second bottle. "This is the same kind of rum as the first one, but it is fifty-five percent alcohol.

"It's got a sweet, sugary smell," Isobel said, sticking her nose deep into her glass. "It's sort of honey-like."

Max nodded.

"La Mauny distillery is maybe an hour's drive from here.

There are eight working, or smoking, distilleries on Martinique, along with a few that stopped producing, but either have their rum made by one of the smoking operations, or else they might still serve as aging facilities, warehousing oak barrels of aging rum.

"Probably the most unique thing about the rhum agricole produced on Martinique is that it has a special designation. Look at this," Max said, pointing to the label on one of the bottles.

"*Appellation d'Origine Controlée Rhum Agricole Martinique,*" Isobel read aloud. "What does that mean?"

"The French are very particular about the quality products they produce. Think about the Bordeaux classifications for wine, or think of Champagne, for that matter. Outside of the Champagne growing region, sparkling wines are just called sparkling wine. They can't be called Champagne unless the grapes are grown in the right place, they are the right varietals, they follow all the rules. Then they can label their bottles Appellation d'Origine Controlée Champagne."

Isobel nodded to let Max know that she understood, as he poured out rum from the last bottle on the silver tray. "Mmmm," she said, giving the V.S.O.P. rum a sniff. "Smells like caramel and a little bit like orange."

"Rhum agricole on Martinique is regulated just like Champagne," Max said. "They have certain areas where they are allowed to grow the sugarcane, a certain method of distillation is required, and the cane must be freshly pressed or crushed to produce the juice within a certain time. There's a very specific process, but the end result is AOC rhum agricole Martinique. And you're surrounded by it."

"Wow," Isobel said, and Max wasn't sure if she was feigning fascination, or if she was genuinely impressed. "Do you work in a rum museum or what?"

"No," Max said coyly. "But there *are* a couple of rum museums on the island. Actually, I'm in accounting."

This time Isobel Greer laughed out loud, in a playful, boisterous way that Max appreciated. "Are you serious?" she asked.

"It pays the bills. You know."

"You are quite the interesting gentleman, Maxwell Craig," she said, twirling a bit of her blonde hair around her finger.

"When I first heard your accent, I instantly thought your hair should be red," Max said, suddenly wondering if it sounded insulting.

"Sure, stereotype me. An' you should have plastic pocket protectors with pens, pencils, and... protractors, and such. Mr. Accountant."

*This girl is so much fun,* Max thought to himself.

"On the topic of pockets, why do you wear this long sleeve black shirt thing?" Isobel asked. "It looks like the proper kind of shirt for the Caribbean. What is that, nylon or rayon? But usually they're turquoise or pink, sorry, salmon—but you've got black, and your sleeves are down to your wrists." She picked up his hand and turned it over in hers. "And you've got it buttoned down like you're going to church or something."

"You know how it is, you lock yourself into a certain look and it's hard to do anything else."

Angelique brought Isobel her food. Isobel appeared very surprised to see the whole fried fish with head and tail still on.

"Bon appetit," Max said, standing up from the table.

"You're leaving?" Isobel said, sounding disappointed. She put her sunglasses back on. "Pity, we were just starting to have fun."

"I've got to catch up with my business associate for a meeting this afternoon," Max said, putting on his tortoise shell wayfarer sunglasses.

"Ooh," Isobel cooed. "Top secret accounting business. How exciting."

"I don't know how you found this place," Max said, tipping his sunglasses down to look at Isobel, "but I'm really glad you did."

"Cab driver brought me," she said. "I think he was looking for a nice, out-of-the-way place to deliver me, to run up his fare as much as he could. Seemed like we drove around in circles first for about twenty minutes, though."

Max chuckled and nodded.

"Hope to see you again," Isobel said.

"I'm in here every day," Max said. "So it's almost a certainty. If you can find it again."

"See you again, then, Maxwell Craig," Isobel said, her bright eyes flickering like stars.

On his way out, Max stopped by the bar, where Angelique was mixing drinks for a group of four young women, likely tourists from the U.S., who filled a table out on the beach. "What's-his-name hasn't bothered you again, has he?"

Angelique smiled and shook her head, before throwing her arms around Max's neck in a sweet embrace.

"You tell me if he comes around you again, okay?" Max looked deathly serious. "You tell me, don't let it slide."

The young waitress nodded. "Merci, Max."

Max headed for the door, almost missing altogether the person who sat in the shadows at Max's regular table. As Max's fingers gripped the doorknob of the door separating Maisie's back wall from the outside world, the man at the table stood up and placed a firm hand on Max's shoulder.

An impulse of reflex made Max reach for his right hip.

"Whoa!" the man said, throwing up his hands with a concerned frown.

Max wheeled around and almost instantly recognized that the man wore the uniform of the Gendarmerie Nationale. He also ascertained that this man was not your typical gendarme sergeant or corporal; this one's shoulder insignias indicated he was a rank much higher up. A major? A colonel?

"I don't know what you have under your shirt, but let's keep it in your pants, no?" the gendarme said with a good-natured chortle.

Max relaxed his arm and let it swing down comfortably to his side.

"Maximilian Craig? I'm Colonel Travere, head of the Gendarmerie Nationale here on Martinique. I've been looking for you."

# CHAPTER 3

MAX OFFERED COLONEL TRAVERE A seat at the small yellow table in the dim corner of Maisie's Beach Café. As they took their seats, Max wondered if the gendarmerie was onto him for the theft of *The Cash Settlement* the night before. It had been a brazen act, stealing the boat, and Max now wondered if it had come back to bite him in the end.

Josue *had* wiped the boat down well and scrubbed it with a long-handled brush, using two bottles of bleach to eliminate any physical evidence he and Max might have left behind them. Then the stealthy Haitian had dumped it at a private dock near St. Pierre, way over on the other side of the island. Other than ripping out some of the expensive boat's electronics, letting the cops blast a hole in the roof, and using up a hell of a lot of someone's gas, the vessel had been returned relatively unscathed.

"Anything he wants," the colonel called to Angelique. The law officer held up his hand like a kid in elementary school. "It's on me."

"Angelique, do you still have that bottle of Trois Rivières 1953?" Max asked the young waitress.

"No," Angelique said, a slight smirk curling her lips. "Some business guy from New York, or maybe it was Newark, bought the last."

"Thank heavens for that," Travere said, taking off his black and white kepi and placing it down on the table. "I didn't bring my checkbook with me."

Max figured the colonel was about fifty. Close inspection of the man's toned arms and a lack of a bulging midsection suggested him to be much fitter than a typical man of his age, even a lawman. Wispy streaks of light gray marked the colonel's short wheat-colored hair, and a roadmap of thin wrinkles in the tanned skin around the man's eyes seemed to be the only things betraying his true age, and likely keeping folks from thinking him a much younger man.

"Just another Ti' Punch," Max said, leaning against the wall and trying to appear relaxed. He checked the face of his Bulova Precisionist in a disinterested fashion.

"Make it two," Travere said to Angelique. "I hear you make a very good one here."

Max noticed Isobel Greer over at her table, trying to make sense of her whole fried fish, picking at it suspiciously with her knife and fork. Once in a while she would shoot a glance in Max's direction, no doubt wondering why this cop was questioning him. Max wondered the same.

"What can I do for you, Colonel?" Max asked, doing his best not to sound annoyed.

"I've heard about you around the island, Maximilian, and I very much wanted to meet you. I suppose, you could say, your reputation has preceded this meeting."

Max couldn't get over how "French" it sounded when the colonel said Maximilian. "It's actually Maxwell," Max said.

Colonel Travere looked Max in the eyes. The gendarme had piercing light green eyes, likely trained to elicit submission from whoever dared gaze into them. "How did your parents decide upon that? Ah, merci," he said, as Angelique handed him his cocktail. She set one in front of Max as well, who quickly took a sip.

"Honestly, Colonel, I think my folks were making breakfast

one morning, opened a fresh coffee can, and said, 'Hey, I know, let's call him Maxwell.'"

It took the colonel a moment, but at last he chuckled. "Ah, yes. Could have been worse; you might have become Folgers Craig."

This time Max laughed. The colonel seemed like a nice guy, a guy whom Max might have been friends with, had the colonel's own mission not have been quite so diametrically opposed to Max's.

"So what of this reputation you've heard about?" Max asked. "Did I file some tax returns for some of your friends or colleagues and they recommended me to you?"

"No, I recently enjoyed some of your wonderful product?" the colonel said furtively, glancing from side to side, as if they were speaking of dangerous and clandestine matters. "It is among the best I have ever had."

"I'm not following," Max said, doing his best to sound cordial, despite feeling his patience running thin.

"The Fleur de Lis brand. I enjoyed a couple of drams with a colleague the other night, at his home in Les Trois-Ilets. What struck me was how your rum was so different than the other rhum agricoles produced on the island, very nuanced, unusually earthy. And yet it's made from cane grown here, cut here, fermented here, distilled here. I simply had to meet the man who made the rum."

"I'm sorry, Colonel, but I work in accounting. I have a home office in my villa. I don't know what you've heard—"

"Very well," the colonel interrupted. "I am not here to threaten you or anything. But perhaps to maybe suggest that you think about making your operation legit."

"Hmmm," Max said thoughtfully, not sure what the colonel's motives were. *Was he actually being nice to him, or was this simply a shakedown?*

"Hey, Max, I've heard other rumors about you swirling around the island, particularly around these parts, and I'm afraid I'd be remiss if I did not ask you about them," Colonel Travere said, slowly swirling the two ice cubes around in his glass.

"Ask me anything," Max said, pretending he had nothing to hide from the gendarmerie commander.

"I've heard stories, like the one about the waitress' boyfriend stalking her," Travere said. "The rumor is you beat the living piss out of the guy, to let him know it wasn't a good idea to keep bothering her."

Max shrugged his shoulders lightly. He looked the gendarmerie colonel square in the eyes.

"There is another account of a drunken fisherman wrestling a young local woman to the ground on a beach near Château Dubuc," Colonel Travere said, peering at Max with his laser-like green eyes. "Apparently, after smacking the girl around a bit, the man was trying to rape the woman when—according to witnesses—a man with black hair and black clothing beat up the man pretty bad, threw the fisherman into his own skiff, and took off with him to destinations unknown. No one has seen or heard from that particular fisherman since that moment," Travere said suspiciously.

Max looked at Travere with a sober expression. He took a sip of his drink.

Travere gave a light nod. "All right, then. Enough about you. I moved here a few months ago from Paris," he said, smoothing out his close-cropped military-style haircut with his hand. "My wife's parents had moved there from Martinique in the fifties. They were native Martinicans. Long story short, my wife inherited some land here, up north. Nothing spectacular, fifty acres of flat land in Saint-Marie—not far from the Saint James distillery, actually. The property has a good-sized villa, but it needs some work. If you were to ask my wife, it is her roots to the island that brought us here."

"That wasn't the real reason?" Max suggested.

"Just between you and me, Maxwell, it was the rum," the

colonel said, easing back in his chair with a satisfied expression, and bringing his glass to his lips.

"The rum?" Max said, surprised.

"Yes, my friend, the rum. My wife and I—her name is Adeline, by the way—lived busy lives in the city, she working in accounting herself, me chasing down terrorists and international criminals in the City. We came to Martinique for a holiday a few years back. I had never had the pleasure of having tasted rhum agricole before. My first sip opened my mind to a whole new world of rum drinking possibilities.

"If you ask Adeline, she will tell you I became obsessed with the stuff. Every Friday I would stop at a small spirits shop at a busy crossroads near my office; I would buy a new bottle of AOC rhum agricole Martinique each time and spend much of the weekend enjoying it. I would sit on my balcony and think about the men cutting the cane, what hard back-breaking work it must have been. I'd think of them crushing the cane, extracting the sweet juice, and fermenting it before distilling it in their big column stills. My mind would go crazy thinking about all of those oak barrels sitting in aging rooms here on the island, just waiting to be uncorked and release their magic.

"I suppose the rum itself made me long for my wife's roots," Travere added. "Funny, no? They are not even my own roots here on the island, but I longed for them as if they were."

"You are a real connoisseur," Max said, feeling a measure of respect for the colonel, "aren't you?"

"I wouldn't say that I have a sophisticated palate for tasting, or anything like that," Colonel Travere said, sounding strangely sheepish, for as powerful a man as he obviously was. "I just know what I like, you know? There is nothing else in the world quite like rhum agricole Martinique."

Max nodded. "It *is* special."

"Angelique," Max said, spontaneously, "would you bring the Colonel and me a glass of Clément 1976?"

"Certainly."

"It's on me, Colonel," Max said, feeling as if he were starting to like the commander of the gendarmerie on Martinique. He was not sure if he was springing a trap that Travere was setting for him, or if he was just being foolish. Yet a small part of him wondered if the colonel might become an asset. Max's underground brand of unregulated rhum agricole could grow exponentially with a powerful gendarme on his side. "But only because I know you can appreciate it."

"Merci beaucoup."

Angelique brought the half-empty bottle of well-aged rum, placing it on the table with a couple of tasting glasses. "Enjoy."

"Honestly, Colonel," Max said, pouring out the scarce amber liquid, "this is a bit more drinking than I usually do before one o'clock. But, if I'm honest, I must admit I feel a sort of kinship with you."

"And I shouldn't be drinking at all, Max. May I call you Max?" Colonel Travere took his glass with relish, lifting it to his nose and embracing the aroma of the spirit made on the island decades ago. "After all, I am on duty."

"Your English is very good, Colonel," Max said. "Your French accent is unmistakable, but you don't mispronounce words the way a lot of non-native English speakers do."

"I studied English all through university," Colonel Travere said, seeming to want to savor the aroma of his rhum agricole forever. "I wanted to master it before I started working. I suppose I thought it could take me places someday."

"Like the States?" Max asked.

"Possibly. But I believe I have found the place that I belong here on the island. It's funny how something can lead you on one path or another, no? Like, one big choice you make, or a major event in your life can change its entire course, you know?"

"Believe me," Max said, before draining his glass, and starting to pour another, "I know."

# CHAPTER 4

**M**OMO GAZED DOWN AT HIS smartphone, its white display shockingly bright against the darkness of his musty bedroom. "He's what?" Momo asked the phone, which was switched onto speakerphone mode.

"Brain dead," the disembodied voice said through the phone's speaker. "Big Flow is brain dead. Turn on channel six!"

Momo walked to his living room, kicking an empty bottle in the darkened hallway. He fumbled around for the remote to his eighty-inch flat screen. He clicked it on, and his eyes strained to adjust to the brightness of the television, but he swiftly toggled through the channels until he heard the words, "suspected leader of an ultra-violent Haitian street gang, died today at Mercy Hospital Miami, succumbing to numerous gunshot wounds, including at least one to the head.

"Pierre Bruno, or Big Flow as he was known on the streets of the Little Haiti area of Miami, apparently engaged members of a rival street gang in a gunfight in the parking lot of a Monty Maximus Pizza restaurant in the Key Biscayne area late this afternoon. Witnesses counted dozens of shots exchanged between gang members, with Big Flow and two members of an unnamed street gang also killed in the altercation.

"Our own Tawny Abernathy has spent several months preparing an in-depth look at the enigmatic and often brutally violent street gang known as Ti Flow."

Momo's eyes were huge and his mind raced as he watched the

investigative news package begin to roll. He stumbled backwards and sat down on his leather sofa. A partial bottle of warm Prestige beer sat on the side table, and Momo absent-mindedly picked it up and drained it.

"In Port-au-Prince, a lot of the guys speak French Creole." Momo recognized the speaker, it was Big Flow, and he was speaking in front of the courthouse, just last year. "And the name Ti Flow is loosely translated from the French word petite, meaning small, and fléau, which means scourge. Ti Flow ain't a big scourge that gonna kill everybody, but a smaller one that takes care of business here, in our corner of Miami, you know what I'm saying. You wanna join Ti Flow, you better have pride in the homeland—don't forget where you, or your parents, or your grandparents come from—and you better be ready to be the scourge."

"That was the charismatic leader of Haitian street gang Ti Flow, who ironically goes by the name Big Flow, speaking about the origin of the gang in his own words after having been acquitted of a laundry list of charges which included kidnapping, murder, racketeering, and torture," Tawny Abernathy said in voiceover as b-roll of several Haitian gang members beating up a member of a rival gang rolled across Momo's TV.

Momo's mind swirled. He knew if he was going to take action, he needed to take action quickly, lest he lose his advantage to another member of the gang. Ti Flow was now a body without a head; it was time to show the rest of the gang who the alpha dog now was.

Momo stepped outside, and walked into the middle of Lemon Street. The hot June night evaporated the rain that had fallen earlier in the evening, causing wisps of ghostly mist to rise up off the graying asphalt, floating toward the streetlights overhead.

Standing at six foot six, and weighing over three hundred

pounds, Momo knew most people in the neighborhood feared him. It was now time to redeem that fear.

Momo pulled the .50 caliber Desert Eagle pistol from his waistband. He started firing it in the air, its muzzle flashing brightly like a flare gun, quickly drawing the attention of everyone in the neighborhood. Porch lights and lamps in windows flickered to life all along the street, as everyone in a five-block radius was shaken awake by the sound of Momo's powerful pistol.

A few people stepped tentatively out of their homes, peering down the street like cautious mice, eager to see what was happening, but willing themselves to maintain their distance. One by one the residents of Lemon Street, seeing Momo standing alone in the street, trudged toward him like zombies in their pajamas, bathrobes, and sweatpants, until a large congregation had gathered around the mountainous gang member.

"Big Flow is dead," Momo said, when he had determined enough of the neighborhood's residents were present for such an announcement. "He dead," Momo reiterated, as he tucked the powerful pistol back into the elastic band of his long Miami Heat shorts.

A couple of people began to sob, and one woman gasped with horror and fell to her knees. A general groan rumbled through the assembly, and Momo knew that every man, woman, and child present felt a great sting at the loss of their leader, Big Flow. It was tough news to bear, as most of the neighborhood residents counted on the gang's leader for everything from protection, to money for groceries, to a steady supply of weed and coke. Big Flow had always prided himself on taking care of his tight-knit community, and he would not hesitate to burn down anyone who dared to stand against him or his people.

"Momo's in charge now," Momo said soberly, looking from face to face, and seeing a wide audience of frowns. He wondered if what he witnessed was the heaviness of loss at the passing of a charismatic criminal leader, or if it was something much worse, dissent.

"Anything you need, you come and talk to Momo. You got a problem? You come and talk to Momo. Somebody mess with you? You come and see Momo. Momo gonna take care o' y'all. You dig?"

One by one, folks began to nod their heads, reinforcing the mental image Momo had of them as zombies.

"Right now," Momo said, hoping he could swiftly turn the tide in his favor, "we gon' have a party. We gonna have a massive blowout. We gotta send out our master Big Flow with as much love as we can muster up, and we gonna celebrate the new sheriff takin' over the town. Momo is takin' over. Dig?"

The zombies nodded.

"Zann, Tiny Deege," Momo said, motioning with his huge hand for two of his cronies to step toward him. "Go in my house, bring out the two folding tables from the back room. Set up one with as many boxes of Don Legado as we got. Zann, you set up shop rolling blunts for everyone. I'll get you the weed, and if anybody wants it, the coke.

"Tiny Deege, you go get all o' the Cristal out the garage fridge, grab as many bottles of Barbancourt rum you can find, and set up a blender on the second table. Momo gonna make some cocktails."

"Yeah!" A couple people in the crowd cheered, at the prospect of receiving free booze and weed. *It's working*, Momo thought. He knew it would.

In moments, Momo stood in front of a blender, haphazardly throwing together a cocktail of Haitian rum, expensive Champagne, lime juice, mint leaves, and ice. Momo was assisted by Tiny Deege, a young undocumented Haitian who was really small—not just short—but a proportionally small man: unusually small hands and feet; smooth bald head the size of a large grapefruit; short skinny legs; child-sized torso. No one knew why he was that way, they just accepted him, and called him Tiny Deege.

"Hey, everyone! Come and get a drink!" Momo shouted to the crowd. "It's like my own kinda mojito. I'm callin' it a Momojito. Come and get a Momojito!"

The crowd of shell-shocked zombies cheered, and crowded the cocktail table. At the other table, Zann, a skinny Haitian refugee with orange hair, thick black horn-rim glasses, and a shiny platinum grill over his teeth, carefully split the Don Legado cigars down their length with a razor, dumping out the tobacco and replacing it with marijuana, packing it firmly and licking it to seal it closed. He handed the finished blunts out like party favors to members of the crowd.

Another one of Momo's associates pulled the four-foot-tall speakers from Momo's living room out onto the lawn of the tiny turquoise house on Lemon Street. Within five minutes, they were listening to a gruff rapper belting out a violently quick staccato burst of vocals about an AK-47 blowing out windows like a hurricane.

Momo switched on the blender to churn another batch of his special concoction, when a stern face appeared across the table from him. It might have been the only person—now that Big Flow was dead—whom Momo actually feared in the world.

"Oh, hey, Mama Dorah," Momo said, trying to sound as if he were happy to see the Haitian-American woman, who wore a colorful blue, yellow, and red karabela dress and matching headwrap. Even though she was only in her late thirties, Mama Dorah was largely considered to be like a mother and spiritual leader to Ti Flow, as well as everyone who lived on or near Lemon Street.

"A word," Mama Dorah said with a deep, striking Haitian Creole-accented voice that invoked more fear in the neighborhood than Big Flow and Momo put together. She turned on her heels and walked directly into the house opposite Momo's, where the door stood open, an eerie red-orange light smoldering inside.

"Yo yo, Tiny Deege, Zann, come with me," Momo said to his cronies, as he followed the colorfully-dressed woman into her dimly lit home. "I ain't goin' in there alone," he whispered to his friends.

A weird smell, like weed, perfume, and sweet incense, assaulted Momo's nostrils as he passed through a wall of strung beads in a doorway to enter the woman's living room.

Mama Dorah knelt by a low table, maybe just a coffee table, and the first thing Momo saw was a dead cat, gutted and sprawled out over a covering of banana leaves, various scattered bones, and a long, smoldering pipe.

"Oh, man!" Momo shrieked, looking at the cat's red bloated entrails contrasted against the animal's snowy white fur. "What you have to go and do a thing like that fo'?" He looked at Tiny Deege and Zann; both of them peered down at the table with moon-like eyes.

"Kneel," Mama Dorah ordered. Momo knelt down opposite her, feeling a sick sensation inside his stomach, like two hands twisting a thick rope. Tiny Deege and Zann knelt with great reluctance.

"I have seen the future, Momo," she said, tilting her head back and inhaling deeply. "I have seen the future of Ti Flow, and you sit at its head. You shall be its leader. You, and you alone."

Momo felt himself relax a bit, despite the gruesome scene which lay out before him. "Thanks, Mama. You know I hoped you—"

"But first there is one thing you must do, Momo," Mama Dorah said, pouring herself a glass of Haitian rum and taking a long swig. "There is a task that you must perform before you can truly call yourself leader. You must finish that which you once begun. You must finish what you started."

"I don't know what you—"

Mama Dorah looked directly at Momo. "You will go to a place where the earth once shook, where a mountain rumbled and spit sulfurous vapors and spewed ash, fire, and steam over an entire city." Her deep voice grew in intensity. Her eyes darted wildly about, and she lifted her arms above her head.

Momo swallowed hard.

"You will go to a place where an entire city of people boiled in their own skin," Mama Dorah shrieked. "All this happened on the day, on the day when the Christian God ascended into heaven. Thirty-thousand lives brought instantly to each one's sudden, terrifying, and painful end."

Momo made a face of disgust. "What you talkin' bout, Mama?"

"You must go to the island. There you will find the boy. The boy who betrayed you, he betrayed me, he betrayed all of Ti Flow. He spat in all of our faces. You must find him. And you must not only kill him, you must make him pay a great price for his betrayal. You must cleanse him through pain. This you must do. You *must* do this, or I swear by the blood on my hands that you should not return. You fail me, you should never again show your face here, lest you be smote down by my own vengeance. Do you hear me, Momo?"

Momo nodded, but he felt like he was going to throw up.

"You will finish what you have begun, or I will destroy you, Momo. I will turn your bones into ash, and I will drink your blood in my rum." Mama Dorah's eyes blazed with frightening fire.

"I'm sorry, Mama," Momo stammered. He wondered if she would curse him or kill him with her mind just for asking a question. "But who do you want me to kill?"

"Do you not remember, Momo?" Mama Dorah's tone was softer now. "Has it been so long that his face eludes you? Did his betrayal not sting enough for you to even remember the betrayer's name?"

Momo shook his head, feeling sick inside. Tiny Deege was crying. Zann was wringing his hands together nervously.

"I shall tell you, Momo," Mama Dorah said, her eyes locked onto his with a sinister gaze. "I shall tell you who you must destroy."

She paused for a long moment, in which all that Momo could hear was the sound of his own throat as he swallowed dryly.

"His name is Josue Remy."

# CHAPTER 5

M AX'S MACHETE CUT THROUGH THE stalk of
sugarcane as easily as if it were cutting through
air. Each stroke of the razor-sharp blade brought a
satisfying *zing* to his ears, and another of the thick, fibrous stalks
toppled free.

With a dexterity that only comes from experience, Max
grabbed the cut cane, quickly lopped off its bright green, grassy
foliage, and tossed the finished stick onto the half-filled cart
hitched to a four-wheel-drive Polaris quad.

The work was hot, sticky drudgery, and it began shortly before
dawn. Prior experience told Max that his back and shoulders
would ache from shortly after he started cutting until days after
he was finished, which would likely be long after the sun had
gone down for the night.

"Another two or three hundred pounds and you can drive
this load over to the shed," Max said, taking a moment to run a
sharpening stone over the length of his machete blade. Keeping
the instrument sharp made for lighter work. It took a fine balance
between keeping the work going and knowing when to stop and
sharpen the blades.

Josue simply nodded and continued with his own task of
cutting. He stood about a dozen feet from Max, and he zipped
through the cane even faster than Max, taking full advantage of
his benefit of youth.

One of the things Max loved about working with his Haitian

friend was the younger man's easygoing demeanor, and the fact that they could work side by side for hours and not feel obliged to fill in the gaps of quietness with too much chitchat. The two worked in near silence for most of the afternoon.

Once, Josue encountered a lancehead viper while pulling out a couple of freshly-cut stalks of cane. The coiled pit viper lifted his head menacingly. Its thick body writhed in a strange, mesmerizing fashion as the venomous snake threatened to strike.

Josue struck quickly, and he struck true. In the blink of an eye, he had separated the snake's head from its body. He continued cutting sugarcane as if nothing had happened, ignoring the unnerving sight of the twisting body of the headless reptile.

Max hoped that by sundown they would have harvested nearly a quarter of an acre; this would produce plenty of juice to fill his five-hundred-gallon pot still.

Josue was now about twenty feet away from Max, hacking away at his section of the small forest of towering sugarcane with a cane knife. Just when Max felt confident in his skill as a cane cutter, he glimpsed his Haitian friend, moving effortlessly through the tall foliage, slashing the stalks down like a demon.

"Boss, water," Josue said, glaring at Max with an expression of concern.

Max realized his partner had stopped just long enough to see him wipe his dripping brow and spit the thick saliva that seemed to be choking him. Max stopped cutting and took a long drink from a two-liter soda bottle half-filled with water, half with ice. The cool water was even more refreshing than Max had expected.

"It's always good to have my mom here with me on harvest days," Max said, laying his machete down on the seat of the quad. He took another drink from the plastic bottle.

Josue flashed his nearly perfect, pearl-white smile. Max didn't know how a man with Josue's background had such perfect teeth, and he never thought to ask. But the man had one of the most likeable, charismatic smiles Max had ever seen.

"You try doing this when you get to forty, Josue," Max said, rubbing his left shoulder vigorously. "It's not the same as doing it at twenty-five."

"I just hope I look so good, I get to be forty." Josue said with a sober expression. Max didn't know if he was joking or not.

"Your flattery is good for a fifteen-minute break, I think," Max said, realizing he had been looking for an excuse to take a breather. "Smoke 'em if you got 'em."

Josue reached into his backpack, which was slumped into the rear cargo rack of Max's quad. He produced a three-fingered leather cigar sleeve and removed two Arturo Fuente Hemingway cigars. He handed one to Max.

"Oh, you got 'em all right," Max said, sitting down sideways on the Polaris' seat. "Good choice, my friend. Got a light?"

The two men lit up and smoked the quality Dominican cigars in relative silence for a time, until Josue exhaled a large cloud of smoke and said, "Thank you for giving me job."

"What?" Max asked, dumbfounded.

"I don't remember if I tell you before. Thank you for giving me job."

Max puffed his cigar and said, "You're my best friend. I didn't give you anything, Josue. You are my partner. Equal. Savvy?"

Josue nodded, but Max still saw the humility in the younger man's eyes. It almost brought tears to Max's. "Thank you, Maxwell. You help me. You save me."

Max stood and placed a hand on his friend's shoulder. "I'm not just being nice when I say this, Josue. You saved *me*. And I owe *you* the thanks."

The two shared an embrace that made Max feel like the most unlikely father-figure in the world. Sure, he had rescued Josue from another life; a dangerous life the kid had not chosen for himself. But Max knew it was no accident Josue had come into his life. Without the young Haitian, Maxwell Craig was certain he would be dead.

"Now get back to work!" Max quipped, picking up his own machete and leading Josue back to the sugarcane field, where a wide swath of cane stumps protruded from the ground where they had already blazed through with their blades.

Max's villa resided on a small island that the locals called an *ilet*. Situated among a cluster of ten similar small islands off the coast of a town called Le Robert, Max's ilet, known as Ilet d'Ombres, translated 'small island of shadows', encompassed a total area of about six or seven acres of overgrown land. The property Max owned occupied only about half of the ilet, with a small resort hotel inhabiting the remainder to the east.

The property had remained on the market for nearly two years before Max took ownership of it. Accessible only by boat, most prospective buyers would have reached the end of the property's long pier to find themselves a hundred feet from the parcel's dilapidated villa, realizing they could not make more than a dozen steps before becoming ensnared in the ilet's overgrown foliage: bamboo, palm trees, banana trees, balatá trees; they all grew together like a living wall, punctuated by bright red anthurium flowers and otherworldly looking bromeliads.

Max had been the first interested party to arrive at the dock armed with a machete and a hard-working Haitian friend. The two had hacked their way through to the villa in about fifteen minutes' time, leaving a dumbfounded realtor standing behind on the dock, holding her briefcase.

The villa was old and had needed work, but was structurally sound. The area around the villa would need some clearing, but otherwise contained some quite beautiful fauna and flora. Max had never lived somewhere that all manner of lizards, geckos and iguanas; scary, but colorful spiders; and a rainbow of unusual birds all roamed free as if on a tiny tropical and very private zoo. It only took about five minutes of poking around for Max to know the property was exactly what he had been looking for.

The real find on the property, though, was the cavern. Josue had been hacking through the tangle of jungly plants, exploring the island, when he nearly fell into the huge hole in the ground about twelve feet in diameter. Closer inspection revealed the hole to be the entrance of a cavern a dozen feet deep, and just over thirty feet in length.

Exploring the cave with flashlights, Max and Josue had discovered a small opening near the darkest recess, about two feet across, just above the lapping, tropical water of Le Robert bay. As he had inspected the opening, Max spotted a continous trickle of cool water dripping into the bay like a tiny waterfall. He traced the stream to its source, finding a miniature freshwater spring right inside the cave.

Max knew right away the cave was the perfect spot to situate his five-hundred-gallon pot still. Each time he made a batch of rum, Max typically needed to add a certain amount of water to the cane juice to get the pH level just right before pitching the yeast. Max attributed the spring's unique mineral composition to the singular quality of his finished rum. And it became an essential element to his brand's *terroir*, and the reason it would be impossible to reproduce the Fleur de Lis brand anywhere else in the world.

The shiny bulbous pot still always reminded Max of that scene from Willy Wonka and the Chocolate Factory in which Gene Wilder fires up the bubble-sputtering soda-powered car with all of its brass and copper pipes and tubes. Max's rum still did not seem so different. Looking like a big mushroom constructed of shiny, hand-tooled copper, the still featured a curvy swan's neck on top and a separate fresh water-cooled condenser on the side.

Max and Josue hacked and zinged their blades until Max's

calculations told him they had harvested nearly ten tons of sugarcane. He kept a little leather-bound notebook that included all of his rum-making calculations, dates, and observations. The small black book was the rum-making holy grail of the Fleur de Lis brand.

But the grueling job of harvesting the cane was only half the work. Max and Josue still faced the next step in the process of creating their own rhum agricole. Max lacked the authority and credentials to call his product AOC rhum agricole Martinique, not to mention his product was one hundred percent unregulated, untaxed, and otherwise against the law.

Max threw a switch in the shed behind his villa. Four powerful sodium lights flashed to life, bathing the massive pile of cut sugarcane, heaped in the grassy backyard of the villa, with warm orange light that steadily changed to a brighter yellow color.

Josue began to hose down the cut cane; it gave the stalks a quick wash before they were fed into the crusher. Max's tool for the job was an old Goldens model #36, powered by an eight-horsepower Honda generator engine, which grumbled to life with a few pulls of its cord.

Max grabbed two stalks of cane and fed them into the crusher. Robust steel gears turned rollers that grabbed hold of the sugarcane and pulled it through, effectively flattening it, and squeezing out the sweet, light green juice that ran off into a fifty-gallon plastic drum. From the drum, the extracted juice would eventually be fed by a lengthy food-grade siphon hose that stretched, snakelike, down the gaping hole of the cavern opening and into the big copper still.

Max drew off the first liter of fresh-crushed juice into a pitcher, and he added ice from a cooler. He poured himself and Josue a refreshing cup of sweet cane juice which they drank from disposable plastic cups.

Josue clinked cups with Max. "Cheers, Boss."

Then the two set their attention back to their grueling task. Max fed the canes into the crusher two or three at a time. Josue stood behind the rollers; he grabbed the compacted, fibrous husks spit out on the other side. He then pitched the spent canes onto a growing pile, about fifteen feet from their work area.

After they had collected the next two liters of juice in another pitcher, Max took it into his small laboratory on the ground floor of his subterranean distillery. He set the glass pitcher on a long stainless steel table next to a glass-fronted medical-style cabinet which contained beakers, Erlenmeyer flasks, hydrometers, thermometers, and all of the other complicated testing equipment he needed to produce his secretly renowned rum. Max added his preferred strain of liquid yeast to the pitcher of juice to make a yeast starter that would grow for several hours until the crushing work was finished.

At the crusher, every hour or so Max and Josue traded jobs. Not so much to give the other man a break—each job was back-breaking work—but rather to split up the monotony of doing one thing for such a long period of time. Max could not believe the sun had not yet come up by the time they had filled the still with cane juice.

"Must be a new record or something," he said to Josue, who rubbed a knot in the thick muscle of his left shoulder. "We cut so much cane, I thought it'd be noon before we were done crushing. Not that I'm complaining..."

"You are animal, my friend," Josue said. "You work as ten men."

"Ten really old men," Max replied. "It's how I feel anyway."

Max and Josue descended a rustic wooden staircase built from the mouth-like cave opening in the yard to the smooth cavern floor. Halfway down, Josue flipped a switch on an electrical box attached to the porous rock of the cavern wall. An elaborate lighting grid, arranged throughout the entire subterranean distillery, flickered with bright fluorescent illumination that filled the entire cave with cool, even light.

Max reached the bottom step and approached the still. He used a chemical test kit to check the pH of the cane juice inside the copper still. He opened his black book and compared the results to previous batches. Then he jotted down some calculations.

Josue carried over several buckets of recently collected spring water, and he poured some into the small opening on top of the still. Max checked the pH level again, and added a bit more spring water. He did this three more times until satisfied the juice was not too basic and not overly acidic, and then he pitched the yeast.

The yeast would grow, feasting on the sugar in the juice, producing alcohol and burping off carbon dioxide gas for the next couple of days before the distilling process would begin.

"Thank God for that," Max said, slapping Josue on the back. "I don't know about you, but I think I need sleep. You might have to carry me upstairs."

Josue responded by rushing up the wooden steps as quickly as he could. *He'll be in bed before I even make it halfway up*, Max thought. *Lazy, lazy, lazy*. Max snorted awkwardly to himself. He was tired to an almost delirious level.

With an excessive amount of caution, Max connected a tripwire across the cavern, about a foot up from the floor, just off the bottom step. Then, he delicately pushed a button on a control panel next to the light switch. An indistinct red light flickered to life on the wall beside the glass-fronted cabinet. The slowly flashing light indicated an armed detonator attached to about forty pounds of C-4 plastic explosive hidden in the base of the cabinet. Should anyone come down the stairs looking for Max's illegal rum operation, they would, along with any trace of the subterranean distillery, suddenly cease to exist.

Max mounted the steps and reached the cavern's mouth, but was startled by a strange sound. The dense foliage around the villa typically teemed with life: squawking birds, clicking bugs, even the geckos would make a strange bird-like chirping sound from time to time.

But the air was still and silent as Max's head broke the surface and he climbed up to ground level. He searched all around him with a watchful gaze, but saw nothing.

Darkness enveloped him. Josue had switched off the sodium lamps on his way to bed. He likely had assumed Max would have been right behind him and not thought twice about cutting the lights.

As he stood in the middle of the yard behind the villa, Max listened. His senses felt prickly and alert. He turned his head, deliberately scanning the entire area for the rustling of a leaf, a stepped-on twig, an out-of-place motion.

Max observed for nearly ten minutes. And though he didn't spot anything out of the ordinary, Max knew full well: someone else was present, and they were watching his every move.

# CHAPTER 6

ESPITE HIS BODY'S PROTESTS, MAX'S senses told him
to wake up. He resisted as long he could, but the smell
of frying bacon assaulted his olfactory senses, and
forced him out of bed. He went downstairs and found Josue hard
at work in the kitchen.

"Smells good," Max said, rubbing his stubbly face with both
hands. "What is it?"

"Creole eggs," Josue said. He was wearing a black tank top
and shorts, and he had a white apron tied around his waist; he
looked like a line cook in a restaurant. All he needed was a really
tall hat.

What Max had thought was bacon turned out to be tasso.
The spicy and flavorful Creole ham sizzled in little cubes inside a
cast iron skillet on the stove. Josue was a dynamo in the kitchen,
sautéing, simmering, and chopping all at the same time. Max
wasn't sure where the enigmatic Haitian had learned to cook so
well, but he was thankful to be the beneficiary of the younger
man's skills.

Josue opened the freezer and pulled out two gallon-sized
freezer bags filled with crushed ice cubes. "Arm up, Boss," he said.
The quiet Haitian unrolled an Ace bandage, and then plunked the
first bag of ice on top of Max's left shoulder. Max cringed.

Josue wrapped the bandage around Max's arm in layers,
securing the ice pack in place before repeating the process on the
other side.

"I think we're about one bitter argument away from being considered an old married couple," Max said, slapping the other man on the back. "Thanks, Josue. Would you call me when breakfast is ready?'"

"Lunch," Josue corrected.

"Oh, jeez," Max said.

"Oh, Boss. I got text message few minutes ago. Serge say he dropped off box on dock."

"I'll get it," Max said, stretching out his arms to ensure he could still move them with his ice bags attached.

Max stepped through the kitchen door leading outside, to the rear of the villa. It was only about ten feet away from where he and Josue had crushed all of the sugarcane, the pile of spent stalks looming like a small mountain close by.

A path bordered by banana trees, tall palms, and dense low-growing foliage connected the villa to the long wooden pier at the south side of the island. The pier, with a wide boat dock on the end, was the lifeline that connected Max's island with the rest of the world. Built over the shallows close to the ilet, the lengthy white pier extended about fifty feet out to the deeper waters where a good-sized vessel could approach the ilet without grounding its outboard motors.

An arrangement Max had made with a grocer in Le Robert meant that a box full of eggs, cheese, fresh baguettes, milk, and cream, was delivered by boat to the dock, two times a week. It also contained whatever produce was fresh and available at the moment; Max always enjoyed the surprise of finding out what was in the box. It only cost him three bottles of Fleur de Lis rum per week.

Max stepped over to the corner of the dock to find the box overflowing with greens: kale, spinach, and arugula spilled out over the top of the box like a volcanic eruption of salad. He dug around inside and found some nice fingerling potatoes and heirloom tomatoes along with the usual stuff. He bent down and picked up the box. "Oof," he said, straining under the weight of the groceries, as his back and iced shoulders reminded him he wasn't eighteen anymore.

As he walked back to the kitchen, Max considered the effort he put into the production of Fleur de Lis rum. He cut the cane himself, crushed it, as well as doing the fermenting and distilling of the juice for every batch of rum he made going back to the very first one, nearly five years earlier. Each time, it took a toll. Recovery time took longer with each batch. Max wondered how much longer he could keep doing it.

Sure, he could hire others to do the manual labor. But Max knew it wouldn't be the same. As far as he was concerned, he needed to do the work himself, to put a little bit of himself into the process each time. This devotion to quality was what made his product special, and it was why people would seek it out every time.

At the end of the pier, Max's eye caught sight of something that stopped him short. The moist dirt near the end of the pier revealed several footprints quite clearly visible in the light of day. Max set down the box and inspected the prints. Close scrutiny showed the prints all had the same shoe style, and appeared to be all of the same size foot.

The foot was small. Max guessed about a size seven. *Or maybe it was about a nine in women's*, he thought.

Max had never seen anyone but Serge from Guillaume's Market dropping off the box of groceries on the dock. And he had never seen the hulking grocer take a single step further than necessary to drop off the box at the far end of the pier. And Serge de Bounevialle's foot was probably about a size fifteen.

*Why would a woman be snooping around my dock?* Max thought. *Where else on the ilet had she been? Had she seen the still?*

Max considered the previous night, the time just before he had gone to bed, with the startling stillness he had experienced around him. He followed the footsteps and discovered they faded away as the soil grew dryer and denser closer to the villa where more of the rocky foundation of the island showed through the earth.

Max's cell phone rang to life in his pocket, startling him. He hardly ever received calls. Max removed the smartphone and saw the name T.L. Wilkinson.

"Sorry, Terry," Max said to the phone, as he pressed the phone's lock button to reject the call. He slipped the phone back into his pocket. "Not today."

"You haven't seen anyone else on the ilet, have you?" Max asked, when he returned to the kitchen.

"No, why?" Josue sounded alarmed. It was out of character for him.

"Nothing. Just stay sharp, okay?"

"Of course."

Max and Josue sat down for a slow lunch to be savored and enjoyed. Their physical efforts over the previous thirty hours or so had taken a toll and would require a great deal of calories to replace the energy spent. They each consumed about six eggs, which were deliciously prepared with onions, peppers, celery, and the crispy tasso, and some hot sauce—along with a whole baguette each. Max had made a large French press full of coffee. He poured Josue a steaming cup, while he trickled his own over ice, before adding a generous splash of heavy cream.

After the replenishing meal, Max fell asleep in his master bedroom until well into the evening. Four Ibuprofen tablets had relaxed his aching back and shoulders just enough to allow him to drift back to sleep.

He awoke, sunken into the center of his queen-sized memory foam mattress, and parted the opening in the mosquito netting draped over the four bed posts. His room was nearly pitch dark.

Max switched on a lamp and let his eyes adjust to the room.

Tropical furniture decorated the large room: part of some sort of Hemingway collection he had ordered from back in the States. The room was orderly, impeccable. *Come a long way from the slob I was when I was married*, he thought. But his life was less complicated now, simple in its purpose.

He walked downstairs and stopped by the door to Josue's room. His young business partner lay sideways on his bed, reading a book in the shallow light from a small bedside lamp.

"Dinner?" Max asked.

Josue nodded.

"Le Homard Paresseux?"

The younger man nodded again.

Within minutes, the two were casting off Max's boat—a Cobia twenty-seven foot center console fishing boat—from the dock. Josue gave the boat some throttle and the twin 225hp outboards propelled the boat forward. The slender dark-skinned man wore black wraparound sunglasses despite the darkness, and the wind did nothing to muss his short, perfectly-trimmed afro.

Max made himself comfortable in the stern, leaning his left arm over the rail to touch the warm spray from the bow, and just enjoying the warm humid air of the evening.

The swift speedboat had proved to be a great way to travel around the island, often proving to be much faster than the roads. The exception would be traveling to the leeward side of Martinique. Max could drive from Le Robert to Fort de France in twenty minutes, while a boat trip would take an hour or so. That was why Max kept a car in Fort de France, one in Saint-Pierre, and another in Le Robert; nothing fancy, just reliable, economical Japanese imports. He also kept a couple of motorcycles and a pair of scooters parked in friends' sheds in various locales around the island. Not the priciest or fastest bikes he could find, but reliable, gassed-up, and always at the ready. Max wanted to be able to get anywhere on the island quickly, and in his business, he never knew when he might need to make a quick getaway.

A fifteen-minute boat ride took them around the Caravelle Peninsula, an area popular with hikers and tourists thanks to its mangrove paths and magnificent views of the ocean, a lighthouse, and the ruins of the seventeenth-century castle called Château Dubuc.

Josue directed the boat toward a beach adorned with the lights and all the activity of a bustling and lively village. He throttled down to an idle. Max grabbed a pair of night vision binoculars from a duffel bag and scanned the shoreline. It was a precaution, but Max knew the one time he failed to be vigilant would be the one time he got burned.

"Looks clear," Max said, and Josue throttled up until he reached the pier, almost identical to the one at his ilet.

Max helped Josue tie off to the pier and secure the boat. The beach at the town of Tartane was one of Max's favorite on Martinique. A lively little fishing community, it was popular with tourists on their way to see all the sights of the peninsula.

Max knew a few of the fishermen from the village, and as he and Josue walked the pier toward the beach, they passed some of their colorful skiffs, often called gumtrees, each bulging with heaping nets and tackle, as the boats rested for the night.

A quartet of musicians: a guitarist, a keyboardist, a djembe drummer, and an alto saxophonist performed what Max decided was their take on mini-jazz outside Le Homard Paresseux, a bustling seafood restaurant specializing in whatever the fishermen dragged in that day. Max threw a couple of Euros in the musicians' hat and Josue opened the door to the restaurant.

"Bon soir, bon soir, Maxwell," the host said. The guy had a craggy look about him that suggested he had grown up casting nets off one of the skiffs outside for decades before opening his restaurant. Now the man stood poised behind a podium, well-dressed in a bright yellow and white striped linen suit with a matching fedora. He embraced Max and kissed him on both cheeks, before doing the same to Josue.

"Bonjour, Alfred," Max said. "Any chance you've got a table for us? I know we should have called first... but we didn't."

"Of course, Maxwell. Un moment." Alfred gestured to one of his wait staff. In seconds Max and Josue were ushered through the crowded restaurant to a big round table in the corner, large enough for about six people. Max knew Alfred kept a table or two open for last-minute VIPs, and for whatever reason, he considered Max to be such a customer.

As Max sat down, sliding himself around the booth-style cushioned seat so that his back was to the wall, facing out into the middle of the bustling restaurant, he felt his breath catch in his throat, as he spotted Isobel Greer sitting two tables down, alone.

Max whispered a few words to Josue and then stood up to walk over to Isobel's table. He tugged on the tail of his black Columbia Bahama shirt to straighten it out as best he could. He looked down at his cargo shorts and flip flops. *Wish I'd known she'd be here*, Max thought. *I'd have worn a blazer, and maybe some long pants.*

Max walked past Isobel, who faced the front window of the restaurant; she seemed to be enjoying the musicians, even though she only saw their backs through the window. Max turned and smiled at Isobel. It took a few seconds for her to notice him.

Isobel's mouth gaped open. Her right hand gravitated toward her hair, and her left hand collected up the ridiculous oversized handbag she carried with her. "Max, right? What are you doing here?" she asked, sounding almost as if she were caught cheating on someone.

"Just dinner, with my business partner," Max said.

"I didn't see you at Maisie's yesterday," Isobel said, suddenly looking rather critical. "Or today. You said you go there every day."

"I'm sorry?"

Suddenly Isobel's countenance changed and she, despite her bright sunburn, began to turn even more red. "I hoped to see you there, but you weren't. At least not while I was there. I mean, I didn't wait *all* day. I just thought I would see you."

"I'm sorry, Isobel," Max said, nodding toward the empty chair across from Isobel. "May I?" Max sat down in the chair. "I shouldn't have told you I go in there every day, the day before the two odd days I wouldn't be there."

"Well, it wasn't as if we had a date, or anythin'," Isobel said, forcing a smile.

"I was... working. A busier workday than I expected, and I didn't make it off of my island all day."

"Your island?" Isobel asked, and he wasn't sure if she was really impressed or not. "I didn't know the life of a tropical Caribbean accountant was so demanding. If you're under so much stress, maybe you should unplug and move to a—oh wait—island or something."

Max was about to get up and go back to his table when Isobel laughed. "It's okay. I'm just playing with you, Max. Relax. Let's get some drinks. Oh, wait, you're with your friend. It's okay if you want to get back to your table. We can catch up another time."

"Would you like to join us?" Max asked. He stood up and offered his hand like a proper gentleman. "I'd love for you to meet my partner."

Max introduced Isobel to Josue, who nodded and stood up to shake her hand politely, before they all sat down around the big round table. "This is Josue," he said, as his friend slid over to make room for the Scottish substitute teacher.

"Did you say, Josue?" Isobel asked, staring blankly at Josue. Max noticed that she looked surprised, but couldn't tell how.

"Yeah, why?" he asked. "You know someone named Josue?"

"No," Isobel said with a wave of her hand. "It's just such an unusual name. Is that Cuban or Haitian or something?"

"Haitian. Josue made it to the states right after the earthquake in 2010. A refugee. I caught up with him in Miami, we partnered up, and we ended up here, in Martinique, eventually," Max said, intentionally avoiding the most delicate details of their past adventures.

"And what does he do for you?" Isobel asked; she twirled her blond hair around her finger as she spoke; it nearly mesmerized Max. "Is he in accounting too?"

"No," Max said with a chortle. "My villa requires a lot of upkeep. Josue just takes care of anything that needs to be done."

"So he's like a manservant or somethin'?"

"He is most definitely not my servant," Max said, sounding a bit more defiant than he had intended.

"I didn't mean it like that," Isobel said, looking at Josue. "Sounds like you're a very good friend. Max is lucky to have you on his side."

They ordered large platters of food with white rice, lentils, fried plantains, whole fried fish, shrimp, octopus, and lobster. Max carefully avoided the octopus; something about the suctioning tentacles had always sent an icy chill up his spine.

"If you'll excuse me, I'd like to go to the bar and get us some drinks," Max said, standing up and smoothing out his wrinkled nylon shirt.

Isobel and Josue nodded, and continued back to their deep conversation. *Good to see them hitting it off*, Max thought. He knew that if he liked a girl but she didn't get along with his partner, there was no going forward with any kind of relationship. He respected Josue that much. It was a relief to Max that things were already off on the right foot.

"Maxwell!" a loud and rather high-pitched man's voice greeted his ears, and Max spotted the bartender Smoky down at the end of the long and nearly overrun bar. Smoky was about Max's age, a shade over five feet tall, and he knew all there was to know about all the unique rums of Martinique. The petite bartender was a native of Tartane, and a person Max considered a trustworthy friend. Max eased himself into an empty space between patrons at the crowded bar and leaned forward, resting his elbows on the wood.

"How about three Neisson planter's punches? And then, in about fifteen minutes, could you send over three Rhumerie du Simon mojitos? And fifteen minutes after that, send out three JM V.S.O.P. Ti' Punches."

Smoky nodded. "Excellent choices, all. Hey, I'm glad I ran into you tonight, Maxwell. I wanted to tell you a woman came in looking for you earlier this evening."

"It's okay, Smoky," Max said, picking up a few cashews from a bowl on the bar. "I caught up with her already. She's sitting at my table with Josue now."

"The blonde?" Smoky asked, craning his neck to look past the throng to see Max's table in the corner of the busy restaurant. "No, no, no. This woman was black, maybe a meter eighty-two."

Max strained his brain to convert the numbers. *That'd be about six feet tall. Wow*, he thought.

"Beautiful, actually," Smoky continued, "but her makeup was kind of subdued and her hair, black, long, and curled, was tied into a ponytail in the back. Almost seemed she was trying to dumb down her obvious hotness."

"Hmmm," Max said, thinking back to the female footprints he had found near his dock. Too much of a coincidence to be coincidental.

"I think she was Martinican," Smoky said, putting a tiny folding umbrella into a drink for a female bar patron.

"What makes you think that?"

"She carried no bag or purse with her, and her clothes were no-nonsense, if you know what I mean. She didn't look like a tourist, and she wasn't dressed to impress anyone; more like just for comfort. Otherwise, she could have been a runway model. And I don't mean that in the exaggerated way people say that to describe a hot chick. This woman had all of those model features: long slender arms and legs, amazing eyes, curves in just the right places—she just didn't seem like she was using them."

"Did she say what she wanted with *me*?" Max asked, feeling a slight unease in his gut.

"No, she didn't say, Max. But she gave me twenty Euros to call her if you showed up here." Smoky laughed. "She thought I would give you up for twenty." Smoky mixed pineapple juice, orange juice, and freshly squeezed lime juice in a shaker as he talked. "You know where my loyalties lie, Max."

"Thanks very much, Smoky. You're a good friend." Max peeled two hundred Euros off his money clip and handed them to the bartender.

Smoky showed Max his palms and shook his head. "Not tonight my friend. I will not take your money for the information. And the drinks are all on me."

Max knew Smoky was just trying to prove to Max it wasn't money that made him a loyal friend. It was one of the reasons Max kept coming back to this crowded restaurant, when he would have rather been at home eating takeout in front of the TV.

"I've got two bottles of Fleur de Lis élevé sous bois in my boat. I'll make sure you get them before I shove off," Max said, as Smoky pushed a small serving tray with three planter's punches toward Max, who picked up the tray.

"Those I will accept," Smoky said, his face lighting up with a huge grin.

Max, Josue, and Isobel enjoyed the local spirits, fresh seafood, and lively company well into the small hours of the morning. Max and Isobel talked for hours, and he felt as though the more she revealed about herself, the more about her he wanted to know. It had been a long time since he had liked someone so much, and somehow, it almost hurt him, deep down.

Before heading back to his villa, Max promised he would meet Isobel at Maisie's for lunch later in the day, and he made certain to get Smoky the bottles of well-aged rhum agricole from his boat. To avoid causing a frenzy among the few patrons left at the restaurant, Max wrapped a jacket around the bottles to conceal them, until Smoky had safely stowed them behind the bar.

Max kissed Isobel on the cheek. She smiled and hugged his neck tightly. Josue held out his hand for a shake, and Isobel hugged him as well.

As they headed back to the ilet, Max asked Josue if he had ever seen a six-foot tall Martinican woman poking around their island. "Apparently she is quite beautiful, and she sounds rather no-nonsense. If you see her, would you tell me?"

Josue nodded. "And if *you* see her, will you send her to find me as quickly as possible?"

Max grinned and pushed away from the dock with his foot. Despite the questions raised in Max's mind about the mysterious Martinican woman who was looking for him, it had been a good night.

# CHAPTER 7

M
AX SNAPPED AWAKE AS SOON as he heard the TV. The flat screen's alarm was set to wake him up every morning at six. After crawling out of bed, Max typically did some pushups, jogged around the rugged terrain of the island, or took out his sea kayak for an invigorating paddle around the ilet. Feeling the residual effects of the previous night's drinks, Max now cursed himself for not having turned off the alarm before dropping into bed.

The channel was always set to West Indies Media Network, and he usually woke up to the audio from in-depth stories about various rum producers in both the Greater and Lesser Antilles, as well as puff-pieces about yachting, skin diving, and fishing in a variety of locales throughout the Caribbean. The network offered typical lightweight newsworthy stuff; it tended to represent much about why living in the Caribbean was so appealing.

It was the tone of the presenter that startled Max, waking him up from his deathly slumber. The drinks had left him slightly hungover, and staying up so late had made him feel groggy and weak. The soreness in his muscles from the cane harvest and all of the crushing still ached deeply in his back, shoulders, and thighs. Despite his mind telling him he could do it and be okay, the reality was, pushing himself so hard over age forty was starting to take a toll.

"… a lot of blood," the female presenter's voice said urgently from the small speakers on the TV. "But, mysteriously, no bodies have yet been found."

Max pried his head up from his pillow. It felt like a dead lift of more weight than he could handle just to get his body upright so he could look straight at the TV. With the curtains closed, the room was very dark, except for the bright, pixelated glow from the television.

He squinted, his eyes struggling to focus on the face of the woman speaking earnestly into the microphone in her hand.

Max rubbed his eyes and blinked about ten times.

"The fifty-five foot Viking yacht is called *Plan B*, and is registered to Jacques Troy Miller, a resident of Grand Cayman. Mr. Miller and his wife, Susan Miller, are co-owners of a popular beach bar called Suzy's Hurricane Hideout on Grand Cayman, and a spokesperson from the bar told West Indies Media Network that Mr. Miller and his wife had been traveling from Trinidad and Tobago to the Bahamas, stopping at as many islands as possible along the way to purchase new and unique rums to serve at their bar. Strangely, no rum was found on board the *Plan B*, leading authorities to believe that Miller and his wife may have become the ill-fated victims of robbery gone very wrong; an unfortunately all-too-real case of piracy in the Caribbean."

Max stumbled out of bed. His forehead burned with feverish heat brought on by a shock cocktail of fear, misbelief, and horror. Clammy beads of perspiration covered his face. *Was this really happening?*

Max tried to stand up, but he tripped and fell, face forward, onto the ground. He picked himself up and shuffled across the hardwood of the master suite's floor. He kicked open the bathroom door.

Max stepped inside and dropped to his knees. For a fleeting second he thought the nausea might pass. Then he lifted the toilet seat, and retched violently and uncontrollably into the bowl.

# CHAPTER 8

MAX STUMBLED DOWN THE LONG pier toward the boat dock when he heard the rumbling sound of outboard motors approaching. His feet shuffled over the grip tape placed on the white boards to prevent slipping as he wobbled his way to the end. Clear turquoise water surrounded the pier, and one could see the coral and the starfish no more than a few feet under the surface of the clear water. Max stumbled on, feeling numb and lifeless.

Josue stepped off the Cobia. Max remembered buying the boat in Miami; he had chosen a paint scheme called Atlantic Blue, and it now served almost as camouflage against the sparkling blue of the Atlantic ocean. Max staggered to reach Josue, to tell him what had happened.

Max's gut twisted as he saw Josue reach toward the boat and offer a hand to Isobel, who was stepping down onto the dock. He didn't want her to see him like this. Haggard, unkempt, heartsick and in mourning.

Isobel spotted Max. She hurried over to him, jogging the length of the pier. "What is it? Are you all right?" Her big eyes looked up at him with deep sadness. It was one of the most stunning sights he had ever seen.

"Something's happened," Max said, staring off the side of the dock into nothing. "Something terrible. It's not a good time for you to be here, Isobel."

"I'm sorry," she said, her cheeks reddening. "I only wanted

to surprise you, maybe take you out to breakfast or something." She frowned and crossed her arms, looking awkward. "I shouldn't have come."

"May I have a word with Josue?" Max asked Isobel. "Alone?"

"Of course," she said. She sounded like she was trying to be understanding. "It is *your* island."

Max walked halfway up the path to the villa with Josue. Then he stopped and faced his friend. "Jacques and Susan are dead. That couple you met on our drop the other night. They've been killed... for the rum."

Josue's lips curled into a frown. He was not one to express a lot of feelings, but Max saw the concern in his eyes. "I'm sorry, Max. Let's get you inside and get you some tea."

Josue walked side-by-side with Max all the way to the front porch of the villa. The younger man made sure Max was comfortable in a cushioned arm chair before going into the kitchen to put on the tea kettle.

"Would you take her back to land?" Max asked. "Don't tell her what happened, just tell her I'll catch up with her tomorrow at Maisie's. I just can't... be around her right now."

"I run into her in town, Boss," Josue said by way of an explanation for Isobel's presence. "She beg me to bring her out here. She wanted to see you very badly. Can't you let her stay?"

"No, you're right, Josue. She should stay." Max considered what a great thorny wall he could put up in order to keep the world out. He liked this girl, and he could tell that she liked him. "Why don't you show her around a bit. I'll go get cleaned up and meet you two on the porch, okay?"

After a hot shower and shave, Max put on a clean black shirt, carefully buttoning down the sleeves over his wrists, and a pair of black pants. He slipped tan leather huaraches over his feet and secured his Bulova diving watch over his wrist. He even slapped a bit of Polo Sport on his neck and slicked his mussy black hair with gel. For a moment, Max sat on his bed and he stared off into the corner. He fought tears again as he saw his friends' faces in his mind. His throat was dry and it was difficult for him to swallow. He would never see their faces again.

As soon as he stepped out onto the porch, Isobel stood up from her chair. "I'm sorry, I shouldn't have just come out here without asking you, Max. You don't have to tell me anything if you don't want to."

"My friends from college," Max said, his voice at first sounding hoarse. Josue handed him a steaming mug of tea from a tray. Max took a good sip. "Jacques and Suze. They were on a yacht. They were cruising up to the Bahamas."

"Oh, no," Isobel said, her facing growing pale, as if all the blood had suddenly left it. "It wasn't that couple everyone's been talking about? The *Plan B* or something?"

Max nodded.

"I'm so sorry," Isobel said. She threw her arms around his neck, and tears welled up in her sparkling eyes. She pulled a bright pink scarf out of her large handbag and rubbed her face with it.

"It means a lot to me that you care so much about my friends you didn't even know," Max said, putting down his tea and wrapping his arms around Isobel.

She wiped her face again with the scarf. "I must look like a wreck," she said.

"Actually," Max said, holding her chin up to get a better look at her face. "You look amazing." His mind tossed back and forth about whether he should show her his rum-making operation; whether he should let her into his world.

"What is it?" Isobel asked, and in her bright blue-green eyes, Max saw a mixture of sorrow, concern, and pity. "You look like you want to say something."

"I don't know how, or even if I *should*," Max said.

"Does it have anything to do with this?" Isobel said. She lifted the front of Max's shirt by his left hip. He instinctively moved his hand down to swat hers away, but he stopped himself.

"What are you doing?" he protested, half-heartedly.

She uncovered the Smith & Wesson 6906 tucked into a holster, just inside his waistband. "Accounting is dangerous work, Max? Isn't it?"

"I..." Max started, but was cut off by Isobel.

"You don't have to tell me anything more than you want to, Max," she said. "I have a secret too: I seem to have an unending penchant for gravitating toward dangerous men. And while I can tell you are a dangerous man, Maxwell Craig—maybe I'm really stupid for this—but I trust you."

Max was silent. He didn't know what to say.

"Only a good man would have helped Angelique the way you did. Maybe it was not the most proper, most legal way to help her, but you helped her. You did what needed to be done, and she has peace now. You're a good man, Maxwell."

"Can I show you something?" Max asked, covering his pistol back up with his shirt.

"Sure," Isobel said, before blowing her nose into a tissue that Josue had handed her, "if it's something good."

Max led her by the hand through the villa, stepping into the kitchen and out the back door. The first thing she noticed was the gas-powered sugarcane crusher, and the massive pile of flattened spent cane.

"What's all this?" she asked.

"It's a sugarcane crusher," Max said, "and these are all the canes that me and Josue crushed the night before last."

"What did you do that for?" Isobel asked, sounding genuinely ignorant about what he was talking about. "Are you going to make sugar or somethin'?"

"Remember when I told you about rhum agricole, and how it is the only rum made out of fresh sugarcane juice, most others being made from molasses?"

Isobel nodded. "You make rum?"

Max nodded. "I make rum. But I don't have approval to make AOC rhum agricole Martinique. My island is not one of the designated cane growing areas, and I don't expressly follow all of their rules. And also, they don't know my operation exists, and I don't pay taxes on my product sales either."

"So, you're like a rum-making outlaw," she said, sounding a bit intrigued.

Max smiled. As empty as he felt at the loss of his friends, this woman shone like a ray of bright sunshine in his heart.

Max led Isobel out to the field of sugarcane, growing almost wild among the other foliage of the ilet, and occupying about half of Max's total property. "There're about three acres of cane here; maybe two and a half since our recent cuttings. Some of it was already growing here when I bought the place, Josue and I planted the rest. The ground is rocky and uneven here, so the idea of harvesting the cane with a tractor is unthinkable. Josue and I harvested all of that cane by hand."

"What did you cut it with?" she asked, sounding interested in the process.

"I use a machete, Josue uses what's called a cane knife. You want to see where the juice ended up?"

Max escorted Isobel down the staircase into his subterranean distillery. He flipped on the lights, and her face lit up as she saw the still for the first time. Her eyes gazed, childlike, as she took in the sight of all of the copper and brass, the tubes, pipes and valves.

"It's like a steampunk time machine, or something out of Willy Wonka," she said with a laugh.

*I knew there was a reason I liked this girl*, Max thought.

Max explained that he was keeping an eye on the cane juice's fermentation progress, and that he would likely begin the distillation process the following morning. The five hundred or so gallons of juice would yield only three barrels of rum. He would age the rum in barrels purchased from a Scotch whisky distillery that had shuttered its doors after two hundred years of business.

"Scotch whisky, you say?" Isobel said, beaming with pride. "I knew there was a reason I liked you."

That was part of the secret to the unique finished product that Max produced; the French oak barrels, once saturated with maturing Scotch, now filled with rhum agricole, yielded a finished product with a distinctive flavor unlike any other.

Max drove Isobel back to her hotel in Tartane on his boat just before sunset. Before heading back to his ilet, the two had dinner at a beach bar where the proprietor grilled lamb chops on a huge outdoor grill, his face lighting up with the blazing orange glow every time the fire flared up. Max caught himself staring into the fire from time to time, burdened by thoughts of Jacques and Susan. But he snapped himself back to the present, doing his best to enjoy his time with the sweet Scottish school teacher.

Max walked Isobel to her hotel and kissed her goodnight. Then he made his way back to the fishing village's pier and fired up his boat for the short leisurely trip back home.

As he neared Ilet d'Ombres, Max acted on a hunch. Rather than driving straight for the dock, he switched off his running lights as he drew close to the small island. He powered the motors down to a relatively quiet rumble and circumnavigated the ilet with purpose, scanning the island through the Armasight night vision binoculars he kept in his duffel bag.

Max spotted a dinghy—a small inflatable raft with a forty or so horsepower outboard tiller motor, tied off to the rocky north shore of the island—on the opposite side of the ilet as Max's boat dock.

*Doesn't get more suspicious than that*, Max thought. He pulled out his smartphone and called Josue.

"Yes?" came the urgent reply.

"There's someone poking around our ilet, Josue. I would like you to quietly and quickly position yourself at the northern end of the island, and keep your eyes open for anything."

"Sure thing, boss," Josue said.

"Do it now," Max said, an unmistakable sense of urgency in his voice.

He docked the boat and walked toward his villa, trying to keep his gait nonchalant. His senses were alive—he had no idea what kind of trouble he was about to encounter—but he was ready for it.

As he reached the end of the pier, Max noticed the island had fallen back into that strange quiet that suggested something was out of the ordinary.

Max walked toward the villa, slower than usual. He detoured from the front door, instead walking around to the back. He stepped right up to the edge of the cavern opening, where the still was located, and stood there for several minutes. He pulled a Cuban cigar from his duffel bag and clipped off the end before roasting the tip, and puffing the cigar until it blazed to life.

Another moment passed, and Max heard a woman gasp in the thick foliage somewhere to his left. He could not suppress a smile.

# CHAPTER 9

**M**OMO, TINY DEEGE, AND ZANN all sat, crowded around the tiny computer desk in Reggie's room, inside Mama Dorah's house on Lemon Street. The small space, packed with so much junk and so many people, gave Momo claustrophobic pangs of panic, and for a moment, he actually considered leaving the room, despite Mama Dorah's insistence that he stay.

"Yo, what is all this crap?" Zann said, jerking his head from left to right, a half-empty bottle of Cristal dangling from his hand between his legs. He adjusted his thick-rimmed glasses and scanned the cluttered room. "Makes me feel nervous, just bein' in here."

"Would you rather go sit in the living room?" Tiny Deege asked suspiciously. Momo remembered the gutted cat and tried to hold back the involuntary shudder that started at his neck, and worked its way down to his right foot.

A small workbench stood near the door, cluttered with a soldering iron, several pairs of small pliers, partially-built circuit boards, along with all manner of other electronics parts and tools. An end table had a variety of gaming consoles stacked one on top of the other, nearly to the ceiling, while an entire corner of the room appeared to contain their various controllers, power cables, and boxes and boxes of game cartridges and disks. Three or four computers in various stages of repair sat on the floor by the unkempt bed, and posters of *Black Ops* and *Grand Theft Auto* were carefully tacked to the wall.

"Yo, Reggie, my man," Momo said to Reggie, who presently occupied the chair at the computer desk directly in front of the thirty-inch monitor. The kid was eighteen years old, and he was Mama Dorah's nephew, which gave Momo enough reason to exercise caution around him. "I gotta ask you somethin'." Momo looked over his shoulder to make certain no one was watching by the door.

"Yeah, what?" Reggie asked, not looking up from the display. Momo noticed he was missing an eyebrow, likely a workshop accident, since the kid loved tinkering with soldering irons and propane torches and stuff.

"Is Mama Dorah's deal for real? You know, that thing she do with the cat and the incense and all that."

"Yeah," Reggie said, adjusting his round silver-rimmed glasses. "It's real."

"It voodoo?" Zann asked, looking over his shoulder as well, although Momo didn't know if he was scared of Mama Dorah or the boogeyman. Zann took a long drink from his bottle of expensive Champagne.

"No, not voodoo," Reggie said. "She always calls it *the sight*, so I reckon that's what it is."

"*The sight*?" Tiny Deege repeated. Now it was his turn to give a shudder. "Don't know why you gotta go and gut out a cat."

"Tell me what she said," Reggie said, looking from one face to the next, finding each one looking more uncomfortable than the next.

"She said somethin' 'bout a mountain top blowin' off its stack," Momo said, recalling the terrifying moment when Mama Dorah had revealed her "prophecy" or whatever it was.

"Sound like a volcano or some such thing," Tiny Deege said, pulling a blunt out of his pocket and sticking it in his mouth.

"Please don't smoke in here," Reggie said.

"What you gon' do 'bout it, chump?" Tiny Deege said, sounding like he might punch young Reggie in the face.

"It's not me," Reggie said meekly. "Mama Dorah doesn't like it."

Tiny Deege stuffed the blunt back in his pocket quicker than Momo had ever seen anyone do anything. "Whyn't you just say that, little man," Tiny Deege said, patting Reggie on the back. "No problem. No problem."

"She said there was like thirty thousand people got boiled in their skin or some sick stuff like dat," Zann said. "Look it up, Reggie. Look for a volcano done killed like thirty thousand geezers, boiled 'em in their skin."

Reginald punched the details into a search engine and waded through the results. One hundred thousand killed in Indonesia in 1815. Twenty thousand killed in Colombia.

"What else she say?" Momo asked the group. "We need more details to refine the search."

"Whoa, whoa, whoa, whoa," Zann said, tossing his empty bottle onto the floor of Reggie's room, where it rolled over to join other trash such as Twinkie wrappers, wadded-up McDonald's bags, and empty Big Gulp cups. "Hold onto the phone, ya'll. Mama Dorah say somethin' 'bout the Christian God? Somethin' 'bout going up to heaven or some such?"

"Ascension Day?" Momo asked. "Was she talking about Ascension Day?"

"Yo, what dat?" Tiny Deege asked. He picked up a Star Wars action figure from Reggie's computer desk and began playing with it, making it fire its tiny blaster at Zann's crotch.

"Ascension Day," Momo said. "It celebrates the day when Jesus wen' up to heaven. After he been crucified. Plug it in, Reggie. See what we got."

"Volcano, Ascension Day, thirty thousand people killed," Reggie spoke as he typed.

"Mount Pelée?" Zann asked. "Where dat?"

"Martinique," Momo said, reading over Reggie's shoulder. "The mountain erupted in 1902. Says that a pyroclastic flow rolled down the mountain into the densely-populated city of Saint-Pierre. Superheated steam, volcanic gases, and dust raced down into the town at over four hundred miles per hour, covering the entire city in a two-thousand-degree cloud, killing everyone in minutes."

Zann's body shivered.

"So what Mama Dorah be sayin' is that Josue is on the island of Martinique?" Tiny Deege asked, placing the action figure back down on the desk.

"Sounds like we goin' to Martinique, boys." Momo said. "How we goin' get there, though?"

"We could fly?" Zann said.

"Ain't nobody can fly, Zann," Tiny Deege said, finding a Han Solo blaster on the floor and holding it up to Reggie's head.

"Tiny Deege, you wasted," Zann said. "We take a plane. You ever heard of a plane befo'?"

Tiny Deege started laughing. It was the kind of laugh only uttered by a drunk person when even the slightest hint of a joke struck one as the funniest words ever uttered.

"You will rent a boat, and you will travel together to the island, where you will kill Josue Remy!" The booming voice from the doorway caught everyone off guard, and a collective gasp erupted from the entire group. It was Mama Dorah. It was hard to say how long she had been watching the proceedings, but Momo felt a cold chill merely at the woman's presence.

"We ain't got passports," Momo said.

"Reginald will help you apply for your passports, and you will follow his instructions to rent the boat you will take to the island," Mama Dorah said sternly.

"Why don't we just fly?" Zann asked, sounding meek, as if he worried he might be smote down at any moment.

"You will take a boat," Mama Dorah reiterated. "It will be much easier for you to smuggle your weapons from here to Martinique. It would be almost impossible if you took a plane."

"Okay, Mama Dorah," Momo said. "We'll go, an' we'll finish off Josue."

"Yes," Mama Dorah said, the fire back into her eyes as before. "You will do it, or you will never lead Ti Flow. You will kill Josue Remy, or you should not come back here again, lest you face my wrath."

# CHAPTER 10

M AX RAN TOWARD THE STRUGGLE, still holding onto his cigar. He fumbled in his pocket for the small yet powerful LED flashlight he had taken from his duffel bag. He clicked it to life, and the cool bright beam cut a wide swath through the darkness, illuminating his way forward through the thick green growth of the ilet.

Max's phone rang in his pocket. He quickly checked it as he stepped through the jungle-like tangle of foliage. T.L. Wilkinson. *Not now, Terry,* Max thought, as he rejected the call, and silenced the phone.

Max had almost reached the rocky northern shore of the island, when he encountered a tall black woman in a black tank top and jeans. He bathed her in the light from the flashlight. The woman *was* quite beautiful, Max decided, though she also looked like she was trying hard to maintain an ordinary countenance. Smoky was right.

Closer inspection revealed that the woman wore Josue's right arm like a scarf around her neck. Her left arm was twisted behind her back; Max would have ventured a guess that Josue held it in a tight vise-like grip. She would be completely incapacitated.

"What are you doing here?" Max asked. "This is private property."

"I got lost," the woman said, her accent sounding French Creole, as if she was Martinican, as Smoky had surmised. "Do you have a phone I can borrow?"

"What are you doing on my island?" Max asked again. "Who are you working for?"

The woman appeared indignant.

"You're not going to say?" Max asked. He stared coldly into the woman's eyes and tugged hard on his cigar, and its tip burned to a brightly glowing orange. He exhaled a cloud of smoke.

"What are you going to do?" the woman said with defiance. Max could tell she was fighting hard to sound unafraid. *Strong woman*, he thought. *Brave.* "Try to burn it out of me?"

Max appeared taken aback. He hadn't even considered such a thing. He dropped the cigar and stomped it underfoot. "Of course not. I wouldn't hurt a woman. But what you tell me will decide whether you go home or if you spend the rest of the night in a jail cell."

The woman struggled to get free, and Josue instinctively tightened his grip on her throat. "Okay, okay," the woman said, gasping for breath and sounding rattled. "My name is Vivienne Monet. I am a private investigator."

"Who's your client?" Max reiterated.

"I was hired by the president of one of the rhum agricole distilleries on the island," Vivienne said, "La Maison de Verre."

Max nodded at Josue, who released the private investigator from his grip.

"Why?" Max asked.

"He wanted to know if you were producing rum here," Vivienne said, rubbing her long, elegant throat. "He is angry that your product has become so popular around the islands when you are not a legitimate producer; he feels threatened by you. He wanted me to find out everything I could about your operation."

"I found this," Josue said, holding up a digital SLR camera, which had been slung over his shoulder by its strap. He tossed it to Max.

Max turned it on and toggled through the pictures. There

were photos of Max, Josue, the villa from nearly every angle, the cane field, the cavern opening. What shocked Max most though were the close-up shots of his still, his mineral water spring, and his laboratory.

"How did you get these?" Max asked Vivienne. "Don't you know my distillery is booby-trapped with about forty pounds of C-4? How is it you, and my whole operation, haven't completely caved in?"

"I was cautious going in, Maxwell," Vivienne said. It was weird that she used his name. He almost felt as if she knew him well, and the sentiment was not mutual. He didn't like it. "The bomb's flashing red light was easy enough to spot, right there, on the wall. So was the trip wire used to arm it. What did you use, piano wire? I was able to see it without my flashlight even. You should think about using a more discreet security system in the future."

"I'll take that under advisement," Max said, feeling betrayed at having his illegal rum operation scrutinized so meticulously. He began deleting the photos off Vivienne's camera.

"No, don't!" she shouted. "I need those. Do you know how many hours of investigation those represent? How am I going to get paid for the job now?"

"A good investigator wouldn't have been caught snooping." Max said.

"You're right," Vivienne admitted. "It was not my best work."

"I'll let you go, but you can't come back here again," Max said.

Vivienne Monet rolled her neck around and looked at Josue, who stood like a ghost amongst a row of guava trees. "I never heard you coming until your arm was around my neck. And once you'd gotten hold of me there was nothing I could do to get free. You are like a jaguar in the jungle. I could use a guy like you—"

"Goodbye, Vivienne," Max said, handing the private investigator her camera. "You're not poaching my best man away from me."

Vivienne stumbled over an unearthed root sticking out of the ground as she took the camera from Max. She grabbed onto his shoulder to right herself. Max put his hands on her hips to steady her.

"Your best man?" Vivienne said with a short laugh, shaking Max's hands off her torso. "He's your only man. You two should think about hiring a few more men. I watched you cutting sugarcane, Maxwell. I almost called for a medic."

Max couldn't help but smile. Despite the fact that Vivienne Monet had walked all over his private land, uninvited, and had intended to give away all of his secrets, he got a kick out of her. He liked that she was cute and playful despite the fact that she was obviously determined and strong.

"Boss," Josue said, "she knows everything about our operation. She tells someone, we're likely going to jail."

"I didn't know you could talk," Vivienne said.

"So what do you think we should do, Josue? Kill her?" Max intended to sound sarcastic, because to him, it was a ridiculous suggestion. "If she turns us in, I guess we're going to jail, because we're letting her go."

"A real gentleman," Vivienne said.

"By the way, Viv," Max said. "May I call you that?" He held the light from the bright LED flashlight on her chest to keep from blinding her. "Sorry about the cigar. I didn't mean for you to think I'd hurt you with it."

"I must admit, I was a bit scared for a moment," she said, placing her hand on her hip. "But you don't have that look."

"What look?" Max asked.

"That dark look a man has in his eyes, when he is a man who likes to hurt women," Vivienne said. "Believe me, I've seen it quite a lot."

"Thanks for saying so," Max said.

"A tip, Maxwell," she said, checking her camera, before

slinging the strap over her shoulder. "In the business you are in, don't ever tell anyone what you won't do. I might know now that you are a nice guy, but I also now know a place where you are weak. And if it came to it, I just might exploit it."

"Thanks for the tip, Viv. Honestly, I am really glad to have met you. I hope we meet again, but not when you're snooping on me."

Vivienne disappeared through the dense plant life near the northern end of Max's property, where he had earlier seen the dinghy. He heard her boat motor start up, and then wind up loudly as the small craft motored away from the ilet.

"Boss," Josue said, in the matter-of-fact way that he said everything, "my wallet is gone."

Max slapped his hand to his back pocket. "Mine too!"

The two ran toward the villa, rushing into Max's accounting office, where he threw back one of his bookcases. It swung forward on hinges, revealing a small room, just behind. "I've got the Benelli, you get the Mini 30," Max said. The two grabbed the weapons and headed toward the dock. Max hoped he had enough time to run her down in his Cobia before she reached land.

"Don't shoot her," Max said, checking to make sure the twelve gauge was loaded with shells, "we just want to give her a good scare. I think she has that coming, don't you?"

Max ran toward the dock clutching his semi-automatic Benelli M4 shotgun, and he chambered a shell as he charged toward the dock. Josue clipped a magazine into the Mini 30 as he jogged beside Max. They had nearly reached the pier when they spotted the police boat driver casting off his stern line as Colonel Travere stepped onto the pier, sixty or seventy feet away, illuminated by the solar-charged lights attached to each piling, lighting up the full length of the pier.

Max stopped running and handed his twelve gauge to Josue. "Get these back in the villa, but be discreet about it. I'll go talk to the gendarme and see what he wants. I'll try to get rid of him quickly."

"Right, Boss," Josue said, holding the weapons in front of his body to conceal them as he walked back toward the villa.

Max continued forward toward the dock as if he were intending to welcome the inspector to his island. "Colonel Travere? Good to see you," Max said, putting on a forced smile and stepping directly toward the commander of the gendarmerie on Martinique. He extended his hand toward the colonel for a shake. "Welcome to Ilet d'Ombre. What brings you out here at this late hour, Colonel?" Max asked.

"Trevor," Colonel Travere said to the boat driver, "hand me that bag." Max recognized the man in the police boat to be the guy who had held the bullhorn while Max was fleeing the police Zodiac while driving the stolen speedboat, *The Cash Settlement*. He hoped Trevor would not recognize him.

"I picked this up in town, and I could not think of anyone else I would rather drink it with than you," Colonel Travere said, pulling the brown paper bag away from a bottle. He held it up so that one of the dock's solar lights caught the tawny liquid inside, and Max was able to read the label.

"Trois Rivières single cask, bottled in 2006," Colonel Travere said proudly.

Max had had a very long couple of days, and his patience was getting to that place where it was about to run out. It made him worried about what he might do. "Colonel, at the risk of sounding rude, I have to ask. What are you really doing here?"

"I bought this in town after work and thought you might want to share it with me, before I head home to have dinner with my wife." Colonel Travere suddenly looked like he might actually be embarrassed. "Was this a bad time for me to come? I can go right now."

"No, Colonel," Max said. "Please, come up to the villa. I've got glasses and maybe we can rustle up some snacks as well."

Max led Colonel Travere through the front double doors to the villa. They walked the main hallway, past the spare room where Max kept all of his scuba tanks, spear guns, and other skin diving gear, toward the sitting room where Max had a bar set up with glasses and a fridge.

As they walked the hall, Travere apparently noticed the light on in Max's office, and he gravitated toward it like a bug. He must have been overcome by that natural curiosity every law enforcement officer was apparently born with.

"The bar is this way, Colonel," Max said.

"Please, call me Edgar," Colonel Travere said. "Is this your office?" The colonel had taken a step inside the cluttered office and his eyes scanned the room. "So this is where you do all of your accounting? I suppose there are worse places in the world that one can be an accountant."

Max noticed that the last bookcase on the wall was still pulled partway forward. If Colonel Travere, Edgar, was to walk over and look, he would see a small room with dozens of pegs secured to the wall, each one holding a pistol, a shotgun, a scoped rifle, a submachine gun. It was very likely that Edgar Travere would take one look inside and arrest Max and Josue on the spot.

"Can I see the bottle?" Max asked.

"Certainly," Travere said, passing the long bottle to Max.

Max scrutinized the label. "These single barrel offerings are pretty special, aren't they?" he said.

"I find that single cask spirits tend to be a bit hit or miss, but so far the Trois Rivières offerings have been excellent." Travere's eyes fixated on Max's desk. His policeman's eyes scanned every article on the desk like a laser.

Max wasn't worried. He had placed every pen, every manila folder, every scrap of paper on the desk to give the illusion it was the messy desk of an accountant who had just stopped for the day with several items in progress.

"Some of these bottles are very old," Colonel Travere said, scrutinizing the half-dozen antique rum bottles which decorated Max's desk. "J. Bally 1952? Clemént, what is this from the 1930s? These are sealed, Maxwell. What are you saving them for?"

"They're just bottles I picked up in shops around the island. I thought they'd make interesting conversation pieces. I never really thought about drinking them."

Travere shook his head as if he were dumbfounded. The gendarme had the bug, that was for sure. Rhum agricole was his drug, and he was a hardcore junkie.

"What is *this*?" the colonel asked, sounding suspicious.

"What?" Max said, maybe a bit too loudly and forcibly. *Be cool*, Max. But Max knew he could not hurt Colonel Travere. If it came down to it, Max would go quietly. He would yell to Josue to give him a sporting chance to get away, but Max could not hurt someone as decent as Colonel Edgar Travere.

"You have an entire box of Don Legado cigars on your desk," Travere said, sounding disgusted. "These are crap, Max. I'll make sure to get you something decent for your desk, some Davidoff's, perhaps some Cubans. Can't have you smoking this Dominican trash. Not that Dominican cigars are bad, some of my favorites hail from the D.R., but these, I wouldn't let my dog smoke these."

"Thanks, Colonel—Edgar," Max said, trying to sound genuinely grateful. "I'm not much of a cigar smoker, so I suppose it was the packaging that appealed to me in the cigar shop."

"What's this?" Travere said, facing the bookshelf which stood askew.

"Oh, Josue and I moved it earlier. We were looking for a mouse that scurried behind it," Max lied.

"A mouse? You have mice on your island? I did not think there were any mice on Martinique."

"Hmmm," Max said, not quite sure how to respond.

"Perhaps it was one of the species of rat that live on the island," Colonel Travere said. "I mean, I am no expert on such things, but I did a bit of research on the wildlife of the island when my wife and I were first considering moving here. I wanted to know what sort of pests and predators might be a problem were I to grow any kind of crops on our land. Here, I will help you put back the bookshelf."

"Help!" Josue's manic, terrified-sounding voice resounded from the kitchen.

Max and Colonel Travere both ran toward the commotion, finding the four-burner stove in the kitchen completely engulfed in flames. Apparently Josue had set some hot canola oil in a pan to heat up when he accidentally bumped the pan and spilled its hot flammable contents onto the gas burner's open flame.

Max rushed out to his shed and grabbed a thirty-pound $CO_2$ fire extinguisher, and in no time, the leaping flames were snuffed out. Thick black smoke spread throughout the villa like phantom fingers creeping from one room to the next.

"I took out some frozen beignet dough to thaw," Josue said, sounding embarrassed. "I was going to make some for a snack. I was careless with pan of oil. Sorry about that, Boss."

"It's okay now," Max said, slapping Josue on the back. "Colonel, this is my good friend, Josue. He takes care of my house and works as my assistant."

Colonel Travere shook Josue's hand. "Pleased to meet you, Josue."

"Say, why don't we grab some glasses and take our drinks out onto the porch?" Max suggested. "Where it's a bit less smoky."

As they walked out behind the gendarmerie colonel, Max whispered to Josue. "Good thinking with the kitchen fire."

Josue flashed his white teeth in a grin.

Max, Colonel Travere, and Josue sat on the cushioned rattan

chairs at the front porch of the villa, smoking the colonel's last three Cohiba cigars, which he had pulled out of a leather cigar sleeve, and finished off the bottle of single cask rum. It had some nice notes of honey, tobacco, and licorice and a very smooth finish.

Travere mostly talked about his inherited plot of land near Saint-Marie. He actually talked a lot less about Max and his illicit rum-making operation than Max would have suspected. Still, Max could not help but wonder just what was the colonel's game.

"I've taken up quite enough of your time this evening," Travere said, standing and extending a hand to Max. "I still have a fifteen-minute boat ride home, and my wife will be wondering what I've gotten up to." Max shook the gendarme's hand and thanked him for the drink. "Very nice meeting you, Josue."

Travere walked down to the dock, where the driver of the police boat powered up the twin outboards, and made ready to shove off.

"What do you think the Colonel is up to, Josue?" Max asked suspiciously. "Do you think he's shaking us down, letting us know that he knows what we're up to? Or do you think he's trying to catch us doing something next-level so he can collar us for something big?"

"Honestly?" Josue said, offering a rare moment of opinion. "I think he was just being friendly."

---

Colonel Travere clung to the powder-coated railing that surrounded the Zodiac's control console. The quick police vessel cleared the shallow waters of Le Robert Bay and the driver opened up the engines, heading flat out toward the tip of the Caravelle Peninsula.

"Sir, if I may be so bold as to ask?" the boat driver, a young second lieutenant named Trevor, said as he steered the boat across the light chop of the Atlantic Ocean. "What are you doing socializing with that criminal?"

"You think he was the guy who stole the boat the other night?" Colonel Travere asked seriously.

The young officer nodded. "I would bet a million Euros on it— if I had a million Euros. Can I borrow a million Euros, Colonel?"

Travere laughed. He struggled against the wind to get a long draw on the last of his Cohiba as the boat rounded the easternmost tip of the craggy peninsula.

"I think he's a good guy, really," Colonel Travere said pensively.

"But he's a boat-stealing, rum-running, criminal thug," Trevor said. "He almost killed me and Pierre."

"As I recall the story," Travere said, sounding unexpectedly fatherly, "you two did a pretty good job of that yourself."

Trevor became quiet for several minutes, until the Zodiac reached a private dock that belonged to a neighbor of Colonel Travere. It was likely the security of knowing the guy next door was the top law enforcement officer on the island, but the neighbor was happy to allow the gendarme to come and go from the dock as he pleased.

"Seriously, Colonel. What are you doing with that guy?"

"Well, Trevor. I suppose I feel for the guy. He has been through a lot, and I believe he is still trying to figure some things out. You see, about five or six years ago he was on a vacation with his family in the Florida Keys. They rented a boat to go fishing and sightseeing. Max stumbled upon a major coke trafficker transferring about fifty kilos of product to a bush league distributor. The trafficker took one look at Max and opened fire with an H&K submachine gun. He killed Max's wife and two very young children. Max himself was hit three or four times.

"I know he is a bit of a criminal, Trevor, but still, I cannot help but feel for the guy."

# CHAPTER 11

MAX OPENED HIS EYES AND gazed at the cloudless sky. A circular canopy of balatá trees and tall palms framed the sky like a pale turquoise painting as far as Max's peripheral vision would allow him to see. The sight struck him as both picturesque and incredibly peaceful.

Josue's face popped in front of him, snapping Max back to his senses. The young Haitian looked down. He furrowed his brow into a deep look of concern.

"You okay, Boss?"

Max turned his head and promptly became aware of his position on a gym mat he and Josue used for sparring. *Must have been choked out again by the wiry Haitian*, Max thought.

They usually trained together three times a week. Max considered the combat training an important part of their readiness for the conflict that was almost certain to be coming soon to their lives. Presently, Max shook off the disorientation and looked back up at Josue, who offered his hand to help the older man to his feet.

After Max had first met Josue in a seedy street in Miami, he had learned that growing up in a small village outside of Port au Prince, Josue had spent his youth studying Jujitsu and *tire machet*, a Haitian martial art focused around fighting with the machete, both disciplines taught to him by a legendary uncle. From Josue's description, Max gathered that the uncle had been a very old man, and also incredibly dangerous.

"Did you choke me out again?" Max said, realizing his voice sounded hoarse and dry.

Josue grinned. "Aye, Boss."

Max stood up and braced himself. He stumbled to a cooler at the edge of the four cushioned mats which were connected together by Velcro fasteners. He grabbed out a yellow Gatorade, old school style, which he drank all at once. Then Max rubbed a dry towel over his face and slick black hair, mopping up as much of the dripping sweat as he could. Even after toweling off, Max felt as damp as if he had just stumbled out of the shower.

"How did I do?" he asked.

"Until you let me slip behind you and apply the Hadaka Jime," Josue said, grabbing a bottled water out of the cooler, "you really impress me."

"The rear naked strangle," Max said, spitting onto the nearby grass. "Well done, mon frère. Glad I have you on *my* side."

Josue took a long drink of his water and toweled off his own face. It sort of caught Max off guard, but he was suddenly struck by how content the younger man appeared to be.

Max thought back to the violent day he had first met Josue; the skinny, frightened Haitian refugee had nearly been executed in the middle of the street, right in front of Max. Somehow—and some days Max still wondered how—he had stumbled into the altercation and managed to prevent it.

The two had been through a great deal together, and Max knew the worst of it likely lay ahead of them. Yet he still hoped for, *longed* for, peace at the end of it all, especially for Josue. The mysterious dark-skinned wunderkind had experienced so many trying days in his short life. Max thought he deserved a generous measure of peace.

"Let's move on to *tire machet*," Max said, stepping over to a table where several wooden training machetes lay alongside some made of carbon steel, their sharpened blades eighteen to twenty inches long.

Josue folded up the Jujitsu mats and stowed them in the storage shed behind the villa, unveiling a wide swath of green grass for them to train upon. They each chose a blade. Like gladiators, they each approached the center of the grass from a different side and circled each other like predatory cats.

Josue took the offense, while Max stepped carefully from side to side, lowering his center of gravity, and moving his machete swiftly to defend Josue's graceful, practiced strikes. The exercise was not one man trying to hack away at the other, but rather it played out more like a dance. The moves took place deliberately and with elegance, a lot like fencing, but instead involving the wielding of a primitive razor-sharp jungle tool.

"Well done," Josue said. "Now change."

Suddenly, Max was on offense. Josue stepped one long, slender leg behind the other fluidly and without perceptible effort as he moved side to side in a dangerous blade-swinging ballet.

"Good," Josue said. "Keep your breathing even. Don't strike too hard. That's it."

After training, Max and Josue made a simple lunch of leftover ham and brie cheese sandwiches on sliced baguette accompanied by strong cappuccinos. As they ate, they made plans for the rest of the day. Max's black leather journal sat open on the kitchen table, and he looked at his notes.

"Should be about time to distill the batch," Max said. "You good to go for that?"

"Ready, Boss," Josue said, before taking a sip of his frothy cappuccino.

"Excellent," Max said, wiping his mouth with a napkin. "Let's make some rum."

After cautiously disarming the C-4 plastic explosive that stood guard over the underground distillery, Josue turned on the cavern lights, and Max ran through a checklist to ensure they had all of their tools and supplies ready for the process of distilling the rum.

Max took a gravity reading of the fermented cane juice inside the still. A small amount of the juice was poured into a long beaker. Then a glass instrument that looked a lot like a long glass thermometer was floated inside. Max gave it a spin and wrote down the reading in his black leather journal.

"Looks good," he said, jotting numbers down into his journal.

While it was often common practice in many distilleries to burn the crushed cane stalks for fuel to heat up the fermented juice in the boiler section of the still, Josue instead switched on a powerful propane boiler that looked a lot like an under-counter dishwasher. The boiler would provide a steady supply of heated water to circulate throughout the still's steam jacket in order to slowly and evenly heat up the fermented cane juice inside.

It would take time, likely a couple of hours, for the still to heat up to Max's target temperature, which was about 178 degrees Fahrenheit. The idea was to bring the alcohols in the fermented juice, often called wine, up to their boiling points, until they evaporated and rose up into the conical bell at the top of the boiler. The vapors would then travel down the length of the graceful swan's neck and into the water-cooled condenser, running out of a valve below, and then drip into a half-gallon mason jar.

Producing rum in a pot still was all about the careful collection of the distillate, and then the meticulous blending of these elements before the distillate was transferred to barrels for aging.

The first collected liquid, called the heads, would contain a lot of harsh components such as methanol and acetone, and it was generally separated from the more desirable hearts, which represented the main portion of the distillate.

Over the next several hours, Max collected the distillate in meticulously labeled half-gallon jars. That way, he could separate each of the delicate stages of the distillate's transitions from heads to hearts; each one had its own unique aromas and flavor properties. Max would later have the option of blending back in some of these transitional collections with the hearts to create a truly unique rum.

The distilling process continued until early in the evening, and at the end of the process, Max had collected about ninety gallons of rum hearts, which he transferred to a two-hundred-gallon stainless steel blending vat. He ended up with about two dozen mason jars full of the aromatic transitional collections from the beginning and the end of the process, each one marked with masking tape and a Sharpie marker, and then catalogued in Max's black book.

Max and Josue sniffed each of the mason jars, deciding if each one should be set aside for blending with a later batch of rum, or if some or all of it should be mixed back into the blending vat. Each time a mason jar of transitions was blended into the batch, Max noted in his book which number it was, based on the order it came out of the still, and how much of the incendiary liquid he blended back in.

Max even went into his glass-fronted cabinet to pull out some of his favorite transitions from prior rum batches which he had thoughtfully saved for future batches.

Any time Max had doubts about adding one of the jars' contents, he consulted with Josue for a second opinion. Every decision would change the finished product when the spirit ultimately came out of the French oak barrels, likely in about three to five years' time.

When Max and Josue were content with the batch of rum they had produced, Max measured the alcohol content, and then poured in previously collected buckets of spring water to lower the spirit's *proof*. Then it was time to barrel the rum.

Max had acquired the barrels from a defunct Scotch whisky

distillery that had aged their own distillate in the barrels to elicit the subtle flavors afforded by the French oak. Josue had carefully re-charred the inside of the barrels with a powerful propane torch, toasting the inside surface to mellow and flavor the finished rum. Some of the residual flavors from the Scotch whisky, such as vanilla, caramel, and peat moss, now embedded themselves in the very grain of the wood. It would give Max's finished rum even more complexity of flavor and character, and would serve to help remove some of the impurities from the rum.

After all of the hard work, the batch only produced three barrels of finished rum for aging. A couple of gallons of spirit were left over: the small portion that wouldn't fit in the fifty-four-gallon barrels. Max and Josue had a custom of making punch out of the remainder each time to celebrate the completion of the batch.

"You are quite an artisan, Maxwell Craig," a silken voice said from the top of the stairs.

Max wheeled around, and instinctively moved his hand to his hip, just as he had when Colonel Travere had startled him at the beach bar. But Max saw Vivienne Monet's face before he drew his FNS .40 caliber pistol from its holster.

She wore a pink and white striped tank top and khaki shorts, and as she stepped down the staircase into the cavern, Max considered how Vivienne's long mocha-colored legs appeared to be almost never-ending. As she neared him by the still, Max saw that she had a wallet in each of her hands. "I was just playing with you boys," she said. Her crooked smirk gave Max a tingle of delight.

"You're lucky," Max said, snatching his wallet out of the private investigator's hand, and then flipping through it in an exaggerated fashion to ensure the wallet's contents were all there. "We were going to come after you for these. If Colonel Travere hadn't shown up with that bottle of Trois Rivières…"

"Who's Colonel Travere?" Vivienne asked. She placed her hand on her hip. Max had no doubt she was just making herself comfortable, but the motion made her appear even more model-like than she already did.

"Travere's the new head of the Gendarmerie Nationale on Martinique; came here a few months ago. He caught up to me at Maisie's the other day. Thought he was shaking me down, but after he showed up here last night with a bottle of Trois Rivières single cask, I think he might actually be stalking me."

Vivienne laughed. *Wow. She has a great smile*, Max thought. *It almost knocks your breath out, like when you're a kid and you fall off of the jungle gym and land flat on your back.* "Hmm, I don't know him. Must have arrived after I left."

"You were a gendarme?" Max asked, now smirking himself.

"I've already said too much, Maxwell." Vivienne flashed her intoxicating smile again and tossed Josue his wallet. "You know you should really think about going legit, Max. If you get caught making illegal rum you could get in a lot of trouble. And the client I am working for is not happy with your presence in Martinique."

"Now you sound like Travere," Max said, closing up his black leather journal and tucking it under his arm. "You sure you don't know the Colonel? Anyway, I'm not too worried about that, Viv. I'll take my chances."

Vivienne picked up one of the plastic gallon-sized pitchers filled with freshly distilled rum and gave it a gentle shake to swirl its contents. "So are we going to go up to your villa and make some punch, or are we going to stand here in a cave talking all night?"

Max, Josue, and Vivienne sat on the porch drinking planter's punches until they lost track of time. At least once, Max fell off his chair laughing; Josue walked down the porch stairs, and then back up on his hands; and Vivienne produced a jar of Creole terrine that she had brought with her. She smeared the meaty spread on hunks of leftover bread and handed them out. Max had not expected to enjoy the pureed spread of chicken and pork, but found it quite nice, especially with a glass of rum.

Max was about to ask Vivienne if she'd like him to call a friend in Le Robert to come pick her up on his boat—he was certain she shouldn't drive her own back to town—when his phone began to vibrate in his hand.

"Who would be calling you at this hour?" Vivienne asked. "A girlfriend, perhaps?"

Max looked down at the face of his smartphone and saw the name T.L. Wilkinson again. "No, it's Terry; guy I used to work for. He calls me at weird times to check up on me."

"Aren't you going to answer it?" Vivienne asked, pouring herself another punch.

"I never do," Max said, and he tucked the phone back into his pocket.

Vivienne handed him another drink.

# CHAPTER 12

"**Y**O, WHO DID THAT!" TINY Deege said, clutching his nickel-plated Beretta by his side. The diminutive bald-headed gang member looked as if he had finally reached his boiling-over point. "Reggie, man, I know that smell is comin' up offa you. An' look at this place, man. We supposed to be livin' large up in here. This is a yacht! And look at it. Looks like Reggie's messed-up bedroom back on Lemon Street in here."

"What's all the noise?" Momo said. He had just stepped down the steep staircase from the flybridge where the catamaran's control console was located, to enter the vessel's living room-like salon. The rear salon doors had been tucked away to create a wide-open rear wall. This afforded an unencumbered view over the catamaran's white foamy wake behind them, as the boat cut through the open Atlantic Ocean.

"Hey, now, if Momo's down here, who's up there drivin'?" Zann said, suddenly sounding panicked.

"The boat is on autopilot," Momo said. "It'll stay on the course I set until I turn it off."

"What if we crash into something?" Tiny Deege said, tucking his pistol into his front waistband. "We all goin' die."

"If something shows up on radar within two miles of us an alarm will sound," Momo said. He was starting to feel like the parent on this trip. "Now what you throwin' yo' piece around fo', and what you bickerin' 'bout, Tiny?" Momo asked; he made certain to inflect his voice with just enough anger to bring a chill into his shipmates.

"Yo, yo, it's this mess," Tiny Deege said. "I feel like I can't find no peace on here, brother. You know what I'm sayin'?"

For a moment, Momo wondered if Tiny Deege might suddenly burst into tears; he *had* at Mama Dorah's house. Indeed, the salon and galley area inside the forty-four-foot catamaran looked like a landfill. Gazing around the normally posh and comfortable space, Momo saw empty Champagne bottles, empty cookie packages, frozen pizza boxes, chicken bones, and other miscellaneous garbage strewn about, making the room—which was occupied by only four people—seem claustrophobic and crowded.

"You brothers are goin' to clean up this room directly," Momo said commandingly. "Feel me? Directly."

Tiny Deege and Zann nodded. Reggie looked up from the screen of the thirty-two-inch flat screen where he was playing an Xbox 360 game just long enough to nod his head. Then he turned back to the game.

"Now, Tiny Deege, if you feelin' like you can't get no peace, why don't you go down to your stateroom and chill for a bit?" Momo decided that reasoning with the others might be the best way to diffuse a potentially explosive situation. "We all got a stateroom. It ain't like we all livin' in the same room or somethin'."

"Yo, Momo," Tiny Deege said, his voice climbing in pitch as he began his protest, "you and Zann got your own staterooms, but I'm doubled up with Reggie, man. We doubled up in a double bed. You feel me? Brother snores, an' you can smell his shoes from here." Tiny Deege made a disgusted face and held his nose. He waved his other hand in front of his face. It made Momo laugh.

Tiny Deege reached for his pistol again.

"Woah, whoa, Tiny," Momo said, straining to contain his laughter. "I feel you, brother, but this is what we got goin' on. There's plenty other places you can chill. You can sit up with me on the flybridge and lay out on the lounge, listen to some tunes. You can lay out on the big deck on the bow. I mean, you got options, man."

"Yo, Reggie, man," Tiny Deege said, barely eliciting the youngest man's attention from his video game. "Why don't you sleep up here in the salon and let me get some peace?"

Reggie hit the pause button on his game controller. "I don't think Mama Dorah would like that. You all get a stateroom and I gotta sleep up here." He hit the button again and returned to killing Nazi zombies on the flat screen.

"Yo," Momo said, sounding more heartfelt now. "Why don't you go down to your stateroom now, and when Reggie comes down to sleep, you can come back up here and chill. That'll be all right, right? And listen up, fools. Ten o'clock is the curfew."

"Ohhh, man!" Zann shouted. Reggie echoed his sentiment.

"No, man, it's just for tonight, awright?" Momo said. "We all gotta refocus ourselves and find our chill. Dig? Now you don't gotta go to sleep at ten, but you gotta go to your stateroom, an' Deege gonna come up here into the salon and chill. Salon gonna be Tiny Deege's stateroom tonight. After you chumps clean it up. Dig?"

Everyone nodded, and Tiny Deege looked genuinely pleased. "Another four hours and you gonna take over at the wheel, Zann," Momo said. He opened a cabinet door under the galley sink. The wide cabinet was cluttered with bottles of Drano, an orange coiled-up electrical cord, a propane-fueled blow torch, and a box filled with various pairs of Channel Lock and Vise Grip pliers. Momo found a stashed bag full of candy and snatched out a box of red licorice, then headed back up the ladder to the helm on the flybridge.

Momo actually found it quite peaceful to drive the boat. The guy at the yacht rental place had seemed reluctant to allow Momo to drive the boat himself. Three times he had asked if Momo wanted to hire a captain. But after fifteen minutes of coaching Momo on how to operate the vessel, it was clear the large man had a good handle on it. Besides, Momo had looked the part in his Ralph Lauren blazer and slacks; Mama Dorah had insisted he wear wire-rimmed glasses to make himself look more intelligent.

*Chump fool,* Momo thought. *Intelligent. If only she knew.* The truth was, Momo hated acting like a thug. Growing up in Georgetown as the son of a lawyer and a lobbyist, Momo had known he stuck out. His size alone had contributed a great deal to the other kids' notion that he was some sort of freak. Momo was called Montgomery back then, and he had always tried to make the best out of whatever situation he found himself in.

Acceptance into Brown University was supposed to be the great step toward having people regard him as something more than what they perceived him to be: a huge, menacing thug.

It was all going well, until that one night when Momo found himself in a microbrew pub just off the Brown campus. It was that night when the loud-mouthed ethics major, whose foot he had accidentally stepped on in class earlier that day, singled him out, and pressed him.

The blond graduate student had played pool with a couple other Brown students. They drank pale ale and did Jagermeister shots all evening, interspersing drinks with finger points and laughter in the direction of Momo, who occupied a small corner table, as he studied for a biology exam early the next morning.

Momo ignored the jeers, for the most part. He knew they were drunk, and he didn't really care about their taunts. But after trying to concentrate for nearly an hour while listening to the bullies' crap, Momo found himself pushed too far when the blond guy shouted, "Hey, Shaquille, why don't you bring us our drinks?"

Momo held quiet until the blond guy left. Then he had followed the belligerent man almost all the way back to his apartment, finally confronting him between a couple of eighteenth-century historical buildings down by the Providence River.

"Hey, man," Momo had said. "Hey, just wanted you to know that my name isn't Shaquille."

The blond guy barely turned around to look at Momo. "Oh, sorry. Is it Anfernee?"

Momo caught up to the guy in about three seconds. He grabbed hold of the blond man's head. He snapped the guy's neck right there by the dark water of the steady-flowing Providence.

Momo had watched the news every night after that, wondering when the police would finally catch up with him. Of course, he avoided the pub where the blond and his friends had bullied him. But after a few weeks, the police had never so much as knocked on Momo's door.

Momo knew he couldn't live with the feeling that the hammer might drop on him at any moment. So he dropped out of school and moved to Miami. His mother was half-Haitian, and the incredibly large young man found quick acceptance in the Little Haiti community. Some of the same characteristics that had made Momo seem like little more than a freak up north were the same ones that gave him near-deity status down in Miami.

Momo, no, Montgomery, was going to major in business acquisitions. And now, Momo had every intention of fulfilling that dream as the leader of Ti Flow. He would grow the gang like a corporation. They would make gains in capital, in influence, in numbers, and as a result, he would gain even more power.

Only one more job stood in his way, and it loomed about a thousand miles to the southeast of Momo's current position. *It will be easy*, he thought. *Easy like snappin' the neck of that blond-headed fool in Rhode Island.*

Momo kicked his feet up on the control console and poured himself a glass of Cristal. He took a long sip of the Champagne, and then chewed on a stick of red licorice. Yeah, he would kill Josue Remy, and then he would go back to Miami and he would rule; like a king he would rule over his kingdom of Little Haiti.

# CHAPTER 13

V IVIENNE MONET PARKED HER CAR in the space closest
to the front door of La Maison de Verre rum distillery
near Le Francois. She slammed the door again and
again at least six times before the latch decided to catch and stay
closed. The '73 Citroen looked like a shuttle bound for another
planet, but Vivienne would not have traded it. Not for a brand
new Mercedes. Except for the failing bits of trim, she kept the
vehicle in excellent running order. It had belonged to her father.
The truth was, it was all she had left to show for him.

La Maison de Verre's distillery had gone through total
restoration at least three times during its long history, with
the most recent having been completed only three years ago.
Vivienne took in the grand elegance of the plantation's main
villa, a massive colonial building with a second floor balcony and
matching window shutters hung in stark white against the red
brick of the structure. The building looked ancient, and brand
new at the same time.

The villa represented so much of the history of rum production
on Martinique, having produced rhum agricole since the 1890s.
To some this place was practically holy ground. Today the palatial
villa lived on as a literal museum of rum… and gift shop.

As she dropped her keys in her pocket, Vivienne caught
sight of a couple of men standing beside a beat-up Ford pickup.
Landscaping equipment littered the bed of the truck: Vivienne
spotted the push handles of two lawn mowers, a weed eater, and

the long handles of what must have been shovels or rakes, all of which stuck out of the truck as if thrown in haphazardly.

The two men, both large and strong-looking island natives, were obviously groundskeepers at the rum plantation. One man was older, maybe late forties, while the other looked to be twenty to twenty-five; she wondered if they might actually be father and son. But the thing that startled her, and drew her attention to them in the first place, was the baseball bat the older man tossed into the truck bed, while the younger man dropped in a splitting axe whose edge showed the glinting, shiny surface of having been freshly sharpened.

*Interesting gear for grooming the garden*, Vivienne thought to herself, as she mounted the steps to the villa's front porch, and opened the door.

The entire first floor of the nineteenth-century villa contained a tidy display of antique rum-making equipment, arranged and displayed proudly: an evolution of old cane-crushing presses, from one generation to the next, took up an entire wall; a tarnished copper pot still that must have boiled only eighty gallons of juice at a time stood next to a placard explaining the rum distillation process; and a colorful timeline of rum bottles, revealing how they had changed through the ages, occupied shelf after shelf, all just out of reach behind a red velvet rope.

Vivienne walked past it all and mounted a staircase, ignoring the posted sign that read: Employés Seulement, or Employees Only. At the top of the stairs, Vivienne found some of the museum's more opulent pieces: silver pitchers and trays for serving rum punches, likely on the villa's grand balcony over a hundred years ago; ancient China vases overflowing with freshly cut torch lilies and red flowering heliconias; some of the finer antique rum bottles, still filled with amber fluid, having been filled many decades ago; paintings of the different generations of the Molière family hung in gold-gilded frames, eerily watching Vivienne as she walked the hallway to a red door.

Another painting on the far wall, this one at least a meter tall and depicting a black man holding a shotgun in the crook of his arm, the weapon's open breach venting wispy black powder smoke. Two hounds stood beside the man, one of them clutching a limp pheasant in his jaws as he looked up at his master with obvious admiration. Vivienne noticed a small brass plaque at the bottom of the frame engraved with the name Vidal Roche Molière.

Vivienne knocked on the red door beside the painting and waited.

"Entrer," a deep voice shouted from within.

Vivienne opened the door and stepped inside. The room was rather dim for a working office. Several pieces of antique colonial furniture crafted in rich mahogany decorated the wide room, extending the museum feel of the building. A huge, cluttered desk sat near a shuttered window opposite Vivienne.

She approached the desk, which was occupied by an obese bald man who sat crouched over the desk holding a Cuban cigar between his thick, knobby fingers. The man's button-down shirt was wrinkled and dirty; probably not the first time it had been worn since laundry day. A bottle of La Maison de Verre fifteen-year-old rum sat beside him, nearly empty, while his glass of rum and ice rested close by, filled nearly to the top. The shiny face of a new smartphone sat on the desk next to the rum bottle, the only bit of evidence that would place the unappealing man into the twenty-first century.

"Ms. Monet," Vidal Molière said, not bothering to look up from an open manila folder which lay on the desk in front of him. Papers and paper-clipped photographs filled the folder. "It is my pleasure to see you again. Please tell me, what progress have you made in the discreet investigation I have hired you to perform? Do you have the identity of the rum runner?"

"Bonjour, Monsieur Molière," Vivienne said, clutching a manila envelope of her own in her left hand. "I have completed my investigation, but I must say I did not uncover as much illicit activity as I expected to find, based on the anecdotal accounts you passed on to me—"

"Do you have a name?" Vidal Molière interrupted. He looked up from the disheveled pile of papers, photographs, and candy wrappers that littered his desk. He glared sharply at Vivienne. "And a location?"

Vivienne knew that Vidal Molière was only forty-three, but he might have been fifty-five, if judged by the wrinkles around his mouth and on his forehead, and the baggy circles around his eyes. *He looked much better on the painting*, Vivienne thought. The private investigator had learned to read people over the years, and what she saw in Vidal's eyes seemed like something devious, something dangerous. Of course it was just a hunch she had, but she was pretty sure this guy was a total creep.

"Look, Mr. Molière," Vivienne said, clutching the manila folder in her hand as if protecting a holy relic. "I was hired to find out the identity of the supposed 'rum runner' who has been rumored to distill and distribute unregulated rhum agricole to a variety of sales outlets throughout the island, as well as a good portion of the Caribbean. But first, I must say, I spotted some of your boys outside, and I can tell they are getting ready to trash somebody. I can only finish this job and provide you with this information if you give me your word you do not intend to harm the named person or persons inside this report. If you wish to give this information over to the authorities, that is acceptable to me, but I cannot be party to any kind of personal vendetta you might have."

"Mademoiselle Monet," Vidal said, standing up from his chair. *Funny*, Vivienne thought, *he didn't get much taller.* "This plantation has been in my family since 1899. My great-great-grandfather,

Herbert Molière, actually worked for Homère Clément for nearly twenty years, cutting cane in the Rhum Clément fields, saving every cent he made until he had finally saved up enough of his own money to purchase the land you are standing on right now. And then, my great-great grandfather built the original distillery with his own hands.

"Perhaps history would recognize Monsieur Clément as the father of rhum agricole, Ms. Monet, but it was Herbert Molière who perfected rhum agricole, and ensured that La Maison de Verre rum would become a lasting legacy, and continue to be enjoyed today, nearly a century after his death."

*Nice speech*, Vivienne thought. *And what has Vidal ever done to contribute to his grandfather's legacy? Drinking his rum? Spending his money?*

"I can appreciate that, Monsieur—" Vivienne attempted to interject, but was cut off again.

"Those of us who run legitimate rhum agricole operations have worked hard to ensure our compliance with the French government to secure our designations so that we can call our products Appellation d'Origine Contrôlée rhum agricole Martinique. This interloper has moved onto Martinique with no regard for the heritage of the very product he produces. His disdain for the rules—which those of us with legitimate products are required to follow—would very likely cause my grandfather to rise up out of his tomb, and go after this charlatan himself."

"The rum runner is not representing his product as AOC rhum agricole Martinique," Vivienne said, surprised she was so quick to defend Max's honor. But this guy was a troll. "His intention is not to infringe on the legacy of rhum agricole, but rather is only trying to create something unique and extremely limited, something for a boutique market."

"Our V.S.O.P. rums and our Master Distiller's Choice line of rums are also intended to appeal to a select, boutique market of rum buyers. This criminal is in direct competition with our most unique offerings, as well as those from other legitimate producers. I have a very real problem with that, Ms. Monet."

Vivienne was about finished with Vidal Molière. "Promise me that you will not send anyone after the rum runner, and I will finish the job," she said, holding the manila folder between her hands. She half expected she might rip it in half rather than hand it over to this rodent.

"You have my word, Ms. Monet," Vidal said, holding out his hand.

"His name is Maxwell Craig," Vivienne said, passing the folder to the wrinkled, pot-bellied heir to the La Maison de Verre rum empire. "He is an American expatriate, and his property is on one of the Le Robert ilets. All of the details are inside."

Vidal Molière opened the folder and flipped through its contents. "There are exterior pictures of the island, and a few of Maxwell and this other fellow… Josue Remy. But there are no pictures of the distillery, his aging barrels, his still, etc."

"I'm sorry, Monsieur, but I lost a fair amount of my collected data," Vivienne said, knowing that she would not replace the photos Max had deleted, not if Vidal paid her ten times as much. She was glad Max had deleted them.

"As such, I will be unable to pay you the remainder of your fee," Vidal said, tucking the folder under his sweaty arm. "The retainer you've already received should suffice as payment. As a small consolation, you may go down to my aging cellar and choose one bottle of La Maison de Verre rhum agricole; my cellar master will assist you in choosing any item you wish."

Vivienne turned and headed for the door without another word. As incensed as she was, she thought she might hurt Vidal Molière if she were to remain in his presence for another moment.

From the ground floor, Vivienne descended a steep spiral of stone steps, arriving into a darkened cellar that suggested a medieval dungeon. It also reminded her of the time she had visited Florida as a child and had ridden on the Pirates of the Caribbean boat ride. She stood surrounded on either side by walls of stone, fronted by stacked-up, carefully stamped barrels full of aging rhum agricole. She half expected she was walking into some sort of ambush. But Vidal had no beef against her, only Max and Josue.

Vivienne met the cellar master, who was waiting for her by a barrel, which stood on end with a large, very old ledger that sat open on top. He was a distinguished-looking elderly man with a neatly-trimmed white beard and spectacles. He wore a crisp white shirt and a neat red bowtie, and he had a kind smile for Vivienne when she approached.

"He said you could take anything?" the cellar master asked, a skeptical look on his face.

"Anything," Vivienne repeated. "You could go and ask him if you do not believe me."

"No, no, that's quite all right," the man said, and Vivienne bet the old man wanted to go into Vidal Molière's office about as much as she did. The cheap slimeball probably couldn't stand to part with any more of his precious cash, while his family's rum was so plentiful that it likely held very little value to him; even giving away his rarest merchandise was of little consequence to him. She would be certain to grab the most valuable bottle she could.

"Go ahead, Mademoiselle. Look around. Some of the older rums are further back. If it were my choice, I suppose a 1944 Réserve de l'Héritage de la Famille would be the one. Only about five or six left, I suppose."

"Wrap it up," Vivienne said. It wasn't Euros, but it was a valuable bottle; she would be able to trade it to somebody for something at some point.

The cellar master packed the bottle carefully in a small,

hand-crafted wooden crate, tucking bits of straw around the bottle for protection. He then placed a flat wooden board on top and gently tapped brass nails into the face with a small hammer. The kindly old man handwrote an adhesive label, identifying the crate's contents, and then made a note in the ancient-looking ledger, likely removing the antique rum bottle from the cellar's inventory. He melted a stick of wax over the crate with a candle, dripping it to overlap the gap between crate and lid, and then he removed a pewter seal from his pocket, pressing it into the molten wax. He then handed the crate to Vivienne.

"It's all yours, Mademoiselle," the cellar master said. "Save it for a special occasion."

"Merci," she said. She went upstairs, and waded through the villa's first floor museum, stepping out onto the front porch outside. The sun assaulted her eyes. She had just gotten used to the dim light of the rum cellar.

Vivienne put on her COACH sunglasses and took a look around. The first thing she noticed was her Citroen, sitting where she had parked it. The second thing she noticed was that the white Ford truck with the baseball bat, axe, and the two rough-looking landscapers was nowhere in sight.

"Zut," she said.

# CHAPTER 14

I SOBEL SAT IN THE SUN at Maisie's, her blonde hair covered by a large straw hat, and her eyes, as well as half of her face, were covered by her oversized sunglasses. A contented expression spread across her face, and she took a tight-lipped sip of her planter's punch. It had not taken long for her to catch on to the quality drinks the island had to offer.

"Hey, Isobel," Max said, grabbing the chair opposite the Scottish tourist, and making himself comfortable. He gestured toward Angelique by making a shaka symbol with his hand and tipping it back toward his mouth like a tipped drink. She nodded.

"There you are, Maxwell Craig," Isobel said, her face lighting up in a dazzling smile. "I was beginning to write you off as a lost cause."

"Are you sure you're going to be okay here?" Max asked, holding up his arm to block the sun from his eyes in a mock gesture, even though he wore tortoise shell wayfarers. "I don't want to see you get sunburned any more than you are."

Isobel reached arm's length into the bottom of her handbag and held up a white tube with a blue cap. "SPF 100," she said with a slight smirk. And then, as if to prove she could handle the sun, Isobel removed her big sunglasses and set them down on the weathered table in front of her.

Max stared directly into Isobel's face, and he couldn't get over how stunning she looked: her lips were glossy and pink, her blonde hair had been carefully curled and brushed out, and her dark eye liner and shadow gave her a beautiful, mysterious look. It all made what he was about to say incredibly difficult.

"I've got to be straight with you, Isobel," he said, looking into her bright, quizzical eyes. "I think it's best if I don't see you anymore."

"Oh, jeez," Isobel said, sounding surprised and embarrassed. She picked up her sunglasses and stuck them back on her face. "You're married, aren't you?"

"No," Max said, clenching his jaw. His mouth felt dry. "Not anymore."

Angelique set Max's Ti' Punch down on the table and he drained it. "Another, please," he said, and the young waitress took away his glass as quickly as she had set it down.

Tears began to stream down Isobel's cheeks.

Max felt bad. She had been so happy just seconds earlier. And now she looked stone-faced, and her lips curled into a frown. He might have ruined her whole vacation.

Isobel sniffed and wiped her cheeks. "Did you get divorced, or did something else happen? I mean, I got to be honest, Max. The way you said that sounded a little bit... ominous."

Max took a deep breath. He folded his fingers together under the table and gritted his front teeth together before speaking. "About six years ago I was on vacation with my wife, Lovelle, and my kids. I had a girl named Lucy, sweet, redheaded, little thing, she was four. And I had a son, named Lionel, with almost pure white blond hair and freckles, he was two."

"Had?" Isobel said, her voice sounding rough and raspy, and the tears trickled down again.

"It happened in Islamorada, in the Florida Keys. At the time I had been an accountant working for a large TV ministry in Orlando. The head of the ministry is a guy named T.L. Wilkinson—Terry—great man. Terry was exactly the same man on camera as he was when they were switched off, just very genuine. Very humble. Kind of a mentor to me."

Max paused and took a sip from the fresh drink Angelique had just brought him. "You can imagine, me working as an accountant, crunching numbers every day, and chasing after two small kids. Well, I guess I got to a place where I was really stressed out. I needed to blow off some steam. I had always wanted to go fishing in the Keys, and when my wife said I should make the trip down, I said 'No, we should all go.'"

Isobel looked ghostly white. It pained Max to have to share all of this with her, but she had to know.

"I'd chased a school of bonefish into a channel that led me deep into some mangroves, hard to see past them, it was like a twisted maze. At first, I worried I'd get the fishing boat we rented into a tight spot where I couldn't turn around. Last thing I wanted to do was to damage it or get it stuck and lose my deposit. But then we came upon two other boats.

"One boat had three guys in it. I remember it, 'cause it's burned into my brain like a Polaroid. There's a tall well-built guy with peroxide blonde hair, I suppose he was only about twenty-five. The second guy looked short and dumpy, but he easily handed over a heavy bundle to an older couple on the other boat.

"I mean, these two on the other boat, they looked like a typical country club-going, tennis-playing, martini-sipping yuppie couple. The bundle they were receiving looked like a bunch of plastic bags wrapped together by duct tape, obviously drugs—a lot of drugs."

"Oh, my gosh, Max," Isobel said. She looked terrified by his account.

"The boss of the two men on the first boat must of been Cuban or Puerto Rican. And he had oily black hair that was white on both sides, pure white. I mean, it was one of the weirdest-looking hair styles I've ever seen. This guy got one look at us and didn't think twice. He grabbed the Heckler & Koch MP5 slung over his shoulder, and he opened fire on me and my family."

Isobel broke down in sobs. But rather than comfort her, Max continued.

"There is no other more sickly feeling one can have than seeing a bullet pierce his toddler's forehead, and blow out the back of his skull. To see his daughter grab her stomach where a 9mm bullet had just ripped into her abdomen, before a second pierced her heart, then her neck, then her face.

"My wife received the worst of it, though: a punctured lung, a perforated bowel, a punctured spleen. It took her three days to die, after knowing that her kids had just been murdered."

"In all, my son was shot five times, my daughter four times, and my wife three times."

"What about you?" Isobel asked dryly.

"I was shot in the shoulder, in my left forearm, in my hip, and in my left thigh. I don't know why my family received all fatal wounds and I was barely touched." Max wiped his eye before his tear fell.

"Barely touched?" Isobel sounded mortified. "You are lucky to be alive."

"I don't know if I would consider it luck," Max said, sounding as if he was speaking to Isobel from some chilly isolated planet.

"Is that why you're so protective of women?" Isobel asked, grabbing a pocket pack of tissues out of her huge purse to wipe her eyes. "Because you weren't able to protect your family, your wife?"

"Probably," Max said, looking off toward the ocean.

"I *am* a dangerous man," Max said, "for a lot of reasons. Ask Angelique's ex-boyfriend. But I'm also dangerous because trouble finds me, Isobel. And if you are around me, it is likely that trouble will find you as well."

"What about the men who killed your family?" Isobel asked. "Do you know who they are?"

Max nodded.

"This was what, six years ago? What has happened to them? Did you go after them?"

"No, Isobel," Max said, taking another drink from his second Ti' Punch. "When the time is right, they are going to find *me*."

"You have a plan?" Isobel asked. "To... kill them?"

Max did not reply.

"Are you planning revenge against the men who killed your family?" she asked. "Because if I were in your shoes, I suppose I would be thinking about doing exactly the same thing."

"I don't know how long until they will find me, Isobel," Max said, twirling the ice in his glass, "but they *will* find me. I've made sure of that. And when they do, anyone I am close to will be at risk. I can't put you in that position. You are the first woman since my wife who I've had feelings for. A part of me felt like it was dead. And then you came into my life and put the paddles on my chest, and shocked me back into life. But I can't put you at risk, Isobel. So, this has to be goodbye."

Max stood up from the table.

"Seriously? *Goodbye.* Just like that?" Isobel protested. "Max, it sounds like we might have something that's worth fighting for, worth putting a little effort into. I'm sorry if you think it won't work. I thought meeting you might be a chance for me to finally get away from—"

Isobel stopped herself, mid-sentence.

"Get away from what?" Max asked, looking down at the Scottish substitute teacher. "Another dangerous man?"

"I... I don't know what to say, Max," Isobel said, dabbing at her eyes with a tissue.

Max's eye caught an odd sight on the horizon. "Do you see that?" he asked Isobel. Max pulled down his sunglasses and gestured out toward the bright turquoise waters of the Atlantic.

"Looks like a yacht," Isobel said, lowering her own sunglasses as well and squinting. "Looks like a big yacht. What do they call that… a mega yacht, or somethin' like that?"

"I'm sorry, Isobel," Max said, dropping two twenty Euro notes on the table to pay for lunch and drinks. "But I've got to go."

Max was torn. He needed to separate from Isobel so she wouldn't get wrapped up in his precarious future. He didn't know what was going on with her, what she was trying to tell him, but he knew that as long as she was close to him, she wouldn't be safe.

"Will I see you again, Max?" Isobel asked. She took off her sunglasses and looked up at him with her sparkling blue-green eyes.

"I don't know," Max said, sounding distant.

Max bolted down the beach, running pell-mell toward the long white pier where his Cobia fishing boat was tied off. He sprinted the length of the dock, jumping down into the stern and firing up the twin outboards as quickly as possible. He cast off the bow and stern lines and pushed the throttle handles forward, and steered the boat out to open ocean, before leaving the helm and unlocking the center console door, grabbing out his big black duffel bag which had been secured inside.

Max dragged it over to the helm and steered the boat while digging through the bag for a pair of Nikon binoculars, which he slung around his neck by their strap. He motored the swift fishing boat toward the end of the Caravelle Peninsula, rounding the craggy easternmost point where he spotted the lighthouse.

Max throttled down to an idle and took off the binoculars' lens caps. He peered through, focusing on the massive black and white yacht, which seemed to be making a beeline toward the ilets in Le Robert Bay.

Max pulled out his smartphone and called Josue.

"Yes, Boss?"

"Check the cams. Search the horizon. See a yacht coming in, a big one?" Max said urgently into the phone.

"A big yacht, you say?" Josue sounded dumbfounded. Virtually all of the big yachts that came to Martinique moored up on the Caribbean Sea side, near Fort-de-France, Saint-Pierre, Saint-Anne. It was extremely unusual to see a vessel of substantial size on the Atlantic side.

Max lifted his sunglasses and sealed the binoculars over his eyes. He centered his field of vision on the rear of the mega yacht and carefully zoomed out as much as he could. He twisted the focus ring on the binoculars until he could read the bright white letters on the back of the yacht. *Snowy Lady.*

"Yeah, I've got it, Boss," Josue said, sounding uncharacteristically excited. "You want me to record and start surveillance."

"Roger that, Josue," Max said, and his lips formed a satisfied grin, even as something churned in his stomach. It wasn't fear. It was more like nervous excitement. "It's time, my friend. They're here."

# CHAPTER 15

V IVIENNE PRESSED HER CORK-HEELED WEDGE into the gas pedal of her Citroen, driving the aged French car hard down the snaky road that stretched between the palm tree-lined rum plantation's driveway and the N6 highway. The Citroen's V6 produced a decent amount of horsepower, and Vivienne used all of it as she powered out of curves, flooring it on most of the long straight stretches of road.

She had taken tactical driving courses back in her days with the Gendarmerie Nationale, and she had enough experience behind the wheel to know that every car had its limits. Her training had also taught her that those limits were easily crossed. She did her best not to lose traction, or to dangerously overdrive the car into the corners. But as she drove, she rode the edge of that fine line between control and disaster.

Vivienne grabbed her phone out of her pocket and fumbled to find Max's phone number. She knew she had programmed it into her contacts recently, that night she had stayed late, drinking punch with him and Josue. She nearly ran off the road while looking at the bright little screen trying to find it. At last, she found the number and dialed. No service.

Vivienne knew that unless she caught sight of the two La Maison de Verre thugs before they reached the highway, she wouldn't catch up to them before they set out after Max. She had to either warn him, or somehow stop them.

She shifted down into third and turned the wheel hard to the right. The carefully crated bottle of seventy-year-old rum from La Maison de Verre slid around on the passenger seat beside her with each twist and turn of the road. Vivienne cursed the bottle. *That little turd sent me down into the cellars to distract me, so he could send his thugs to go beat the piss out of Max*, she fumed to herself.

As she made speed toward the highway, the silver Citroen hurtled like a bullet past pedestrians, other cars, and surprised-looking motorists on motorbikes. She shot past serene villas and peaceful hotels spread out throughout the lush countryside.

The two brutes from the distillery would need to access Max's ilet by boat. Vivienne knew the groundskeepers would likely be boarding theirs anywhere between La Vauclin and Le Robert; finding them would be virtually impossible. So the course Vivienne took was the most direct route to the private dock near Le Robert where she had secured her inflatable dinghy.

The drive would normally have taken about twenty minutes. Vivienne arrived at the boat dock twelve minutes later. She fumbled with the car keys to get the Citroen's trunk open. A beat-up old softball bag filled half the trunk. As a teen Vivienne had used the bag to carry all of her sports gear: softball bats, a mitt, balls, a batting helmet. Now the faded black bag bulged with a lot of the equipment Vivienne used in her sometimes perilous work as a private investigator.

Vivienne threw the bat bag into the bow of her black inflatable and yanked a pull cord to fire up the rubber boat's 40hp outboard. It took a few tries, but at last the motor growled to life with a small cloud of white smoke and a whiff of gassy exhaust. The determined private investigator untied the boat from the dock, twisted the throttle on the tiller, and headed out across the sparkling bay toward Max's ilet.

The bow of the twelve-foot dinghy began to porpoise up and down a bit as it skimmed over the rough water of the bay. A windy day made for choppy conditions, but Vivienne threw caution to it and opened the throttle all the way, racing toward the ilet, which loomed ahead of her, looking like a big craggy rock overwhelmed by an overgrowth of lush vegetation.

It was impossible to know whether or not she could head off the ruffians from La Maison de Verre, but Vivienne was determined to make every effort possible. She couldn't help but feel responsible for these thugs' pursuit of Max, even if it had been his illicit business practices which had made him a target in the first place.

She tried to raise Max again by phone. Straight to voicemail. "Zut alors," Vivienne grumbled.

She reached the rocky edge of the ilet, on the northern side of the island, opposite the long pier and boat dock. Vivienne knew she was outnumbered, and she fully intended to stack the deck in her favor, and use the art of surprise as her ally. She pulled the boat as far as she could onto the wet rocks, and then tossed her sports bag onto the shore.

With a quick tug, the bag's zipper ripped open, and she removed a SWAT-style tactical body armor vest. She threw it over her head, and secured the hook and loop fasteners at her sides, then proceeded to pull on wool socks and hastily laced up a pair of Bates desert combat boots.

Vivienne grabbed out the Mossberg twelve-gauge from inside the bat bag and made sure it was loaded with shells. She liked the 590A1 because the twenty-inch barrel was thicker than Mossberg's standard barrels—it made a good striking weapon when push came to shove—and the nine-shot capacity gave her an extra measure of comfort. The 590A1 had also passed the U.S. military's torture tests, which proved it could endure the worst conditions on earth and keep firing shot after shot.

Vivienne retrieved a fifty-shot bandolier from the bag, each loop filled from a variety of different shotgun shells, mostly 00 buckshot for defensive purposes, but also some rifled slugs, and a couple of different sizes of birdshot for other things, like blowing off door hinges.

She slung the bandolier over her shoulder and across her chest like the most deadly pageant sash in the world. Then she nimbly tied her long, curly black hair in a high ponytail, and slipped on a pair of polarized shooting glasses. Vivienne was ready for action, and God help anyone foolish enough to stand against her.

She pumped a round into the chamber and carried the weapon at the low-ready position, with the barrel aiming toward the ground several feet in front of her. She stepped with agility through the dense foliage of the ilet; she'd done it before when she had been surveilling Max and Josue, and it had been pitch dark then.

Now, facing a potential threat, Vivienne kept her eyes moving, side to side as she advanced. After finding the large grassy clearing behind Max's villa deserted, except for a large piled of crushed sugarcane, she quickly made for the rear corner of the building.

Her adrenaline was jacked, and Vivienne steadied her breathing to keep herself calm. Ever since police training she had loved the feel of the twelve gauge in her hands. It gave her a greater feeling of power than a pistol, and Vivienne felt she had more control and patterning options as well.

Presently, she spotted an unfamiliar boat—a beat-up 1930's era black fishing boat—tied up at the boat dock beside Max's Cobia fishing boat. Vivienne knew that Max did not like company on his island, and she guessed the visitor who had arrived in the old boat was likely an uninvited guest.

She tried the doorknob on the kitchen door at the rear of the villa. It turned, and she crept inside, crouching low and holding her shotgun at the ready. She cleared the kitchen and moved down the hall, sweeping left and right to clear each room along the way. When she had swept the entire ground floor, finding the place as desolate as the yard, Vivienne slowly made her way upstairs. She cleared every room on the second level before exhaling a sharp breath.

"Where the hell are they?" she whispered to herself.

Vivienne parted the curtains of the second floor master suite and peered out onto the grassy back yard with the dry cane pile. She spotted the craggy opening of Max's subterranean distillery, the place where his large still and barrels of aging rum were located. The dark hole in the middle of a wide swath of verdant, ankle-high grass looked like a gaping mouth opened up in the earth. She wondered if Max and Josue were down there.

The shadowy cavern entrance suddenly flashed bright white-orange, and Vivienne heard the distinct crack-crack of repeated gunfire. She bolted from the room and down the staircase as fast as she could without tripping.

Vivienne rushed back through the kitchen, kicked open the door, and rushed out into the yard. Her pulse raced as she considered what she might find in the cavern, but she did not hesitate.

She reached the edge of the cavern mouth and shouldered the Mossberg, her finger covering the trigger. It was dark, and Vivienne switched on the light on the shotgun's foregrip.

From the side of the cave's opening, Vivienne looked down into the shadowy depths of the underground distillery. She spotted a hulking form lying flat on his back on the cavern floor. As she took in the scene, Vivienne realized the limbs of another person wrapped around the first guy in some sort of martial arts grappling hold.

With a gasp, Vivienne felt something clench around her own throat. With a painful jerk, she felt herself tugged backward. She struggled, throwing elbows into ribs, stomping heels toward insteps. She slipped free from her assailant's grasp just long enough to see the seven-inch blade of a military-style bayonet stabbing down toward her chest.

Vivienne used her arm to deflect the strike, which sliced across the front of her vest. Another lightning-quick strike of the blade flashed. She blocked again. This one glanced off her side, slicing through the straps of her vest, and cutting her skin over her ribs.

"Aaah!" she shrieked from the shock of it, more than the pain, which she hardly felt.

The third knife strike was the last straw. Vivienne caught the attacker's wrist and twisted it, bending the six-foot-tall guy over at the waist, and forcing his face down toward the ground. She followed the defensive move by striking the man hard on the right side of his face with bone-crunching force from her fist. She brought her knee hard up into his chest and stomach over and over again, until he flopped onto the ground, gasping for breath.

Vivienne's attacker was the younger of the two groundskeepers she had seen at the distillery. It surprised her that he had escalated the violence to lethal force so quickly. She cursed herself for letting her guard down. But the guy was down.

Six thick plastic zip ties hung from her vest, and Vivienne used one to tie the guy's hands behind his back. She bound the guy's ankles as his struggled gasps for breaths turned into deep, rhythmic breathing. Then she turned her attention toward the dark cavern, where she had heard the sound of hideous grunting and the gunshots from the darkness below.

Vivienne took a step down the wooden staircase to the cavern floor below and paused. She was almost afraid of what she would find. The lights suddenly flashed on, and the bold private investigator gasped.

# CHAPTER 16

"B OAT COMING, BOSS," JOSUE SHOUTED, his voice echoing down the main hallway of the villa to Max's accounting office. Max sat at his desk with a towel laid out across the hodgepodge of papers which normally covered the surface. On the towel lay all the parts of his field stripped Smith & Wesson 6906 pistol, like all the pieces of a very dangerous puzzle. Max used a brass brush to carefully clean the barrel of fouling. "Boat comin' in hot," Josue added.

The slight stress in the Haitian's voice told Max that he took the matter seriously. They did not get visitors on the ilet; not uninvited ones anyhow. And that made Max feel stress as well.

"Looks like Chris-Craft, one of those old wood boats," Josue shouted. "Real fancy." Max knew the young Haitian was monitoring the property's surveillance cameras from a large touchscreen tablet from his seat at the kitchen table. With the swipe of his finger, Josue could toggle through the outputs from each of the cameras.

They were mounted all around the villa, as well as at the top of the viewing platform Max and Josue had built into the tops of the ilet's tall slender balatá trees. From the tablet, Josue could also operate the controls for some of the cameras' pan, tilt, and zoom functions.

Max gave the barrel of his pistol a good wipe with a clean rag and dropped it into the pistol's slide. He replaced the guide rod and spring and reassembled the weapon, attaching the slide to the frame. Max replaced its magazine, the one he kept loaded with only three 9mm hollow-point cartridges. He stood up from his desk, racked the pistol's slide, and then holstered the weapon, smoothing his long sleeve black shirt over it to conceal the weapon.

"I'm ready," Max said with resolve. "Josue, are you ready?" Max checked his other pistol, the .40 caliber FNS compact, which was a small double-stack semi-automatic with an extended magazine; it gave him fourteen shots in the magazine, and one in the pipe. Max checked the weapon, confirming it was loaded to capacity with fifteen hollow-point cartridges.

Josue stepped out of the kitchen, and walked down the hall carrying a Ruger SR556, with black military-style Interceptor body armor strapped over his torso. He pulled back the charging handle of the Ruger and let it go. The handle snapped forward and loaded a 5.56 round into the chamber. The rifle's Leupold VX-6 scope would make the sporting rifle precise and deadly from his perch in the lookout. Then Josue slung the rifle over his shoulder. "Ready, Boss."

"Stay out of sight if you can, Josue. If I bring anyone up to the porch, don't let them know you're covering them with a rifle. The lookout platform should be enough out of sight they won't even see it." Max felt the blood coursing through his veins. He couldn't believe that zero hour had finally arrived. He had waited so long to look into the eyes of Everest Walsh and each of his men, and now it was all about to go down.

"Remember," Max said, "what we're selling them is me as a mild-mannered bootleg rum distiller, not a man whose fire has been slowly burning for years, waiting patiently for them to arrive so he can burn them down to the ground."

"Steady, Boss," Josue said. He placed both hands on Max's shoulders. "You'll be okay. Breathe."

Max took a deep breath. This moment had been far too long

coming for him to relax. He was so wired he felt like a walking grenade begging for someone to set him off. "Okay," he said, shaking some of the nerves out of his hands. He made sure his shirt covered both pistols. "I'm going down to the dock."

"Wait," Josue said. He reached into his pocket and produced a small aluminum box. He flipped it open and removed a tiny earpiece embedded into a foam cutout. Josue made sure the diminutive device was switched on, and Max screwed it into his ear. The miniature communicator virtually disappeared into his ear canal.

"Check, check, check," Max said. "You read me."

Josue nodded. The clear wire of a communication earpiece coiled between Josue's ear and a radio Velcroed to his vest. He turned away from Max and whispered. "Read me, Boss?"

Max gave Josue a thumbs-up. "Show time."

Max's feet made a steady, rhythmic pace as he walked down the villa's porch steps, and onto the dirt path through the trees leading to the pier. He strode with purpose, all the time running various scenarios through his mind. What if they opened fire on him? How would he respond to that? One pistol? One in each hand? How many of them could he cut down before they killed *him*? *Calm down, Max.*

The boat that approached the dock was a fully restored 1930's era Chris-Craft. Its mahogany sides and deck looked as smooth as glass, varnished and polished to deep, shiny perfection. The red, white, and blue flag of the Dominican Republic rippled above the boat's rear deck as it cut through the warm tropical wind. The boat seemed as if it belonged in a museum, yet here it was pulling up to the dock at the end of Max's pier.

Max waved at the two men in the boat, as if he were happy to see them. Truth was, Max did not like the look of either man. And his familiarity with them was both unsettling and disheartening, like a dark cloud that had just rolled into his life. Max promised himself he would become the dark cloud to these men; the fact they didn't know that would prove to be their undoing.

The first guy was maybe six-foot-four and built like a UFC fighter. His thick head of peroxide-blond hair gave one a sense of confusion: at first glance one might assume he was Caucasian. But a second glance in which one observed the man's bronzed skin and dark brown eyes suggested he was actually Latin American: Dominican, Puerto Rican, or Cuban, most likely. The guy looked tough, and he appeared to be around twenty-nine or thirty years old. Tattoos crept like a growing organism up the man's neck, giving Max an unsettling sense they might suddenly grow even more and choke the guy to death.

The other man, the one driving the boat, was squat, maybe five-two, although he appeared to be made up almost entirely of thick sinewy muscle. He was one of those guys you would write off as a fat guy, only to find out too late he was the strongest man you'd ever encountered. This fellow appeared Latin American as well.

UFC hopped out of the boat and grabbed the bow to keep it from slamming into the dock until he and the short, dumpy guy could tie it off. They made quick work of the task and then UFC walked right up to Max.

"You Maxwell Craig?" the statuesque blond asked.

Max's heart pounded in his ears. His throat was bone-dry. He knew he had seen both of these men before. And there was only one place in time he could have seen them. Max thought about his pistols.

"Yeah," Max managed. "I'm Max. How are you guys doing today? You come in off that big yacht? Pretty impressive vessel."

The tall man handed Max a white envelope, which featured Max's full name printed in silver lettering. The tall tattooed man summarily hopped right back on the boat. In seconds, the two visitors had untied the show-quality vessel, and were motoring away from Max's dock as quickly as they had arrived.

Max wasted no time. He ripped open the envelope to find an expensive-looking invitation card inside. It reminded Max of the invitations you picked out for your wedding and sent to all your family and friends. Except this one read:

You are cordially invited to dine as a guest of Everest T. Walsh this evening onboard his yacht the *Snowy Lady* Transportation will be provided by boat; pick-up time 7:00 pm sharp Business casual attire is expected

No contact information was provided for an R.S.V.P. Max wondered what the protocol would be if he couldn't make it. Maybe that was the point; perhaps Walsh was telling him in a subtle way that he didn't have any choice in the matter.

As the Chris-Craft grew smaller in the distance as it neared Everest Walsh's massive yacht, Max wandered back toward the villa, meeting Josue beside the porch. The agile younger man had climbed down from his perch at the lookout platform, and now stood by with his rifle still slung over his shoulder.

"Walsh wants me to meet him for dinner," Max said, still peering down at the silver letters.

"That is good, no?" Josue asked.

"Yeah," Max said. "I suppose it is exactly how I hoped things would play out these many years. It just seems surreal now that it's actually happening."

"Instructions?" Josue looked like a soldier at attention.

"I want you back up in the lookout," Max said. "Gather as much data as you can before the boat arrives back here at the dock. You have the 400mm super telephoto?"

Josue nodded. "Two Canon DSLRs set up to shoot video *and* stills, and I'll be shooting thermal imaging video from the FLIR as well, just in case."

"Good," Max said. "Boat's coming at seven. We'll be ready. I'm going down to the cave and see about grabbing something special to take to Walsh."

"I suggest the 2013 élevé sous bois," Josue said. "You remember? Aged in cognac barrel. Very good bottle."

"Yes," Max agreed. "I am rather proud of that myself. I think there are still a couple of bottles of it socked away, behind some of the barrels."

Josue nodded and headed back into the dense underbrush, where he would find the partially concealed steel cable ladder he would climb back up to the lookout platform. Watching the young man climb—his effortless movements were like liquid, as if he were slowly defying gravity—Max suddenly felt a pang of guilt for involving his friend in everything they had planned. It *was* Max's family who had been cut down by the gunfire of Walsh's man, not Josue's. The young Haitian had never even met Max's wife and kids. Yet here he was, ready to face a dangerous pool of enemies for the honor of Max's family.

Max stepped lightly down the wooden steps into the ilet's cavern. He was so familiar with his rum-making operation, he could have found his way around the humid, subterranean distillery without a light. But he threw the switch and time seemed to freeze.

Max found himself face to face with a towering black man who stood in place, holding up a machete, cocked back, ready to strike. After the initial split second of shock, Max let his countless hours of training with Josue take over.

Max let the intruder swing the blade down toward his neck. Max blocked the machete strike, hitting the man's right wrist with the side of his left hand, fingers tucked down, bladelike. The machete clattered to the floor, and Max flipped off the cavern lights, enrobing them both into shadow.

In the first instant of darkness, Max used the mental

photograph his brain had taken of his environment to strike his right fist square into the assailant's face. A sickly sound of crunching cartilage, and possibly bone, echoed throughout the cavern.

Next, Max slithered around behind the man like a deadly python. Before the invader even had a chance to think about the pain in his wrist or face, Max slipped his arm around the man's thick neck, locking it down with his other arm. He twisted and brought the heavy man down to the ground.

Max's powerful choke hold subdued the massive man, whose body writhed and twisted as he struggled to get free of Max's viselike grasp.

As Max wrapped his legs around the man's torso, further restraining his aggressor, he became concerned about the intruder's free hands.

The huge, wounded man reached his arm far around Max's body. Max cursed as the man fought to get his hand on the FNS pistol holstered on Max's right rear hip.

"Uggh," Max grunted as he wrestled the uninvited behemoth.

He pulled harder and harder on his choke hold. Then Max felt his pistol slip free from its holster.

Max released his hold on the man's throat. He grasped the intruder's wrist of the arm holding the gun.

The pistol went off twice with shockingly loud, echoing reports, and two stabs of blinding light.

A sickening snap resounded as Max broke the man's right wrist, pulling it back against the front of his shin. The gun tumbled to the cavern floor.

Max fumbled for the gun and retrieved it, holstering it. He clicked the light switch on.

As quickly as he had holstered the weapon, he reached for it again as he caught sight of someone standing at the top of the stairs above him. He saw the barrel of a shotgun.

"Easy, Max," Vivienne Monet said. "It's me. You okay?"

Max turned to the guy he had just bested, and was sickened by what he saw. The large black man rolled on the ground in agony, reeling from the pain in his wrist. Max guessed his right radius and ulna were both likely cleanly broken. The guy's face was awash in blood from his crooked, broken nose.

"What the hell are you doing here?" Max shouted at the man. "Who sent you?"

The beaten man hesitated at first, but said, "Molière paid us to come here and trash your still, your barrels of aging rum. He told us not to get caught."

Max looked past the wounded man and saw that his still and aging barrels, as well as the rest of the rum-making equipment, appeared to be intact, except for a pool of rum below an aging barrel which sat at the top of the stack, slowly trickling the sweet liquid from a gash on the side. An axe lay on the ground next to the barrels. He was relieved that he had encountered the man before he had done any more damage.

"This guy will need medical treatment," Vivienne said, covering the fallen intruder with her shotgun. "I took care of the other guy."

"Other guy?" Max said, surprised. He looked at Vivienne's outfit. *What an intriguing woman*, he thought, as he took in the sight of her bulletproof vest, shotgun and bandolier, as well as her military-style combat boots. And still the lovely Martinican looked as if she had just stepped off a private jet on her way to a photo shoot. She wiped away beads of sweat from her face and let out a big sigh.

"I like this look on you, Viv," Max said. Then he noticed the trickle of blood that ran down her side, staining her pink tank top above her hip. Closer inspection showed him the long gash in the private investigator's side. Max's blood boiled.

He rushed up the steps to find the other intruder writhing

on the grass, just outside the cavern's mouth, his arms and legs bound with crowd control zip ties. Max pulled a SOG spring-assisted folding knife out of his pocket and slashed through the ties. He tossed the knife aside and grabbed hold of the man's shirt and pulled him up into a sitting position. Max crushed his fist into the man's face. He let the guy fall back onto the ground. And then Max hopped on top of him and began to pummel his face.

"Max, stop," Vivienne said. She stood beside him; she placed her hand onto his shoulder. "It's okay."

Max pounded the man again, and the guy's face looked blank, as if he had lost consciousness with his eyes open. Max struck him again, and again.

"Max, it's over," Vivienne said, trying to push Max off the guy. "He's done."

Max continued to maul the thug in the face.

"Stop it, Max," Vivienne shouted.

Max turned his head and saw the barrel of Vivienne's twelve gauge inches from his face. His lips spread into a smile. "You're gonna shoot me? To save this guy, who tried to kill you?"

"I handled it, Max. He's done. Now get off of him!" Vivienne looked surprised herself to be covering Max with the shotgun. But Max knew she couldn't stand by and watch him kill the guy, even if he was a criminal and a trespasser, and he had cut a woman with his knife.

Max rolled off the guy. He stood up, and spat on the grass. His breath came in quick panting breaths, and his face dripped with sweat.

Josue rushed onto the scene. "Boss, Boss, you all right?"

"I'm fine, Josue."

"Oh, boy," Josue said, looking down at the pummeled intruder. "He in bad shape, Boss."

"These men are groundskeepers from La Maison de Verre distillery, near Le Francois," Vivienne explained. "I gave the distillery owner my report about you, Max, because that's what he hired me to do. But before I gave him my report, I made him swear he wouldn't come after you. His pants were obviously on fire."

"What?" Josue asked.

"I think she's saying that the distillery owner is a liar," Max offered.

Vivienne smiled. She unstrapped her bulletproof vest and dropped it on the grass.

"Get the other guy up here," Max said to Josue.

Josue helped the wounded man up the stairs, as Vivienne threw a bucket of cold water and ice she had filled in the kitchen onto the other man's face. The unconscious man came to after a few seconds, though he seemed rather disoriented at first. Josue forced the older man to kneel.

Vivienne held her shotgun at low ready as Max addressed the men. "You guys got some cojones coming onto my property. You're lucky you're leaving this ilet alive today. Period." Max did his best not to lose control and start yelling at the men. He knew an icier tone would resound in their heads with much greater impact.

"You came here to attack me? To wreck my distillery operation? You attacked this woman? You cut her?" Max's voice started to rise. "Where's that guy's machete?"

"No," the huge man who had grappled Max in the cave protested. Josue rushed down to retrieve the weapon from the cavern floor. He returned and handed the long-bladed weapon to Max. "Please."

Max stuck the tip of the machete into the dirt. He used his foot to press on the side of the blade, starting a deep bend in the blade. Then Max used his hands to fold it the rest of the way over. He grabbed the machete by the handle and threw it as far as he could. It splashed into the turquoise water, just beside the ilet's long pier. The machete-wielder looked relieved.

"You fellows look like you're related," Max said, smoothing

out his nylon shirt. He was dismayed to find a long tear by one of the chest pockets. "Father and son?"

The younger man nodded. The older man gave his son a stern look, as if he shouldn't have offered such information.

"I'm not calling the police on you," Max said, this time making his voice sound explicitly chilly. "I'm letting you go. But if I ever see either one of you on this property again, you're done. Do you understand?"

The bloody-faced man held his shirt up to his nose; he clearly was in a great deal of pain from his swollen wrist. But he nodded with obvious reluctance. The younger man did so as well.

"And I will tell you this, not as a threat, but by way of giving you my solemn word," Max said, peering directly into the father's eyes. "If I hear that you went to the police about my rum operation I won't just come for you." Max drew his FNS pistol and aimed the muzzle directly at the son's face while he stared into the father's eyes. "I'll come for him first. Then I'll find you. Then I'll look for anyone else who might so much as know your names. Do you understand?"

The groundskeepers both nodded.

"A word of advice," Vivienne said. "Stick to cutting the grass and pruning the flowers. Maybe go and work for one of the other distilleries. Vidal Molière is a human worm. He sent you here and almost got the both of you killed. Life is too short to take the short path. Know what I mean? End of lecture."

Max and Josue helped the men to their feet and escorted them to their boat, making sure each of them could climb across the gunwale of their old fishing boat. The father wouldn't be driving, or likely much else, for some time. The son was about a tick away from delirium, but he seemed to be able to walk a straight enough line, and Max guessed he could drive the boat.

"I recommend you both go and get checked out at the hospital," Max said, as the son powered up the boat. "*You've* got a broken wrist and a broken nose. And *you* almost certainly have a concussion. Don't let these things go untreated, okay?"

The beaten son gave one last confused look at Max and Vivienne on the dock as the weathered fishing boat motored away. Max figured the guy was probably surprised by both the violence he encountered on Ilet d'Ombres, and the civility. But the boat drew away, and Max's thoughts almost immediately drifted back to his dinner with Everest Walsh.

"You are bleeding, Max," Vivienne said, putting her fingers on his cheek to check a wound.

Max looked down at himself. "No, all of this blood is probably theirs."

"No, you have a deep scratch on your cheek," she said. "You should get cleaned up and get some antiseptic on that."

"Forget that," Max said. He grabbed hold of Vivienne's shirt and began to lift it. She grabbed his hand to stop him. "No, Viv, I need to check the wound. It looks serious." He lifted the side of her shirt up to the side of her bra. A four-inch slice appeared across her rib cage, and a thin stream of blood trickled from the wound.

"It's just a scratch," Vivienne said, trying to pull her shirt back down. "Should've bought the armor with the side plates."

"No," Max said. "You need stitches. Josue has first aid training. He'll get you bandaged up, but you need to get to the hospital and have it sewn up. Josue could do it, but it won't be a very straight line." Max unbuttoned his shirt and pulled it down to show Vivienne his left shoulder: a zig-zagging, lighting bolt-like scar showed in pink scar tissue directly over his scapula. "That's as straight as he can do."

Vivienne smiled. "Okay, I'll go."

"Boss, we gotta get you ready for your dinner," Josue said.

He took in the sight of Max's blood-splattered face and

winced. "We gotta get you cleaned up. An' Walsh will ask you about scratch on your cheek. Better think of good story."

Max nodded. It would be an eventful night to be certain. He wasn't sure what would happen. But Max hoped with all the strength left in his body that he wouldn't kill someone with his bare hands before the night was over. He had to bide his time; the killing would come later.

# Chapter 17

"YOU ALMOST GOT US FOUND out, Tiny," Zann protested, as he and the others watched the police boat motor away from the catamaran. The rented yacht rested at anchor with the stern facing a sumptuous palm tree-lined beach hemmed in by protective rock jetties.

Standing on the rear deck of the catamaran, Momo felt as though he was witnessing a living postcard: behind the wide span of white sand, restaurants and shops clamored with sunburned tourists clad in bright tropical shirts and dresses; blue chaise lounges lined the sand outside of a boisterous beach bar; and the distant sound of a local island band's combined steel drums, horns, and guitar reached Momo's ears, giving him a profound and unexpected sense of relaxation. He closed his eyes and breathed deeply of the aromatic smoke of flame-grilled, exotically-spiced meats that drifted into his nostrils like a thin fog of tempting island witch doctor medicine.

The boat's anchorage was near Les Trois Ilets, Martinique; at least that's where the boat's GPS told Momo they were located. The Customs officers had approached lightning fast, before Momo even knew they were coming, in their swift Zodiac speedboat.

Zann had stood by the entire time, ready to discreetly cut a length of rope tied between the catamaran's bow rail and a dry bag filled with guns and ammunition the gang members had brought to the island for their important task. The bag also contained heavy barbell weights; Momo had figured they could cut the bag loose at any sign of an inspection. The loose bag would settle to the shallow bottom of the harbor and go undetected by Customs; they could always retrieve their weapons later. But being caught with unregistered Uzis, Glocks, and Berettas would likely get them locked up in an island jail for a very, very long time.

But the Customs men had seemed much more interested in paperwork and checking passports, than in invading their space or taking up too much of their time. Momo was thankful. The last thing he wanted was to get into it with the police. Besides, all of the papers and passports the fellas had brought were all aboveboard.

"I just wanted them to think we ain't got nothing to hide," Tiny Deege said, opening the fridge and rifling through looking for another bottle of Champagne.

"By asking them if they wanna look around," Zann said. "What the hell is *that*?"

"Where's the Champagne?" Tiny Deege complained.

"Ain't no more cold ones," Reggie said, munching on some pretzel sticks and mashing buttons on his Xbox 360 controller.

"Didn't you think to maybe put a few mo' bottles in the fridge when you noticed we was out?" Tiny Deege fumed as he dug into one of the galley's cupboards, finding an unopened case of Veuve Clicquot. "Gettin' low on bubbly now too."

"You worried 'bout the bubbly when you practically begged those cops to find our contraband," Zann said, angrily. "Why'nt you just say, 'Come on in! Come in and look for some o' the stuff we got hidden. You wanna see some of our weed? Some of our coke? Or maybe you'd be more interested in our weapons horde.'"

"Easy, now," Momo said, pulling the .50 caliber Desert Eagle from his waistband.

"Whoa, whoa, whoa," Tiny Deege said, holding his hands up. He stared at the powerful Israeli pistol through huge bulging eyes. "Chill, Momo, chill. We all right. We just working things out between us is all. Ain't no need to go slingin' lead around."

But Momo just placed the pistol on the galley's granite countertop and stripped off his long Miami Heat jersey. "We in paradise boys. Might as well make the most of it." He strode through the open rear of the catamaran's salon and did a back flip off the deck into the crystal clear blue-green water.

"Yeah," Zann shouted, as he and Tiny Deege clapped. Reggie looked over from his video game, semi-interested.

It didn't take long for Zann, Tiny Deege, and Reggie to join Momo in the warm water of the harbor. Momo climbed back onto the boat and retrieved a mask and snorkel from his stateroom. He hadn't ever really found time to go down to the beach, even though he lived in Miami. But now, despite being here for a purpose, Momo intended to find at least a little time to chill.

He ripped the diving mask out of its plastic packaging and pulled it on over his head, adjusting the strap. He secured the snorkel through a loop attached to the mask and jumped off the catamaran's bow. Then he dove down into the pure water, finding the depth to be less than twenty feet. He spotted brightly colored tropical fish swimming in schools all around him: bright white and yellow butterflyfish; the occasional curious trumpetfish or pufferfish; a cluster of yellow and blue Spanish hogfish. Momo even watched a huge sea turtle swim by, obviously unconcerned by the large gang member's presence. As he swam back to the surface, Momo couldn't believe how peaceful a place he had found; he hadn't even set foot on the island, and now he wasn't sure he ever wanted to leave.

Momo's head broke the surface to the sound of screaming. "Ahh. Agghh. Ahhhhhh!" Tiny Deege was shouting over and over.

"Yo! What happened?" Momo asked. He climbed on board the yacht. He and Zann helped Tiny Deege on board, while Reggie watched passively. As Tiny Deege's foot cleared the water, the source of his screaming became evident. A small spiny red and black sea urchin protruded from the bottom of the pint-sized Ti Flow member's left foot.

"Get it out, man! Get it out!" Tiny Deege screamed.

Momo reached down and gave the sea urchin a good yank. It pulled free from Tiny Deege's foot, leaving half a dozen needlelike spines behind, protruding from his flesh.

"Oh, man, it still hurts!" the wounded man shrieked.

"Shut your mouth, fool," Momo scolded. "You be whinin' like a punk little sissy girl. Man up an' act like you belong in the Flow, brother!"

Tiny Deege collected himself and sat down on one of the waterproof seats on the catamaran's rear deck. He picked up his foot and examined it carefully. "Why there all those little blue spots on my skin? Ain't natural. An' them black spines be in my foot still."

"Zann," Momo said, "grab some pliers an' see if you can help pull them spines outta Deege's foot. It's like I'm babysittin' or somethin' bein' with you fools. Can't get a moment's peace, can I?"

"Sorry, Momo," Tiny Deege said, looking up at the gang's would-be leader with a pathetic, scrunched-up frowning face.

"I'm goin' up to the flybridge, dig?" Momo said, tucking his .50 caliber pistol back into his wet shorts. He picked up his smartphone from the galley's counter as well. "Gotta send a text."

Momo grabbed a packet of beef jerky out of one of the snack-filled galley cupboards and ripped off the top. He stuffed a big piece of dry stringy meat in his cheek and mounted the steep ladder to the catamaran's flybridge. There was a control console inside the yacht's salon, so that one could operate the vessel in climate-controlled comfort. But Momo found he was often left alone on the uppermost deck of the vessel, and he liked that very much.

Besides the command console, the flybridge had lots of cushy lounge seating, a separate refrigerator, and a BBQ grill. Other than the fiberglass canopy that shaded him from the sun's harsh rays, the top deck was completely open, allowing the warm tropical breezes to blow in Momo's face as he sipped a cold beer or glass of Champagne.

Momo sat down on one of the cushioned seats. The large white horseshoe of thick padded seats might have accommodated up to a half-dozen people in a party setting. Now, Momo stretched out his legs, taking up an entire side, and he switched on his smartphone.

He found the contact he wanted to text and began to type out his message by tapping on the little virtual keyboard with his index finger.

*We're here. In Martinique.*

Momo chomped on the beef jerky as he awaited a reply. A minute or two later, the messaging tone sounded on his phone.

*Come to Le Robert Bay. Josue Remy nearby.*

"All right," Momo said, as he placed the phone down on the seat next to him. He lay back with his eyes closed and tucked his hands behind his head, interlocking his fingers. "Reckoning's coming, boy. Time's up, Josue."

# CHAPTER 18

"**Y**OU COULD TELL THEM YOU were spearfishing and cut your face on reef," Josue said. "Sounds adventurous, but not too daring."

Max looked into the mirror at the long thin scratch that ran from his chin to his left ear; a gift to remember his tussle with the man from La Maison de Verre distillery. "I like that," he said. "Sounds believable. And it adds a little island color, which I think Walsh will enjoy."

Max wore one of his long sleeved black Columbia Bahama shirts—one that wasn't freshly ripped from a brawl—along with a brand new pair of charcoal gray chinos. He improved his look by slipping on a black blazer with stainless steel buttons. Max didn't own any fancy clothes, but he hoped he could fake it by wearing stuff that was all brand new.

"I wish you could carry weapon," Josue said, sounding rather somber. "I don't like it this way."

"I can take care of myself," Max said confidently. "You remember what to do, right?" He checked the blazer pockets just to be sure he hadn't left any knives or ammunition inside. He knew Walsh's men would pat him down, and he didn't want to rouse their suspicions.

"I will be as close by as I can get," Josue said. "I bring the dinghy out, and maybe a fishing pole, so I look low key. I watch the boat and shoot some video."

"Don't take any chances, Josue. You get made, you bolt. Right?"

The slender Haitian nodded. "You gonna be okay, Boss?"

"Honestly, my friend," Max said, checking out his completed ensemble in the mirror, "I'm more excited than I've been in years. I can't wait for this."

Max checked his Bulova Precisionist. "Ten minutes until go time."

Josue had prepped the ten-foot inflatable dinghy with his scoped 5.56 rifle and lots of loaded magazines. He also had a DSLR camera, fishing gear, a couple of GoPro cameras, and a spear gun. The inflatable was equipped with a fifty-horsepower outboard tiller motor, but Josue would more than likely be using the twelve-volt trolling motor to move as silently as possible on the water. Josue wore a black shorty wetsuit with a blue button-up over it for a more casual look.

Max intended to bug Everest Walsh's yacht. He carried with him two self-contained tiny wireless video cameras with forty-eight-hour batteries, along with four audio-only bugs. They were concealed inside secret compartments in the heels of his shoes, accessible only by removing the shoes and slipping his insoles out. Max had had years to concoct his plan, and he had spent many hours modifying the shoes.

Josue would try to attach a wireless satellite receiver somewhere on the yacht's hull, so that the tiny camera's images, as well as the other bugs' audio feeds, could be forwarded to the surveillance tablet Josue fiddled with in Max's kitchen.

"Va avec Dieu," Josue said, placing a hand on Max's shoulder.

"You as well, my friend," Max said.

Max was waiting on the pier when the Chris-Craft showed up. He didn't know how they had done it, but the instant the tall UFC-looking guy stepped off the boat onto the dock, Max's watch read six fifty-nine and fifty-three seconds.

"I'm Tito," the tall Latin man with the peroxide blond hair said. "If you don't mind, Mr. Walsh would like me to pat you down for weapons. He... has a few enemies."

"No, not at all," Max said, holding his arms up directly at his sides. He noticed the man's demeanor had changed quite a bit since they had first met. Max wondered if it had to do with acceptance; maybe Walsh had told his men that Max was a friend, and that his men were to treat him as such. Tito patted Max down loosely, but thoroughly. It wasn't a deep search, he was likely just checking for the obvious bulge of a pistol or some kind of bladed weapon.

"After you," Tito said, holding out his hand toward a seat near the stern of the fine-looking 1930's era vessel. "Watch your step, sir."

"Nice boat," Max said, unbuttoning his blazer and sitting down on a cushy leather seat.

"Mr. Walsh commissioned the runabout's restoration just a couple of years ago," Tito said. "It had once belonged to his grandfather. This is Chuy, by the way." Tito nodded toward the driver of the boat. It was the same thick-necked, muscular man who had driven the boat earlier in the day.

Chuy nodded and forced a smile. He throttled up the boat and motored the yacht tender away from the dock. Walsh's mega yacht loomed ahead of Max like a cruise ship against the otherwise stark eastern horizon.

As the Chris-Craft drew nearer and nearer the port side of the yacht, Max grew somewhat concerned that Chuy might drive the antique boat right into the two-hundred-and-three-foot yacht's black hull. Just before Max spoke up to sound the alarm, two doors opened in the side of the massive vessel, opening wide to reveal a cavernous water-filled "garage" built right inside the hull of the *Snowy Lady*.

The sleek runabout idled into the cramped mini-harbor inside the yacht. The narrow space reminded Max of a ship lock that would flood with water to raise and lower boats and ships between two larger bodies of water. But this confined space did not lead to another section; rather it was flanked by a big white steel bulkhead on one side, and a wide opening into a dim, elegant room on the other.

The Chris-Craft bumped into a padded rail at the far wall, opposite the outer doors the boat had come through. Chuy reached his arm outside the boat to press a large green button on an electrical panel beside the boat. Hydraulic rails under the water lifted the boat up, securing it in place. He flipped a switch and the outer hull doors closed behind them and the waterline under the boat subsided until no water was visible beneath the craft.

"If you would step out to your left, Mr. Craig," Tito said, standing up in the boat to face Max. He extended his arm toward the darkened room beside the boat, "Mr. Walsh will be waiting to meet you at the bar."

Max stepped out of the boat and slipped his sunglasses inside his blazer pocket. The huge yacht's bar was about twenty feet by twenty, and featured rich, darkly-stained wooden paneling that covered the walls and added to the dim ambiance of the space. A long bar, constructed of some kind of reclaimed wood—replete with worm holes, nail holes, and knot holes, all sanded to a glassy finish and sealed in a clear lacquer—stretched from one wall of the bar almost all the way to the other. A hand-carved wooden sign over the bar read *Rum Lord's Reef*.

Three small tables with chairs were situated around the space, a candle burning on the center of each despite each one being vacant. Two men sat in stools leaning up against the bar, while one man—the bartender—stood opposite them, smiling and resting both hands on the bar top.

Everest Walsh stood as Max entered. He was a tall, heavy man with droopy jowls and puffy bags around his eyes, and a long cigar tucked deep inside his cheek. Max figured him to be about fifty-five. The filthy-rich cigar magnate wore a loud, wrinkled black and blue Hawaiian shirt, maybe a size or two larger than he was, no doubt to cover his unflattering, middle-aged body. His camel-colored hair was buzzed close to his skull; the short cut helped him evade the otherwise obvious fact he was balding pretty thin on top.

"Maxwell Craig, I presume," Walsh said with a huge grin. "Welcome to my humble home away from home. Everest T. Walsh. You might have heard of me."

"Of course, Mr. Walsh," Max said, shaking Walsh's hand. "I've read all about you and your cigar plantation in the Dominican Republic in GQ, Esquire, Playboy. Your appetite for small batch rum is legendary; probably unmatched by anyone I've ever heard of before."

Walsh chuckled. "And I'm sure you read all those publications just for the articles."

Max smiled. The truth was, he had studied Walsh like a book. The exhaustive research Max had performed after his family's murders had unearthed everything there was to publicly know about the man, and a few things less than public. In addition to owning a cigar plantation in the Dominican Republic, Everest T. Walsh was one of the biggest smugglers of cocaine between Bogotá and Miami.

Max's brother-in-law, Chase, had once worked for NOAA. After his sister was gunned down in the Florida Keys, Chase had been more than happy to help Max secure satellite data from the exact time and place Max's family was murdered. Max had studied the satellite images thoroughly, frame by frame, tracing the course of the boat driven by the man who had killed Lovelle and the kids. He had tracked the boat all the way back to a massive mega yacht that sat at anchorage a few miles away from the murder scene. A yacht owned by a suspected drug trafficker, and well-known international playboy. A yacht brazenly named the *Snowy Lady*.

"What the hell happened to your face, Maxwell?" Everest Walsh asked, staring directly at the long scratch on Max's cheek

"Oh, I went out spearfishing this afternoon," Max said. "I like to do my part by skewering as many lionfish as I can; not bad eating either. Afraid I got a bit too close to the reef, and I left with this souvenir."

"At least you got a good story out of it," Walsh said, slapping Max on the back. "Hey, I'd like you to meet my right-hand man, Marquise de Losa." Walsh stepped aside so that the other man at the bar could stand up and face Max. "He's a good man. If you ever need anything, you just ask Marquise."

The man extended his hand for a shake, and Max noticed the black tattoo on the man's arm which showed a long black trident and an octopus with its tentacles wrapping all around the trident's shaft.

Max froze. His eyes locked with the blank black eyes of Marquise de Losa, a man of about fifty years of age with rough, clay-colored skin weathered by countless hours spent in the sun and salt spray. De Losa wore a long olive drab coat with sleeves rolled up, and black shorts over leather huarache sandals. The leather scabbard of a long machete protruded out from underneath the coat.

The Cuban man's black hair seemed unnatural; as if the top had been dyed black and combed through with some kind of shimmering oil, in stark contrast to the feathery, pure white hair on both sides of his head.

The first thought in Max's head was that he might throw up. His second thought suggested that, if Max did not project the utmost friendliness and tact, the entire situation would unfold, badly, in the next minute or so.

Against every instinct his brain screamed at him, Max's lips formed a cordial smile. He robotically lifted his hand to meet de Losa's in a firm, and outwardly friendly handshake.

"Marquise, was it?" Max asked. "Great to meet you. Are you a rum aficionado as well?"

"Marquise doesn't drink alcohol," Walsh said, slapping de Losa on the back with a bright snapping sound. "I believe he's a Mormon, or something like that." Everest Walsh laughed hard; a wheezing full-bodied laugh one would expect from a six-foot-three expatriate Texan, made fat and crass by old family money, likely never having really worked a day in his life, chain-smoking his own terrible cigars, and guzzling way too much of the finest rums in the world. "No, de Losa's a teetotaler. He just goes out and gets the rum for me."

"I bet he always gets his rum," Max said awkwardly. He wondered if de Losa recognized him, even if only a faint sense of familiarity. Max's hair had changed since the last time Marquise had seen it; once blond, and kept very short, it was now longer, mussed-up, dyed black. Max knew his eyes had changed since de Losa had last seen them; once bright, naïve, and likely about as innocent as a grown man's eyes could appear, and now cold, hard, devoid of life.

"Yeah," Walsh laughed. "You got that right. Like a Texas Ranger who always gets his man, Marquise always gets his rum."

Max thought about Jacques and Suze. What it must have felt like to have had Marquise de Losa cornering them on their Viking yacht. The sheer terror they must have felt as he approached them, machete in hand, before ending their lives, and spilling their blood all over the floor of their stateroom.

Though he tried to force himself not to allow such thoughts to creep in, Max's mind began to dwell upon memories of his young children, his wife, as de Losa cut them down with his 9mm submachine gun. What callous disregard he had for their lives. The temperature in Max's blood rose in his veins as he stood before the man, pretending to be a friendly new acquaintance.

Max's conscience wrestled with itself like the fiercest Jujitsu sparring session he and Josue had ever engaged in. On one hand he knew he had to remain cool; any false move and Walsh might have him shot. More importantly, he would lose his chance to get even with Walsh and de Losa for his family's sake. On the other hand, Marquise de Losa's throat was right there, and nothing would have given Max greater pleasure in life than grabbing onto it, and choking the life out of the man who had taken everything away from him.

"This is Coyo," Walsh said to Max, while stabbing his thumb over his shoulder toward the bartender. "Best rum slinger in all of the islands. He must know how to mix every rum drink there is. Bunch I don't even know about too. Always surprising me."

"Hi, Max," Coyo said, shaking Max's hand. The slick-looking bartender wore a silver silk shirt unbuttoned to the middle of his tanned chest, and crisply ironed black slacks. Coyo's hair was black, and as slick as the rest of his appearance.

"It's always a pleasure meeting the man behind the spirits," Coyo said. "Your 2012 V.S.O.P. is possibly the best rhum agricole I've ever sipped."

Max handed the bartender the bottle he had brought. "This one is pretty good too," Max said. "At least that's the feedback I've gotten."

"Oh, man," Coyo said. "No way. The 2013 élevé sous bois is legendary. Hey Max, since I've got you here, would you tell me something? What would you say it is that makes Fleur de Lis so different from the others? Something about the water you use or something?"

"I make the rum inside a cavern, under the ground behind my villa," Max said.

Walsh burst out into boisterous, breath-gasping laughter. "You make the rum in a cave?" he asked, his old Texas accent resounding through; it suggested to Max a rowdy drunk from a bar scene in a Western. "I knew there was something special about the Fleur de Lis rum. Didn't I?" Walsh threw his elbow into de Losa's bicep, compelling the man to force a half-smile.

"Hey, Coyo," Walsh said, after blowing a big lungful of cigar smoke into the bartender's face. "Make Max one of those strange mojitos you make with the smashed-up mint and the ginger stuff."

Coyo adroitly dropped a half-handful of mint leaves into a glass, along with a spoonful of raw sugar. He used a wooden muddling stick to mash the coarse sugar into the leaves, pulverizing them and releasing their fragrant oils. Next, the suave bartender squeezed a lime wedge into the glass before dropping it in, and adding a scoop of ice. From behind the bar, Coyo produced an open bottle of Fleur de Lis rum, and poured a generous shot into the glass. Max recognized it to be one of the first bottles he had ever produced; it was extremely scarce.

*That would be just like Everest Walsh,* Max thought, *using some of the finest single cask rhum agricole in the Caribbean to make a mojito.*

"The secret to the drink is to use really good quality ginger beer," Coyo said, twisting the cap off a fresh bottle and pouring it into the drink. He stirred the drink with a swizzle stick and handed it to Max.

Max took a sip of the drink, realizing that all eyes were locked on him. "Wow, that is *good.*"

Walsh slapped Max on the back. "Bring it with you. I want to show you around before we have dinner." The wealthy drug-trafficker led Max down a long hallway lined with doors. "These are all staterooms for the staff. I've got a captain, first mate, cook, housekeeper, and stewardess, and a couple of deckhands for good measure. Coyo serves as bartender, wine steward, and sometime cigar cutter."

Max chuckled and nodded.

"I don't have a huge staff on board because I don't like having more people around than I need," Walsh explained. "The folks I have here are here because they are necessary, they are trusted, and they are fiercely loyal."

Max, Walsh, and de Losa mounted a steep stairway—likely one designated for the staff—up to the next deck, and entered a short, narrow hallway with only a couple of doors, one of which hung open. Chuy stood inside the medium-sized stateroom, shirtless, curling a stout dumbbell. Walsh pulled the door closed; he looked pissed. "Chuy's room," he said. "Tito's across the hall."

They reached the end of the short hall and stepped into an expansive room that spanned the full width of the yacht. Wide windows covered almost every inch of the outer walls, running the full length of the great space. Several seating areas occupied the space, with sofas and arm chairs situated so that one might best observe the views outside the windows. An incredibly long, oblong cherry dining table with twelve chairs occupied most of the other side of the room.

"Incredible," Max said, stepping up to one of the port side windows, and peering out toward Martinique. He took a sip of his drink. "I've never actually seen the ilets like this before. And Le Robert looks breathtaking."

"Cigar lounge is upstairs," Walsh said, leading Max to the far end of the great room. The two men ascended a beautiful, carpeted spiral staircase, entering another wide open space, almost as large as the one they had just left. This room featured two matching sitting areas, one on the port side and one starboard. Each one featured three large white sofas situated in a horseshoe fashion with a big, square, stone-topped table in between.

"I could get used to this," Max said.

"My stateroom through those doors," Everest Walsh said, nodding toward a pair of smoked glass doors at the front of the room. "Other end of the boat is the bridge and captain's quarters. But we've got one more deck to go." Max and Marquise de Losa followed Walsh to the uppermost deck, called the sundeck.

Max stepped out into what looked like one of the most elegant living rooms he had ever seen, except it was outside, covered only by a hardwood-lined metal awning with recessed LED lights.

"Dining room's a bit formal for me," Walsh said, cutting off the end of a Don Legado cigar and handing it to Max. He trimmed another for de Losa, and finally one for himself. He pulled a torch lighter out of his shirt pocket and blazed up each man's cigar. "Dinner will be served up here. Hope you like seafood. Chef's been delivered a whole crate of little bitty octopuses, octopai, octopao, whatever they're called—he got a whole crate of 'em."

"Sounds delicious," Max said. "Reminds me of Marquise's tattoo. I've never seen one like that; with the octopus and the trident. Does it stand for anything?"

"Marquise used to be with the Cuban Revolutionary Armed Forces," Everest Walsh said before taking a drag from his cigar. "Before he decided to become a capitalist. Used to lead an armored brigade; each of his men got the same tattoo."

Marquise de Losa glared at Max with an expression that suggested, "How dare you ask questions about me."

*I've got something really special in mind for you, my friend,* Max thought to himself as he smiled pleasantly at the vile murderer.

Walsh led Max to a table at the stern of the yacht. It really was an impressive vessel. Max played the awestruck tourist the best he could. He grabbed onto railings and peered over, he looked down inside hatches and pawed at every piece of opulent furniture along the way, generally acting amazed by almost everything he saw. In truth, Max was trying to get a better lay of the land.

Josue had printed the actual blueprints of the *Snowy Lady* from a yacht sales website that had sold Walsh the vessel eight years prior, so they already knew where everything was; as long as Walsh hadn't changed them. It helped that Walsh had pointed out where Chuy's, Tito's, and his own staterooms were located.

DANNAL NEWMAN

Max wondered if de Losa's room were on the bottom level, near the staff quarters.

A modest, round, wooden patio table sat under a fabric covering which reminded Max of a sail. It allowed a great deal of light to pass through, but blocked out the full strength of the sun, which would soon be setting.

A generous hot tub that must have been twelve feet across occupied the rear of the sundeck, surrounded by handsome hand-placed stonework. The elaborate spa featured a cascading waterfall which trickled down over smooth river rocks on either side of the pool-sized spa.

"The water from the tub is pumped through the waterfall and then back down into the tub," Walsh said, sounding rather proud. "You can sit on one of the rocks and let the warm water from the waterfall trickle down over your body. Feels especially nice when you're someplace cold, like Norway or Alaska."

"Impressive," Max said.

Walsh offered Max a seat at the table, and then he and de Losa sat down across from him. "How long have you lived here in Martinique?" Walsh asked.

"About five years." Max took a long puff of his cigar and tried not to choke on the dry, acrid smoke of Walsh's foul cigar. "I used to be in accounting."

"Accounting?" Walsh almost choked out. "Why would you ever give up accounting to move to the Caribbean and make rum?"

Max laughed along with Walsh and de Losa. He was bonding with these men. It was sickening. "*Why* is right. Why did I ever give up the paper cuts and the fast-paced dynamic of crunching all the numbers on some ignorant wretch's 1040EZ?"

The chef brought each man a large platter brimming with all kinds of claws and tentacles. Max ate as much as he could stomach, before asking, "Where's the nearest head?"

"One deck below. Head toward the bow, through the cigar

lounge, and it's the first door on the left," Walsh said, barely looking up from the lobster claw he was sucking on, his chin shiny and slick with melted butter.

Max slipped down the spiral staircase. He found himself at the end of the cigar lounge, with all of its off-white decor, near Walsh's stateroom. The room was deserted. For a split second Max thought about opening one of the smoked glass doors and poking around Walsh's room to see what might shake loose. But he realized the doors might be alarmed. He wasn't ready to get shot quite yet.

Max found the head and shut the door behind himself, making sure it was locked. Max put the toilet seat lid down and sat, taking off his shoes. He removed his tiny cameras and miniature microphones. Just before leaving, Max made sure to flush the toilet and run the sink for a bit. He stepped out and looked around the cigar lounge for a spot to place a video camera.

Double-checking that no one was around, Max hastily stuck a video camera under an end table at the end of the cigar lounge, near the door to the vessel's bridge. It wasn't ideal, but the ordinary table with a vase of flowers on top would not draw any attention; it was out of the way and would capture a wide span of the room.

Max next placed an audio bug under each of the stone-topped coffee tables on either side of the cigar lounge. That way, even whispered conversations could be recorded no matter which side of the room someone decided to sit.

Max stepped softly down the spiral staircase to the main deck below, looking sharp for anyone who might see him. He found a bookshelf at the far end of the great room with the dining area, and he carefully secured the second video camera under a low shelf, facing toward the opposite end of the room. He placed one of the microphones nearby.

Then Max made a beeline for the uppermost deck. He found

Walsh and de Losa arguing about something, but they ceased as soon as Max approached.

"Find it okay?" Walsh asked.

"Yes, I did. But I must admit I couldn't help taking another look out the windows in your cigar lounge. Please tell me it doesn't ever get old living on a yacht like this." Max said, before taking a sip from his third ginger mojito, despite never having asked for one in the first place. Walsh must have just assumed it was his new favorite drink.

The wealthy cigar plantation owner and drug trafficker shook his head. "Nope, hasn't gotten old yet. Don't expect it to any time soon."

Everest Walsh guzzled down almost a whole ginger mojito in one gulp. "I would give about a million pesos to see your underground distillery, Max," Everest Walsh said. "Any chance I can come and take a look around?"

"I'd love to have you," Max said. "Why don't you have Mr. de Losa, Chuy, and Tito come out as well. I'd love to show you all the same hospitality you've shown me here."

Max had a sudden image in his head of all four of these criminals walking into the depths of his underground distillery. Max would push one button on his smartphone and the C-4 bomb in his cabinet would detonate; his family would be avenged in less than a second.

"How about I come and see you around eleven o'clock," Walsh said. "I like to sleep in," he added with a raucous guffaw. "That work for you, Marquise?"

De Losa nodded.

"Eleven it is," Max said. "Can't wait to show you around."

"In the meantime, Marquise is gonna deal some cards," Walsh said. "You play Texas hold 'em?"

"Of course," Max said, forcing himself to take another draw on his cigar.

Walsh used his cell phone to call Tito and Chuy, to have them come up and join the poker game. Marquise de Losa stepped away from the table and called someone on his cell phone. Max hadn't studied Spanish since tenth grade, but he was pretty sure he heard de Losa calling the person on the other end *mi reina hermosa*. My beautiful... queen?

Chuy and Tito came up and sat at the table. Marquise finished his call and sat down at the round patio table as well.

"How about ten thousand, Max," Walsh said. "I know you're good for it."

Max nodded, and de Losa pushed a pile of chips across the table toward him.

"Somebody tell Coyo to get some of Max's rum up here," Walsh said, almost sounding irritated that he had to ask. "Maybe some daiquiris or something."

The five men played cards for several hours. None of them saw Max stick the microphone bug to the underside of the table. Of course they wouldn't. They were too drunk, too high on coke, and too comfortable with Max to notice anything.

It was two a.m. when the Chris-Craft dropped Max on his dock. "Thanks, Tito. See you, Chuy," Max said, as if he were speaking to two of his new greatest friends in the world. He exchanged waves with the other men as they motored away back toward the *Snowy Lady*.

Max reached the porch of the villa before he encountered Josue. The young Haitian still wore his tight-fitting black wetsuit. He looked somber. "Are you all right, Boss? You look very pale."

Max leaned forward, doubled over like he was about to throw up. He placed a hand on the wall by the villa's front door. He looked up at Josue, seeing the concern in the younger man's eyes.

"I shook the hand of the man who killed my family," Max said.

# CHAPTER 19

MAX WANDERED INTO HIS OFFICE as if he were lost. Josue stayed close by, walking no more than two or three steps behind his shell-shocked friend and business partner. Max stepped up to his desk and placed both palms on the cluttered desktop. His head dropped, and his breathing became shallow.

"You okay, Boss?" Josue asked. He placed his hand on the other man's shoulder.

Max took a deep breath and let it out slowly as he turned to face Josue. "I met de Losa," he said, his voice holding back all of the rage, the sadness, and the sheer gravity of his encounter with the violent murderer. "Marquise de Losa is the name of the man who shot my babies; the man who put bullets in my wife's body; the one who took away all of their lives."

"Boss," Josue said.

"And I shook his hand!" Max screamed. He pulled the Smith & Wesson pistol from his holster and held it flat by the side of his ear like a cell phone.

Josue stood by with moon-shaped eyes, likely wondering what Maxwell might do.

"It's going to be okay," Josue said, and Max figured he was probably trying to talk him down from harming himself. "We have plan. We follow plan."

Max set the pistol down on his desk.

Bitter tears of rage welled up in his eyes, but they didn't

fall. "I shook his hand," Max said, this time in a frightening and hushed whisper.

Max drew his FNS .40 caliber pistol from his right hip and began firing.

Crack, crack, crack. Ear-splitting eruptions of thunderous sound echoed inside the confined space, as bullets ripped holes through a red silk armchair. They peppered the wall. They exploded an antique vase, showering the floor with its jagged shards.

Max squeezed the trigger until the last shot left the smoking barrel, and the pistol's slide locked open. He threw the pistol down onto the floor.

Josue clearly didn't know what to do or say, but Max didn't care. He grabbed hold of a floor lamp with a long lathe-turned maple base. He gave it a yank and ripped the cord out of the wall.

Max broke the wooden body of the lamp over his leg. He used it to bash the antique bottles of rum which sat on the desk. Sixty-, seventy-, eighty-year-old bottles of JM, Saint-James, and Clemént rum shattered, their antique glass raining in all directions, their sweet ancient liquid spilling into nothing more than a priceless stain on the office's hardwood floor.

Max grabbed the underside of the heavy oak desk and heaved with an explosion of power only a man coursing with adrenaline could accomplish. He threw the desk, toppling it over on the floor. Max's box of Don Legado cigars tumbled over spilling the foul cigars all about the space.

"Boss?" Josue asked.

Max put his hands against the wall to support himself. He bowed his head deeply. "I feel better now, Josue," he said. Max gasped, panting for breath. "I feel better."

"Come," Josue said, leading Max to the bathroom halfway down the main hallway of the villa. The Haitian rifled through the medicine cabinet, reading the labels on several orange, white-capped prescription bottles. He handed Max two Ambien tablets and drew him a glass of water. "Take these. You feel better, get sleep."

Max didn't argue, he just took the pills, and drained the glass.

"Come," Josue said, suggesting that he was more of a mother than a friend and business partner to Max, "we'll sit and have a punch. Then you sleep."

Max just nodded. He and Josue sat on the porch sipping glasses of Ti' Punch Josue had made with La Favorite rhum vieux. Max held quiet for a time before he finally said, "I'm sorry, Josue. I lost control. How did you make out with your surveillance of Walsh's yacht?"

"No one was standing guard," Josue said, showing bright white teeth in a broad smile. "I brought the dinghy alongside and boarded yacht."

"You boarded the yacht?" Max asked, incredulous. "While I was eating dinner?"

Josue nodded. "I poked around, found the engine room. The cases of rum stolen from Jacques and Susan were in small utility room next to engine. Also found piles and piles of bundles of white powder. Cocaine, maybe? I took two bundles, think they were kilograms. I found a bag in the room of the heavy fellow."

"Chuy?" Max asked.

"Yes, that's correct. Bag full of clothes, soap, deodorant. Overnight bag. Figure he going ashore at some point to spend night. I place two kilos of cocaine in bag. Then use diver knife, punch hole in bottom of bag, through bundle. When he tries to go ashore, he leaves trail of powder."

Max burst out laughing. In spite of the strong sedative starting to work on his brain, he leapt out of his wicker chair and grabbed Josue by the ears. He kissed him on the forehead.

"Awww," Josue said, facetiously wiping his forehead with his sleeve.

"You're a ninja, my friend," Max said. He felt energized. Things were finally set in motion. "Great thinking on your part. Walsh suspects Chuy tried to steal his snow, well… I shudder to think."

"Hope this help, Boss," Josue said in his usual tone of great humility.

"It will help a lot, Josue," Max said. "I'm certain of it. The whole crew, I'm assuming; Walsh, de Losa, Chuy, and Tito will all be coming, they'll arrive around eleven. I'm going to offer to make special rum drinks for the group. That's when I'll slip the ricin powder into de Losa's drink. By the time he realizes he's sick, it'll be too late to save him."

"What about the others?" Josue asked.

"Honestly, my friend, I've been considering for years what I would do to each man. Now that things are happening, I think we'll improvise. Just be ready when I give you instructions, all right? Oh, and call Maisie in the morning, have her bring over lunch at noon. Pay her whatever she wants."

Josue nodded. "Bed now for you."

Just as he turned onto his side in his bed, having just fallen asleep, Max felt two hands pressing down on his arm. His hand slipped under his pillow and reached for his FNS pistol. He pointed it toward Josue, who was shoving Max, trying to try to wake him up.

"Easy, Boss," the slender Haitian said. "Boat will be here soon. Time to get up."

Max looked at the gun. He thought back to the previous night. "Did you put this here? Did you reload it?"

Josue nodded. "I clean and reload."

"Wow," Max said, dumbfounded.

He got out of bed and got dressed as Josue rushed downstairs to prepare a tray of breakfast and coffee. Max looked down at his right forearm before he buttoned his black shirt over his wrists. The reckoning was coming for de Losa. And it was coming soon.

Max checked both of his pistols and holstered them. He didn't care if Walsh had him patted down today. This was his own domain. And Max would be damned if anyone tried to disarm him on his own property.

He sat in the kitchen and ate breakfast with Josue, who kept a keen eye on the large tablet's bright display. Josue toggled between several cameras, doing his best to ascertain what he could of Walsh and his men's current movements.

"Oh, almost forget. I have surprise for you, Boss," Josue said. He tapped the tablet's screen and brought up an audio clip that had been previously recorded only hours earlier. "Listen."

Josue played the audio clip which featured silence for about ten seconds before Everest Walsh's voice could be distinctly heard, saying, "What the hell is *this*, Chuy? There's white powder spilling out of your bag. Is this—?"

"This recorded shortly after you got home and boat got back to yacht," Josue explained.

"This is blow!" Walsh's voice could be heard screaming as the audio clip continued. "Where does this trail lead? It leads all the way back to your room. Give me the bag, Chuy." Walsh sounded livid. Two sharp gunshots cracked on the recording.

"Now look at this," Josue said. He showed Max a video from the small camera Max had placed on the bookshelf in the yacht's great room. The camera pointed across the room toward the hallway where Chuy and Tito's rooms were located. As they watched the video, Walsh appeared from the darkened end of the hall, looking at the ground all the way. He was following the trail of powder, and he walked right into Chuy's room, followed by Chuy himself, who looked as much confused as anything. Then two bright flashes of light illuminated the hallway, and Everest

Walsh stepped out into the hallway, swinging a small pistol by his side.

In the video, Marquise de Losa and Tito rushed down the hall to investigate the commotion.

"He ordered them to get rid of Chuy's body," Josue explained. "Look." He rolled another video, but this one came from a FLIR thermal imaging camera. The yacht appeared as a hulking gray mass in the video. Suddenly a door opened and two white, glowing forms appeared on screen. The brightness showed their body heat, and as they approached the railing at the rear deck of the *Snowy Lady*, it was clear they were carrying a long bundle, wrapped up tightly, that was quickly changing from dull white to bright gray as it was being dumped into the ocean.

"They dumped Chuy's body into the Atlantic," Max said, his eyes peeled as he watched the surveillance footage. "Chuy's body is sitting there, just below the yacht. They must have wrapped it tight and weighted it down. They only need it to stay put until they leave the island. If the body washes up on shore down the road, I doubt they would even care."

Max wasn't sure how he would feel when the men responsible for the deaths of his family met their ultimate fates. Now that the first one was dead, he was still not certain. There was a hint of relief, but also a tinge of remorse. Max guessed it had something to do with the sense he got at a life being wasted, even if it had been Chuy who had chosen to waste his by associating with Walsh and de Losa.

"Well that's one down," Max said, matter-of-factly. "Three to go. The most important is de Losa. I don't much care what happens to Walsh or Tito compared to that black-and-white-haired demon." Max pulled a small metal twist-top vial out of his pocket. It was the kind heart patients used to keep their nitroglycerine tablets undamaged.

"The ricin?" Josue said.

Max nodded. He had grown his own castor bean plant to harvest the toxic seeds in order to produce the highly poisonous powder that now resided inside the stainless steel vial. "Once de Losa realizes something is wrong it will be too late. He'll be dead within three days."

Josue's body gave an involuntary shudder. "Cold way to kill someone."

Max tucked the poison back inside his pocket.

"Nearly eleven," Josue said, turning his attention back toward the video feeds on the tablet. He adjusted one of the pan, tilt, zoom cameras on top of the lookout to zoom in tighter on the outer doors of the Chris-Craft's "garage." He took a sip of his coffee, and then bit a croissant. Almost as if it were an ordinary day.

About ten minutes later, Josue slapped Max on the arm. It was good, because Max had nodded off; likely the aftereffects of the sedative that had put him to sleep the night before. "Boat's coming out, Boss."

"Who's on it?" Max asked severely.

"Looks like... Walsh, Tito... that's it," Josue said. "De Losa's not on the boat."

Max brought his fist down so hard on the kitchen table, a small stress fracture appeared where his hand had been. "Can you run through last night's footage? See if you can spot de Losa going anywhere? It's possible he stayed behind to guard the yacht."

Josue set about reviewing all of the surveillance video from the last twelve hours, as Max prepared himself for his meeting with Walsh. "I'll be at the dock," he said. "If you find anything you can pursue, then pursue it, but don't do anything dangerous without me."

Max and Josue clasped hands. "I promise, Boss," Josue said, showing his brilliant white teeth. "You don't want me to hang around? Shadow you?"

"No," Max said, frowning as his mind drifted into deep

thought. "No, I'll be all right with Walsh. He just wants a tour of the distillery, and I'll give it to him. I intend to string him along as long as I can. I want to play his men against each other as best we can. Getting Walsh to kill Chuy was priceless."

Max opened a little box on his kitchen table and took out the earpiece he wore to send and receive communications to and from Josue. He screwed it into his ear.

"You don't think it's too risky to wear a wire?" Josue asked.

"No. I'm Walsh's new best friend."

Max headed down to the dock. He slipped on his tortoise wayfarers as he walked the length of the long white pier. At the end, he leaned on a piling as he waited for Walsh's boat to arrive.

Max looked down into the pure tropical water by the dock. Little fish swam by under his very feet. *It was so beautiful here*, Max thought. *Such a sad waste of beauty.*

Everest Walsh's highly-polished runabout approached and Tito pulled it up close to the dock. Max helped keep the boat from hitting the dock, and he tied off the bow, while Tito tied off the stern. Everest Walsh stepped out of the boat. He wore a long, bright yellow shirt with rolled-up sleeves and a white newsboy cap that made him look a bit like Chef Paul Prudhomme. The rich plantation owner also wore wide wraparound sunglasses, the kind you got when your pupils were dilated by the optometrist.

Max offered Walsh a firm handshake and was even bold enough to reach in and give the wealthy cocaine trafficker a manly half-hug. He did the same for Tito. *We're like family now*, Max thought. *As dysfunctional as a family comes.*

"Where's Chuy and Marquise?" Max asked.

Walsh didn't skip a beat. "De Losa had some other business today. And Chuy had to run back to the D.R. Mama's in the hospital. Cancer. I'm afraid you won't be seeing anymore of him this trip."

Max laughed inside his head. *And unless he is resurrected*

*from the bottom of the Atlantic, I suppose he won't be seen much on his next trip either.*

"Yeah, he's a good man," Walsh said. "Real shame he had to go."

"Let me show you around, Mr. Walsh," Max said.

"Everest."

"Everest," Max said, trying to contain his fox-like grin. "My distillery is actually underground out behind the villa. If you and Tito would like to follow me, I'll give you the two-dollar tour."

"You're not gonna show us the villa first?" Walsh said.

Max's mind raced back to the night before. In a moment of utter meltdown, Max had trashed his office, turned over his desk, and shot holes in his walls and furniture. He knew that if Walsh were to see it, he might find it at least a little bit suspicious.

"Certainly," Max said. "I just didn't think it would interest you much. Seems rather pedestrian compared to the *Snowy Lady*."

Walsh smiled. "I love these old Martinican buildings. Ripe with history. Looks like you did an outstanding job fixing it up. Did you do the work yourself?"

"Yeah, most of it," Max said. "With the help of my business partner, Josue."

"Is Josue around?" Walsh asked. "I'd like to meet him."

"No, he had to run some errands in town, and he won't be back until late," Max almost kicked himself for mentioning Josue's name. He didn't want to endanger his friend by getting him involved with the likes of Everest T. Walsh.

"Cigar?" Walsh asked. He pulled out a leather cigar sleeve and slipped out a couple of Don Legado cigars.

"Sure," Max said. "My favorite brand."

"Now Max," Walsh said, placing his hand on Max's shoulder and gripping down firmly. "Don't go and say a thing like that if you don't really mean it. I only surround myself with loyal people because they aren't going to go and say something just because they think it's what I want to hear. Do you get me, son?"

Max nodded.

"Good. Now let's get on with that tour. I'm eager to get a glimpse of your setup." Walsh tucked his oversized sunglasses into his shirt pocket.

Max led Walsh and Tito into the front door of the villa and began to show them around. When they reached the kitchen, Max tried to emphasize the view of the backyard through the kitchen window. "The distillery is just out there," he said.

"What's down here?" Walsh asked, pointing down the hall toward Max's office, where the door hung slightly ajar.

"Oh, that's just my old accounting office," Max said. *First Travere, and now Walsh. What is it with my office?* "I don't actually do any accounting in there. It's sort of a… front… in case anyone comes poking around. I'm an accountant, not a rum runner."

Everest Walsh laughed with deep belly-rippling laughter. "Well, all right," he said. "You got it all figured out. Well done. May I take a peek?"

"Sure," Max said. He wondered if he should escalate things now. He could take out both Tito and Walsh in two seconds with his FNS pistol. Instead, he followed Walsh and Tito down the hall.

Everest Walsh stepped into the room ahead of Max. "Wow," he said.

Max's stomach buzzed with nervous energy. He stepped into the office behind Tito. His jaw dropped.

The mammoth desk Max had toppled now stood upright, its top covered with a smattering of disorganized papers. There were even some antique rum bottles to replace the old, broken ones. Max's eyes gazed around the room. The broken floor lamp was gone, along with the bullet-riddled armchair. Even the bullet holes in the walls and floor had been carefully filled with either spackling putty or wood filler.

While Max had been asleep, Josue must have spent hours fixing the room for this very moment. And now Walsh looked at Max with a broad smile.

Max was curious. What was he smiling about? Max looked down at his desktop where a half-empty box of Don Legado cigars sat open with one half-smoked and stamped out into a glass ash tray.

"You're all right, Max," Walsh said, slapping Max on the back with a skin-tingling crack.

"Enough of this mundane crap," Max said, rolling the dice. "I am absolutely on pins and needles to show you my distillery."

"Well, let's go see it, son," Walsh beamed.

Max led Walsh and Tito through the kitchen and out onto the grass behind the villa. "This cane pile is all that's left from the batch me and Josue distilled a few days ago," Max said.

He led Walsh down the wooden steps into the subterranean distillery. Max noticed a smidgen of blood on the cavern floor, where Max had broken the nose of the thug from La Maison de Verre. He hoped the drug trafficker wouldn't notice.

Of course, the tripwire for the C-4 bomb had been disarmed and removed for Walsh's visit.

"This is absolutely incredible, Max," Walsh said, with what sounded like genuine admiration. "This still is a piece of art, my friend. And you've got barrels aging and cases and cases of Fleur de Lis everywhere."

"Thanks, Everest," Max said. "I'm glad that a real rum connoisseur like you approves."

"I want it all, Max," Walsh said. Max noticed that he wasn't smiling or giving any sense that he was joking.

"What?" Max asked.

"I want all of the rum. Name your price."

"Well, I don't know," Max said, having strange feelings about the rum. It had always been just a means to draw Walsh and the others to him, but now, now that he was faced with the thought of letting all of it go, Max realized that it might actually mean something to him. The thought of selling all of his rum to Everest Walsh made him sick. But he could not let his feelings interfere with his end game.

"I usually get about one-fifty a bottle," Max said.

"Done," Walsh said. "You'll get cash as soon as the product is loaded onto my yacht."

"I'm having a lunch catered for us at noon," Max said. "There's a beach bar nearby with great food, and I convinced them to deliver lunch directly to my dock. It only cost me two bottles of rhum vieux."

Walsh chuckled, and looked back over the stack of rum barrels and cases of bottled rum. "I hope you already paid 'em, 'cause all of this is mine."

Max laughed good-naturedly. "If you fellows would like to head up to the front porch, we can have a cigar and a glass of rum while we wait."

Walsh, Tito, and Max headed up the steps into daylight. Max heard a voice crackling in his ear. His instincts told him to say, "What?" but he resisted the urge. Walsh and Tito didn't know he had a communication device in his ear.

"I found de Losa," Josue said. "He checked in at hotel in Le Francois."

Josue was trained to know that if he heard no reply from Max, it meant that Max was unable to speak.

"He visited woman in the hotel," Josue continued. "I think is his mistress."

*Mi reina hermosa*, Max thought.

"De Losa just left, actually," Josue added. "Taxi driver told me that he checked in about four a.m. Just the mistress is in the room now. When you can talk. Let me know what you like me to do."

Max made Everest Walsh and Tito comfortable on the porch.

"Food should be here in about ten minutes," Max said. "Meantime, I'll get those drinks."

Max headed into the kitchen, and pulled a pitcher of orange juice and a bottle of pineapple juice out of the fridge and placed them on the hardwood island. "Read me, Josue?"

"Yes, Boss."

"See if you can distract the mistress, maybe get her out of the room," Max said in a low voice, always keeping his eye out for someone coming through the kitchen door. "Do you think you can get into the room? Poke around, see whatever you can find out about her."

"Roger that," Josue said.

Max mixed up planter's punches made with Dillon Rhum Blanc 50° and placed them on a silver tray. It burned him that de Losa wasn't present so that he could drop the powdered ricin into the man's drink, sealing his fate. *Guess that'll have to come later,* Max thought.

He took the drinks out to Walsh and Tito, who were seated on the cushioned wicker chairs on the porch, then he sat down with them.

Everest Walsh took his glass from the tray. "I want you to deliver the rum to my yacht tomorrow morning," he said. "Is that going to be a problem?"

Max took a sip of his drink and shook his head, "No, sir. Josue and I can start bringing them out first thing in the morning. It will likely take a few hours, and several trips with my boat."

"That works for me," Walsh said. "I'm not sure when we will be shoving off back to the D.R., and I would like to have the rum loaded up and ready for when we decide to do so."

Max nodded.

"I promise. Come morning, Josue and I will be ready."

# CHAPTER 20

"**D**ID YOU SEE POWER CATAMARAN anchored off of Ilet Boisseau?" Josue asked. He had returned from his surveillance of Marquise de Losa and his mistress, and now sat at the villa's kitchen table with Max, nibbling on some of the leftover charcuterie, cut fruit, and freshly baked bread that Maisie had had delivered for Max's catered lunch with Everest Walsh.

"No," Max said. "Suspicious?"

"Don't see as many tourists anchoring boats on this side of island. Strange to me their anchorage is right between us and big *Snowy Lady* yacht."

"Show me," Max said, his eyes narrowed with concern.

Josue tapped, pinched, and double-clicked on the big tablet that lay on the kitchen table. He controlled one of the cameras, tilting it and zooming in tighter until he was locked on to a forty-five-foot or so diesel-powered catamaran, anchored just off the coast of the ilet nearest Max's.

"Can you zoom in a bit more?" Max asked. "On the bow."

Josue controlled the camera until it had zoomed in tightly enough that three black men were visible, sunning themselves on the catamaran's wide bow area. Josue tapped a button to start the camera recording.

"Well, keep an eye on 'em," Max said, popping a slice of cheese in his mouth. "Hopefully they're just pleasure cruisers. Report anything you see that's out of the ordinary. Okay? Don't keep anything to yourself."

Josue nodded and refilled his coffee cup from a half-empty French press.

"Walsh bought all of the rum," Max said.

"Seriously?" Josue asked. "All of it?"

"Aging barrels and everything," Max said. "We're delivering it tomorrow morning, early. We should try to get it done before Walsh even wakes up. Probably won't get up until ten or eleven."

"What is our next move with these men?" Josue asked, before taking a sip from his steaming cup. "Besides delivering them a bunch of rum."

"What did you find out at the hotel room of de Losa's mistress? Anything we can use?" Max, at first, didn't realize that he rubbed his hands together vigorously under the table as he asked. When he did, it made him feel a bit like a cartoon villain.

"Oh, that was fun," Josue said, a mischievous grin taking over his face. "I pull fire alarm in hallway of hotel. Everyone evacuates and I slip into her room. She leave her purse in the room. From what I can gather, she is cocktail waitress at nightclub in Fort de France. De Losa must have called her to meet at hotel in Le Francois since that is close to *Snowy Lady*."

"Wow," Max said with a grin. "I've always wanted to do that, pull the fire alarm. What was in the purse?"

"I check her phone. Mostly recent calls from de Losa. Seem to call her every couple of hours. Phone actually rings when I'm holding it. Funny ringtone. It was a country western song, *I'd bet my boots, I was meant for you...* or something silly like that."

Max stared out the window for a moment, lost in deep thought. "Do you think you could get back there and steal her phone?" Max asked. "I've got an idea, and it involves the phone. But you've got to take it as closely as possible to the time when we deliver the rum tomorrow. Do you think that will work?"

"I make it happen," Josue said. "No matter what."

"Good man," Max said. "If my plan works, we'll just have de Losa and Walsh left to worry about. I'm planning on slipping the ricin powder into de Losa's drink after we deliver the rum. The entire situation should all be done and dusted by the time the sun goes down tomorrow. Then, it'll be Miller time."

"Miller time?" Josue asked.

"Miller time. It's an American expression."

Butterflies fluttered in Max's stomach. Now that all the action had started, he didn't know if he was ready for it to be over. Six years had passed since his Lovelle, Lucy, and Lionel were gunned down on that hot and fateful Florida afternoon. He had only just met Walsh and his men. It was hard to believe one of them was already dead, and the rest would not be long in following.

Max's phone rang. *Who the hell would call me now?* he thought. He looked at the smartphone's display and saw a picture of Isobel Greer. *When did I add her to my contacts?* Max decided the free-spirited Scot must have grabbed his phone when he had stepped into the men's room at dinner the other night, snapped the picture, and added herself to his list. *Cute girl.*

Max tapped the answer button. "Yes?"

"Max?"

"Yeah, it's me. What's up, Isobel?" Max thought he had made it clear that the two of them had no future. He didn't want their situation to drag on and become even more complicated.

"Max, I don't like how we ended our last conversation," Isobel's Scottish accent sounded thicker today, Max guessed it had to do with the stress apparent in her voice. "And there is something important that I need to discuss with you. Is there any chance I could meet with you, so we can talk? I really think we need to talk."

"I've got a lot on my plate right now," Isobel. "Maybe I can get free and meet you in a few days."

"No, Max," Isobel protested. "It has to be now, today."

"Why don't you just tell me who you're running away from, Isobel," Max said, leaning back in the cushioned seat of his kitchen's breakfast nook.

"What?" Isobel asked, sounding surprised.

"Isobel, you told me all the places you've lived, the fact that you have a penchant for getting involved with dangerous men. I know you came here to get away from somebody. But I can't help you if you don't tell me about them." Max's volume was getting louder as his patience grew shorter.

"I... I don't know," Isobel said. "Can't we meet and talk?"

"Isobel, if you can't answer my question now, then we have nothing further to talk about."

"Please. Just—"

"Who is it? Are they here now, on Martinique?"

"I can't tell you. You'll kill him, or he'll kill you."

"Goodbye, Isobel." Max tapped the red button to hang up the call. He'd be better off without the burden of another person in his life whom he had to protect. Because, what if he couldn't? Max didn't think he could take it if he let a woman like Isobel into his life, only to lose her as he had lost everyone else. The pain and loss would be too much to bear.

"Sorry, Boss," Josue said.

"It's all right," Max said, setting the phone down on the kitchen table. "Sometimes you just have to let go."

# CHAPTER 21

MOMO STEPPED OUT OF THE head in his stateroom, followed by a cloud of steam that whooshed out the door behind him. He toweled off and got dressed in black basketball shorts and a fitted Under Armor t-shirt. He placed a Florida Marlins baseball cap on his head and checked his Desert Eagle. After seeing the shiny brass in the chamber, he tucked the weapon into his waistband and climbed through the companionway to the catamaran's salon.

"What the hell is this?" Momo asked, stepping out into a thick cloud of marijuana smoke so dense, he could barely see a foot in front of his face. "Open a window, fools."

Zann opened the doors at the rear of the salon so that the rear of the galley was wide open to the outside air. A rush of fresh air flowed in and dissipated the thick smoke as Momo stepped through to the rear deck and picked up a pair of binoculars he had bought at Walmart on 79th Street before they had left Miami.

Darkness had encompassed the cluster of small islands that littered the bay in front of Le Robert, except for a smattering of lights from the sloping city itself. A sliver of moon offered some light, but Momo wondered if they'd even be able to see a thing before the sun came up in a few hours.

"I can't see squat," Momo said. He twisted the zoom ring and the focus ring until he had acquired the long white pier that stretched out from the densely overgrown ilet they surveilled. It loomed not two hundred yards away.

"You ain't usin' 'em right, Momo," Tiny Deege said. "You gotta take off them lens caps afore you look through."

"I'm usin' it right, chump," Momo scolded. "There just ain't nothin' to see. The trees and bushes and whatnot is makin' it impossible to view *anything*. Suppose our only hope is to keep an eye out an' wait till he gets on that blue boat to go somewhere."

"Yo, Momo, that's how we should travel on our next trip," Zann said. He pointed through the windows in front of the catamaran's control console inside the salon. A massive yacht sat anchored a few hundred yards in front of the catamaran, dominating the horizon like a huge monolith of shiny white and black. Bright white LED lights on board the vessel illuminated its magnificence, making the imposing vessel look almost unreal. "That's cruisin' in style, dig?"

Tiny Deege clasped hands with Zann. "Yo, that's what I'm talkin' 'bout."

Momo was ready for this trip to be over. Close quarters with Zann, Tiny Deege, and Reggie were definitely taking a toll on Momo's peace of mind. Between the constant arguing, the untidiness, the general smell created by the group of men, Momo was certain he had had just about enough. He couldn't wait to get rid of Josue Remy for good, and to move on with his life as the leader of the gang.

Maybe he would send the others back to Miami with the catamaran while he stayed behind and established a presence for Ti Flow on Martinique. There must be some kind of legit work he could get his hands on here: slinging coke, armed robbery, maybe he could even get a human trafficking line set up between the island and Little Haiti back home. Now that he had gotten a taste of what living in paradise was like, Momo didn't know if he *could* go back.

"Listen up, fellas," Momo said, addressing the entire group. Tiny Deege and Zann had sat down at the bar in the galley facing the rear deck. Reggie, sitting in the salon playing video games, barely looked up. "We take turns watching the dock. Four hours at a time, then we change. You see movement, you come and get me. Dig?"

Everyone nodded.

"Josue leaves the island, me and Zann gonna take the Sea-Doo and follow him," Momo said, commandingly. The catamaran rental had included the use of a personal watercraft to transfer between anchorages and the shore. The Sea-Doo hung suspended out of the water behind the rear deck by an electric winch. "We get a chance, we gonna approach Josue, we Tase him, then we grab him. Then we bring him back here. Any questions?

"Tiny Deege, I'm puttin' you in charge of getting everything ready for when we get back here with Josue," Momo continued. "Put down the plastic sheeting in my stateroom. You get out the ropes we gonna tie him to the chair with, the extension cords we gonna whip him with, the Drano and the funnel, the hammer, and the vice grips. Oh yeah, don't forget to have the blow torch ready to go too; check it to make sure the propane tank full. We gonna make this sucka pay for his disloyalty. And then we gonna smoke him. This is what happens you dis the Flow. Dig?

"Reg, you even listening?" Momo asked, irritated by the apathetic teenager's uninvolved detachment. "Yo, man, I'm gettin' real tired of your attitude, young buck. You think you ain't gotta pull no weight on this crew, you is mistaken, my friend. You gonna take the first watch. Dig?"

"I don't think Mama Dorah would want me to participate in this," Reggie said, after pausing his game. Momo was a bit surprised he did even that. "She said it was you that let Josue get away, and it was you that needs to take care of him."

"Why she even send you along then?" Momo asked, exasperated. "What you here fo'?"

"Mama Dorah wanted me along to keep an eye on everything

you do," Reggie said, looking Momo square in the eyes. The petulant young man wielded the only power he knew gave him the upper hand against Momo—fear of Mama Dorah. "She said I was supposed to tell her if you did anything that didn't make progress toward ending Josue Remy. She said she wanted me to call her."

"I'm getting real tired of yo' high and mighty complex you got goin' on, Reg," Momo said. "Now you gonna get yo' ass out on that deck, an' you gonna keep yo' eyes peeled for any sign of Josue Remy. You don't do what I say, and even Mama Dorah's *sight* won't be able to find where I bury you. Dig?"

Reggie jumped up from the sofa in the salon and bolted for the rear deck. He hung the binoculars around his neck and plunked himself down in one of the deck chairs. Despite the teen's sulky attitude, Momo knew he had gotten through. But he didn't know how much more he could take from the kid before he snapped, and did something he might regret.

Then Momo heard Reggie mumble something in his direction.

"What?" Momo said. "What you say?"

"I said Mama Dorah's gonna put a curse on you, Momo. A hex," Reggie said. "She's gonna make you wish you ain't never been born."

Momo strode toward Reggie as a walking fireball of anger. His jaw clenched, his teeth crushed together, the huge would-be gang leader stomped toward Reggie and grabbed hold of his shirt front. Momo pulled the Desert Eagle from his waistband and stuck it in the teenager's face.

"Open yo' mouth," Momo said. "Open yo' mouth. I ain't playin' now. Open yo' mouth or you gonna get smoked right now."

Reggie opened his mouth, and Momo pressed the thick muzzle of his Israeli-made pistol into the younger man's mouth. Momo could hear Reggie's teeth scraping against the nickel plating of the Desert Eagle's frame and slide. "Now listen up, Reginald,"

Momo said coldly. "You gonna tell me all about Mama Dorah's powers. *The sight* you called it. Tell me about *the sight*, Reggie. It ain't real, is it?"

Reggie's eyes betrayed his terror. He seemed too afraid to answer.

"It's okay, Reggie," Momo said softly. "I know you can't talk now. So you just nod your head up and down, or shake it side to side. Mama Dorah's a fraud, isn't she?"

Reggie nodded his head gingerly.

"*The sight* ain't a real thing, is it, Reg?" Momo said, sounding menacingly cold. "Don't lie to me. Just tell me the truth. Right? *The sight* ain't real, is it?"

Reggie shook his head slowly from side to side.

"Aww, what?" Tiny Deege said, sounding indignant.

"Now I'm gonna take my piece out yo' mouth an' you gonna tell me all about it," Momo said to Reggie. "Dig?"

Momo removed his pistol from Reggie's mouth and wiped the slobber off on Reggie's shirt. "How she know all that stuff? How she know where to find Josue Remy?"

"I found it for her," Reggie said. "She knew I did a bit of hacking now and then; she made me do searches and find Josue. Took a couple of *years*. I hacked into police mug shot databases, traffic cameras, ATM cameras, grocery store cameras. I ran programs that searched the web for photos, videos, and automatically ran them through a facial recognition software I stole. Took a single frame from an ATM camera in Sainte-Anne, Martinique, to identify Josue. Hacked the bank, traced him to Le Robert, Martinique. Mama Dorah figured that was enough to send us on this trip."

"When all this is over," Momo said, standing and tucking his pistol back into his waistband, "and I take over Ti Flow, you and Mama Dorah gonna be movin' out the neighborhood. Dig? Don't want to see you two in the 'hood again, lest I do something *you* might regret."

Reggie just nodded. He was likely too terrified to do anything else.

"Good," Momo said. "I'll be up on the flybridge." He climbed the steps from the rear deck to the open cockpit area overhead. Momo sat down at the cushioned captain's chair at the helm. He leaned back with his eyes closed as the catamaran swayed gently in the tropical breeze that lightly roughed up the water of Le Robert bay.

Momo didn't realize he had drifted off until he felt the gentle tug on his snug-fitting shirt. At first he had thought that some kind of bug or creature was crawling on him. He slapped at it, then opened his eyes and saw Reggie's eager, bespectacled eyes peering down at him.

"What is it?" Momo mumbled. "What time's it?"

"Hey, Momo," Reggie said. "Looks like someone be leavin' from the boat dock. Thought you'd wanna know."

Momo grabbed the binoculars again and swiveled in the captain's chair. He pressed the cushioned eye cups into his eye sockets.

"It's Josue," Momo said, sounding aghast, despite his grogginess. "He's leavin' the island."

Momo checked the face of his TAG Heuer chronograph watch. Nearly two hours had passed since he had nodded off at the helm of the anchored catamaran. He shook his head to clear the fog he felt in his brain.

"Reggie, go tell Zann he comin' with me," Momo commanded. "And grab me a can of Rockstar. Make it two. We gonna catch us a traitor."

# CHAPTER 22

T HE SUN HAD BARELY BREACHED the horizon when
Max finished inventorying the rum in his underground
distillery. He had eighteen fifty-four-gallon barrels of
rum aging in the cavern. That did not include the hundred and
twenty plus cases of bottled rum stored in the dark recesses of the
humid cave.

Transferring all the rum above ground promised to be an
arduous chore. Max intended to make lighter work of the job
using a sturdy garden cart to move the boxes across the cavern
floor, and then lift them above ground using a makeshift crane
built from tubular steel scaffolding. His Polaris quad would
provide most of the muscle.

As soon as Josue returned from his errand in Le Francois—
attempting to get his hands on the cell phone of Marquise de
Losa's mistress—they would begin the grueling task of delivering
all of the rum to Everest Walsh's yacht. And then Max would
get on with his plans to deliver his poison into Marquse de
Losa's bloodstream.

Max stopped to take a moment to look around at everything
he had built. A strange feeling irritated him deep down. He had
to admit: he was sorry to see it all go. He even wondered if he
would ever make rum again. Would he even need to, now that his
efforts as a rum producer had fulfilled their intended purpose?

Max heard shuffling footsteps near the top of the wooden

steps ascending from the cavern floor to the surface. Max drew his FNS pistol. It wasn't like Josue to make so much noise.

"It's okay, Boss," Josue said, showing his bare palms. "Don't shoot," he added in a jesting manner.

"You better be ready to move some rum," Max said. "A lot of rum."

"Ready, Boss," Josue said, kneeling beside the opening of the cavern's mouth. "And look at this." He tossed a smartphone with a hot pink protective case down to Max, who caught the phone with two hands, careful not to drop it.

"You've got light fingers, my friend," Max said. "Good work."

"It was easy," Josue said. He pulled a small credit card out of his pocket and held it up. "I use this to jimmy the door. Didn't take much, small hotel had old-fashioned locks."

"Is that... a McDonald's gift card?" Max asked, squinting at the writing on the bright red plastic card.

"Don't leave island without it," Josue said, flashing his bright white grin that was impossible not to appreciate.

Max chuckled. "Josue," he said, shaking his head, unable to wipe the smile from his lips. "You are a force to be reckoned with."

Max and Josue leaned into the job of transferring the rum as if they were well-seasoned stevedores. It only took a short while for the two men to find a rhythm: lower a barrel from the stack, letting it fall onto a sparring mat placed on the cavern floor to keep the cask from breaking; roll the barrel over by the staircase and strap it to the quad; have Josue run up the steps and drive the Polaris to lift the heavy cask; roll the barrel down to the dock, and load it onto Max's Cobia fishing boat. They performed this same exercise over and over again until the fishing boat sat questionably low in the water, and the rest of the barrels stood upright at the end of the pier.

Max eased the twenty-seven-foot boat across the bay until the relatively small vessel drew up into the wide shadow of the

*Snowy Lady*, being dwarfed by the fortress-like yacht. Max noted the presence of Marquise de Losa, who stood peering down from the sundeck, looking like a sentry in his militant-looking olive green coat and mirrored sunglasses.

Max navigated the Cobia gingerly to the exterior swim platform at the massive yacht's stern. A man in a white, short-sleeved uniform with white shorts and black epaulettes greeted Max and Josue as they arrived.

"Mornin', gentlemen," the dapper crewman said, speaking with a thick Texas accent. He looked about thirty, with perfectly combed, neatly-trimmed brown hair. "Eric Pepperdine, first mate of this vessel. Captain Bartholemew sent me to assist you in getting your cargo stowed aboard the *Snowy Lady*. Hope you don't mind if I pat you down?"

Max stood with his hands out to his sides so the crewman could check him for weapons. Just like the day before, Max had opted to leave his weapons at home when traveling to Walsh's yacht, lest he draw too much suspicion. Eric Pepperdine made short work of his pat-down, and then he shook Max's hand. Then he quickly patted down Josue.

Max was relieved when the first mate operated the controls of the *Snowy Lady's* davit and winch—tools that might normally be used to hoist a yacht tender onto the wide swim platform for transport—to hoist the heavy rum barrels out of Max's boat and onto the yacht's stern deck where they could be rolled into submission.

It wasn't long before Max and Josue had finished unloading the barrels, and the Cobia's throttles were wide open. The boat cut through the fresh morning air toward the long white pier at Ilet d'Ombres, so that they could pick up another load.

The two men worked hard loading the boat a second time. It took three trips to get all of the barrels out to the *Snowy Lady*, and another three boat trips to transport all of the cardboard cases of bottled rum. With just a dozen boxes still sitting on Max's dock, he sent Josue back with the boat to retrieve them.

"I'll square up with Walsh," Max said, standing on the teakwood-covered rear swim platform. "When you get back I'll help you unload the boxes. Then it'll be Miller time."

Josue nodded in an almost solemn way, visually recognizing the gravity of what was about to take place. Max would finally have settled his score with Marquise de Losa.

Max didn't care how he would have to do it, but he convinced himself he *would* be placing the powdered ricin into a drink and Marquise de Losa would be draining it, even if Max had to pour it down the crazy-haired murderer's gullet.

As Max watched Josue drive the boat back to the ilet, his mind drifted toward thoughts of his wife, thoughts that now haunted him every day: how Lovelle had always longed to see the islands someday; how she had loved sweet, gooey rum drinks like daiquiris and pina coladas; how beautiful she was. And he couldn't stop thinking about the cute little fleur de lis tattoo she'd had done on her wrist, just because she loved the way the little French lily looked so much. It now made him sick to realize how much she had meant to him, when he had scarcely ever said a word to let her know that while she was still alive.

Max also recalled how his wife had once joked, "We should sell all our stuff and move to St. Croix—we'll make rum for a living, and spend our days on the beach." He laughed a little as he looked out over the pristine water that faced the scattered buildings of Le Robert in the distance. "Lovelle would have loved this," he said softly to himself, fighting against the tears that threatened to fill his eyes.

Then Max remembered the pink-cased cell phone he had in his pocket. He had the forethought to mute the phone, lest he draw any dangerous attention to himself in the event that de Losa placed a call to his mistress while in Max's presence. But when

Max spotted Tito driving Walsh's Chris-Craft runabout into the yacht's harbor-like garage, he got a sudden urge for a drink.

"How do I get to the bar from here?" Max asked Eric Pepperdine, who happily escorted him through a short passageway that led to a door into the dimly-lit bar Walsh called *Rum Lord's Reef*. "Actually, I could sure use the head first," Max said, letting go of the doorknob.

"Two doors down on the left," Eric said, and Max stepped past him to the yacht's bathroom. He opened the door and the lights flickered on automatically. The tiny bathroom was elegant: all of the wood was curly maple; a countertop of Italian marble; even the toilet was chiseled out of some kind of stone. Max removed the cell phone of de Losa's mistress from his pocket. He turned it on and boosted the volume to the maximum. Then he flushed the toilet and strode down the passageway to the bar, entering just in time to bump into Tito, who had just finished docking the boat, and was stepping into the bar.

"Tito, my man," Max said, clasping hands with the powerful, bleached-blond henchman. Max leaned in for a half-hug and with his left hand, discreetly slipped the cell phone into the right pocket of the lightweight Tommy Hilfiger jacket Tito wore.

"Hey," Max said, plopping down on one of the barstools. "I was just going to get a drink and then head up to the main deck to see if Mr. Walsh is available. I gotta get paid for all this rum," Max said with a sly smile.

"I'm gonna grab a beer," Tito said, waving at Coyo behind the bar. "Then I'll tell Walsh you're coming."

"Thanks, man."

Tito stepped through the door, and disappeared down the lower deck's passageway.

"Morning, Coyo," Max said to the bartender. *This guy must live here*, Max thought. "Too early to get a Ti' Punch to go?"

The slick bartender made Max's drink with a rare bottle of

rhum Galion single cask from 2002, and then Max was on his way up the spiral staircase at the very heart of the vessel, connecting all of the yacht's four decks. Max stepped out into the opulent décor of the upper deck's cigar lounge and found Everest Walsh, standing in his bathrobe with tousled hair. He and Marquise de Losa appeared to be engaged in a deep, serious conversation.

*Is that all they do?* Max thought to himself. *They're like an old married couple.*

Tito sat comfortably at one of the elegant off-white sofas that wrapped three sides of the big stone-topped coffee table on the port side of the stylish lounge. He sipped his bottle of Presidente Beer and gazed out at Le Robert Bay.

"Hey, Max," Walsh said, waving at de Losa in a manner that suggested their conversation was over. "Oh, yes, I almost forgot. Marquise, get Max the cash for his rum. Came out to…" Walsh pulled an iPhone out of his robe pocket and flipped through a couple of pages of apps, before opening one, "$792,200. Oh, hell, just give him eight hundred even." The wealthy cigar plantation owner and cocaine trafficker didn't even bat an eyelash at the amount. It seemed inconsequential to him.

"I've got some business to take care of up in the hot tub," Everest Walsh said, glancing toward the spiral staircase behind Max. Max turned around and saw two bikini-clad women, likely Martinique natives, heading up toward the sundeck.

"Max, you and me are gonna have some brunch later," Walsh added, patting Max on the arm. "I'll tell Claude to get it ready. About an hour?"

Max nodded. "Yeah, sure."

With that, Everest Walsh disappeared up the stairs like Hugh Hefner. Max was left standing in the center of the cigar room with the foul murderer, Marquise de Losa. The steel vial of deadly poison seemed to be searing a hole in Max's pocket as his eyes locked onto those of his nemesis.

Max felt his hands begin to shake involuntarily. He wondered if he should remove himself from the room before de Losa suspected something was wrong. Max looked away and turned around, stepping toward the stairs.

"Wait," Marquise de Losa said. The only word Max could think of to describe the man's voice was small. It reminded Max of the soft, childlike intonation of Michael Jackson's voice; no wonder the enigmatic murderer hardly spoke. The man's accent sounded strangely American. Max had always imagined a deep, gravelly growl, laced with a thick Cuban accent. "I've been wanting to talk to you for awhile, apart from Walsh."

"Yes?" Max asked, legitimately intrigued. Part of him wondered if Marquise de Losa might have finally recognized him from that horrible day in Islamorada six years past.

"I have been looking at some land in Pinar del Rio, back in Cuba. I want to start my own distillery," Marquise de Losa said, looking at Max with a strangely hopeful expression that surprised Max; he hadn't thought a cold-blooded enforcer, like Marquise, was capable of such an expression. "I wonder if you would indulge me, and listen to me talk about my plans for a short while. I ask because I know I will be needing a master distiller to join me."

*Is Marquise de Losa, the man who killed my wife, my son, and my daughter—who took away my world—offering me a job?* Max asked himself, feeling puzzled.

"Well, I'm intrigued, Mr. de Losa," Max said, rubbing his chin.

"Marquise," de Losa said expectantly.

"Yes, Marquise," Max said. "Why don't we go and grab a drink? I'd love to hear all about your plans. The idea of distilling Cuban rum sounds very interesting." Max's hand was in his pocket, and he twisted the vial of ricin between his fingers. He felt impatient, as if his body was urging him to pour the poison down de Losa's throat.

"I'll do you one better," Marquise de Losa said. He pulled

his cell phone out of his coat pocket and tapped on the screen a couple of times.

Max's heart raced. He looked down at Tito, wondering if the purloined smartphone in his pocket was about to ring to life.

"Coyo, bring us up a bottle of HSE V.S.O.P. and a couple of glasses," Marquise said. "Yeah, bring it to the cigar lounge." Marquise put away his phone.

The murderer offered Max a seat at the cushioned sofa that faced the tall port side windows. Max took his own sofa, the one beside where Tito was sitting, sipping his bottle of Presidente. Marquise took the sofa opposite Tito. The three men were situated on three sides of the large coffee table, affording each man an unencumbered view out over the bay. Max noticed the suspicious catamaran halfway between the *Snowy Lady* and Ilet d'Ombres.

De Losa leaned back on his couch and threw his arm over the back cushion. His coat slipped open, showing the 9mm submachine gun the criminal wore on a sling. Max's eyes homed in on the firearm; his mind raced. He couldn't escape the feeling he was seeing the same weapon that had taken his family away from him.

"The property I'm looking at is growing tobacco at the moment," de Losa said. "I wonder how difficult it would be to cultivate sugarcane in its place."

"How many acres?" Max asked.

"A hundred and twenty," de Losa said, pulling an aluminum tube out of his coat pocket. He unscrewed the cap from the bottom of the tube and gave it a light shake, releasing the fine Cuban cigar trapped within. He snipped the end with a razor cutter and blazed it to life with a torch.

"Sorry, would you like one?" Marquise de Losa asked.

Max shook his head. "It shouldn't be too difficult to convert it over," Max said, "if you have enough manpower." Truth was, Max knew very little about horticulture. And it didn't matter what he told the violent criminal; he'd be dead in a few days anyway. "Sure, sounds completely doable."

Coyo ascended the grand spiral staircase from the lower deck. He carried a silver tray laden with a decanter bottle of the very fine rhum agricole from Habitation Saint-Etienne, three glasses, a bucket of ice, and a small rectangular tray filled with assorted snacks: nuts, dried fruits, various cheeses. He placed the tray down on the stone-topped table and set an old-fashioned glass in front of each man at the table.

"Ice, gentlemen?" Coyo asked, flashing a charismatic grin.

Tito nodded, Max and de Losa both shook their heads. Coyo dropped two square ice cubes in Tito's glass and poured the rum.

"If that's all, gentlemen," Coyo said, bowing slightly. Then he made his way back down the staircase to the nether parts of the mammoth vessel.

"What time do you have?" de Losa asked.

Max looked at the face of his Bulova timepiece. "Eleven seventeen."

"Oh, I've got to make a call." Marquise stood up from the table and strode toward the windowed walls on the starboard side of the mega yacht's sunny cigar lounge. The skunk-haired thug pulled the cell phone from his pocket and began to tap on the screen, as he peered out toward the open Atlantic Ocean.

Max looked impatiently at Marquise de Losa's unattended glass of HSE rum. He nosed his own glass and noted the candied fruit and vanilla notes in the V.S.O.P's aroma. He took a sip, and instantly loved the vegetal, alcoholic taste imbued with a peppery spiciness and a strong overtone of French oak. If he could divert Tito's attention away, just for a moment, Max would seize the opportunity. He would lace Marquise de Losa's drink with the deadly toxin and be done with it.

"Tito," Max said suddenly. "Any chance you could run down to the storage hold, the one near the engine room where we unloaded all of that Fleur de Lis rum, and grab a bottle that's marked with two Xs? I'd like to give Marquise a side-by-side comparison with the HSE." Max really just wanted Tito out of the room so he could lace de Losa's drink with the lethal ricin.

Tito's coat pocket screamed to life with the tinny, electronic sound of a woman's twangy voice singing, *I'd bet my boots, I belong to you. I'd bet my boots, you were meant for me.*

Marquise de Losa glared at Tito. Unadulterated rage blazed in his eyes. The cold-blooded Cuban took two steps toward the strapping, peroxide-blond-haired man and stopped.

Tito tried to respond. He stood up and said, "Wait, Marquise, I don't even know how this—"

Tito never finished his sentence.

De Losa whipped his machete out of its scabbard under his coat. The vicious killer drew the long blade back with blurring speed, ready to strike down with fury.

Tito put up both hands in front of himself in protest, but it was of no use.

The first blow from Marquise de Losa's machete killed Tito. The black-and-white-haired killer brought the long razor-like blade down hard at the intersection of the man's sinewy, tattooed neck and his shoulder.

De Losa needed two hands to retrieve the blade, as deeply as it had sunk into Tito's muscular frame.

And then Marquise de Losa went bananas. He drew the blade back, striking it down on Tito's body again and again. The machete continued to strike long after the unfortunate man's limp corpse had fallen back, sprawled over the back of the off-white fabric of the cigar lounge's sofa.

Bright crimson splatters of blood rained everywhere. Max felt Tito's warm lifeblood sprinkling his face and peppering his clothes as Marquise de Losa struck the dead man with his primitive weapon over and over again.

By the time Marquise de Losa was finished, standing and spitting on Tito's lifeless and mutilated corpse, the entire sitting area of the cigar lounge had suddenly transformed from a soft eggshell color to a shockingly bright stain of red.

Everest Walsh descended the spiral staircase and stepped out into the cigar lounge. "What's this?"

Marquise de Losa didn't say a word.

"Marquise! Just what in the *hell* is this?" Walsh shouted, holding his hands out to his sides, palms up, as if in disbelief. "You stupid bastard. What did you do to my boat?"

"I... ," Marquise de Losa said, trying to find the words to explain a situation that defied explanation. "He just..."

"I don't care what you do with your men, Marquise," Walsh said. "I really don't." The cigar magnate's face turned redder by the second, giving Max the mental suggestion of a tomato in a microwave oven; he wondered how much heat it would take until the man's head finally burst. "But you just can't go and do a thing like this in the middle of my lounge. Look at this mess. There's blood on every surface. And look at Max, for crap's sake. He's soaked to the gills."

Marquise de Losa looked at Max, an embarrassed expression on his face. He appeared more as a kid caught with his hand in a cookie jar than as a cold-blooded murderer who had just brutally dispatched one of his own friends.

"You're gonna clean this up," Everest Walsh said, and he began to pace back and forth on the line of demarcation on the floor where the splattered blood met the lush unspoiled portion of clean white carpet.

"Max," Walsh said, turning his attention away from de Losa, "you've got a boat. Would you help us out here? Let's say you haul all of this furniture and carpet over to your island and throw it on a burn pile, make it like it never happened. And let's say I make your rum total nine hundred large instead of eight hundred. What do you say? Help a brother out?"

Max looked at Marquise de Losa, who appeared eager for an answer as well. His face still dripped Tito's blood.

"Why the hell not," Max said.

# CHAPTER 23

"**H**OW YOU LOSE HIM?" MOMO asked Zann, a quizzical look on his face.

"How'd *I* lose him?" Zann said by way of defending himself. "You were there too. I was waitin', ready to put the bag over his head the whole time. Didn't help that Tiny Deege called, askin' me if I would pick him up some nachos and some kinda spray or balm for his jacked-up foot."

"Whyn't you put your gear on vibrate, chump?" Momo asked, wondering how much more incompetence he could stand. "An' you know how much the roaming charges are down here. Cell phone bill gonna be outta sight, brother. An' you be careful with that hood, fool." He looked down at the black backpack containing all of their gear. It sat on the floor next to Zann's chair. "Get it too close to your face and *you* gonna get knocked out by them fumes."

Zann looked sheepish. He shrugged his shoulders and scratched his orange afro.

The two men occupied an outside table at a café overlooking a picturesque turquoise bay near Le Francois. The place had the typical vibrant décor Momo seemed to see everywhere he went, along with the same pleasant laid-back vibe. Water lapped gently at the stones bordering the restaurant's deck area, just a few feet below their table.

Sailboats with barren masts rested at anchor here and there, populating the pure blue-green water of the bay. Zann sipped café au lait from an oversized mug, while Momo drank a bottle of Biere Lorraine.

Momo and Zann had followed Josue Remy under cover of darkness from the ilet where he lived, near Le Robert, to a small hotel in Le Francois whose faded white and black sign read Caline Hotel Ours. At first, Momo had assumed the punk weasel, Josue, was meeting a woman. But it soon appeared more likely that Josue was stalking or surveilling the woman, who happened to be a tasty, dark-skinned local in a bright red floral dress.

Some guy, a real badass, like a military rebel or something, came knocking on the woman's door shortly after Josue had arrived, the latter crouching low and hiding between two cars in the hotel parking lot. Momo and Zann hid in an alley across the street, watching, until the woman and the military guy left the hotel an hour or so later—probably to go get breakfast or something. Josue broke into the sweet honey's hotel room by jimmying the door to the room. Made short work of it too.

"Didn't know Josue was gonna sneak out the back," Zann said apologetically.

Momo and Zann had stood waiting for Josue to come out the same door he had forcibly entered for nearly another hour before they thought to go take a look around the backside of the tiny hotel. There they found the back window of the girl's room wide open, curtains flapping in the tropical morning breeze.

"*You* know he gonna slip out the back way?" Zann asked Momo before taking a sip of his milky mug of sweet coffee.

"Nah, man," Momo conceded.

"So what we gon' do now?" Zann asked Momo. "Who you gotta know to get a scone 'round this place." The nervous gang member waved through a wide window opening with no glass on the front wall of the café, flagging down a young waitress who stood behind a long glass pastry case filled with baked delights. "Yo, yeah, you. You gotta scone or donut or somethin'?"

"We goin' to go back to the cat, and we gonna sit an' wait for our next chance to grab that slippery black back-stabbin' creep," Momo said, as he gazed out over the tranquil bay. "We gonna grab him, and we gonna mess up his whole day."

The waitress brought a big plate of freshly fried beignets, liberally coated in a ridiculous amount of powdered sugar. Zann snatched one off the tray and took a big bite. "Oww!" he shouted, instinctively spitting the searing bite of pastry onto the rocks beside the bay. "Damn thing's hot. Burned my tongue."

After Momo paid the waitress for breakfast—a small argument ensued about the U.S. currency Momo had tried to pay with, before he ultimately whipped out his Visa card to square up the check—the two gang members asked where they might buy some gasoline, and then headed back to the spot on a nearby beach where they had secured their personal watercraft.

"Yo, Zann," Momo said, unable to hide the stress in his voice. "Where we leave the Sea-Doo?"

"We left it right here, under this tree with the little green grape-lookin' things," Zann said, his own voice betraying a sensation of panic.

The sand underneath the tree was smooth and flat, in contrast to the rough and uneven sand covering most of the rest of the beach; it suggested that their watercraft had been slid away from its parking spot in the cool shade of the tropical tree.

"I'm gonna..." Momo gritted his teeth and reached for his waistband. He didn't know who he was going to shoot, but he wanted to be ready to shoot someone.

"Hello," a skinny old man wearing a red Speedo said from where he was sitting nearby on a spread-out beach towel. It took the white-haired man awhile to get up, but he trotted over to where Momo and Zann stood underneath the seagrape tree. "Hello, young friends."

"What you know, fool?" Momo said in a threatening way.

"You'd best not know anythin' about this situation or you gonna have a bad day too. An' put on some shorts or somethin.'"

"Hello," the old man reiterated. He struck Momo as a bleached prune that had been somehow stretched into the shape of a stringbean. "May I help you find something? You look like you and friend are lost."

The man spoke English, but it sounded broken, as if he was French or something. "What I know is I parked our ride over here, under this weird grape tree," Momo said in an escalatingly irritated tone. "Now me an' my compatriot come back to the spot an' our ride ain't here. You seen who took off with it?"

"No," the old man said. "I see nothing. But I have seen another seagrape tree down the beach. There is a motorcycle boat under it. It says something... Sea-Doo... on the side. Does this help you?"

Momo didn't say a word. He pulled out his wallet and slipped out a hundred dollar bill, handing it to the skinny sunbather, and then proceeded a hundred yards or so down the beach to where he and Zann had parked the Sea-Doo.

Once back on the water, Momo felt Zann's hands wrap around his waist until the platinum-grilled gang member's fingers interlocked in front of Momo's stomach.

"What you doin', fool? This ain't the Titanic."

"I don't wanna fall off, Momo," Zann said, in a slightly distressed voice. "You know I don't know how ta swim."

"Why you think you wearin' that lifejacket, Zann?"

"Still don't feel safe back here is all." Zann released his grip on Momo and felt around for another spot to hold on.

Momo piloted the Sea-Doo to a small marina in Le Robert the waitress at the café had given them directions to. At a narrow inlet, he spotted a slightly rusted sign on a piling with an image of a bright red gas pump and an arrow. Momo's eyes followed the arrow to a dock with two gas pumps; he piloted the Sea-Doo to the first pump.

"Bonjour," the attendant said. "Comment allez-vous?"

"Can I buy gas?" Momo asked. "I wanna buy gas for my Sea-Doo."

"Ah, American," the man said. "Welcome. Yes, I'll get you topped off. Credit card?"

Momo handed the attendant his Visa card and unscrewed the gas cap on the watercraft. He stretched his arms out over his head and looked around. A long black inflatable police boat pulled up to the other pump directly in front of them.

Momo looked away at once, feeling a sudden sense of panic. But then he tried to be rational. What had he done that was illegal in Martinique? He had passed through Customs without issue. Other than the .50 caliber pistol tucked into his waistband, he and Zann were legit. He looked down at his waist. He adjusted the baggy Miami Dolphins jersey he had put on earlier so that it covered the bulge of the pistol's substantial grip.

"Hello," a strong voice spoke from the dock. Momo gazed up, seeing a very official-looking man in a powder blue uniform with black and white striped patches on his shoulders. The man stepped down the steps toward Momo and Zann, kneeling next to them on the concrete dock.

The guy looked like a fancy-dressed policeman, or a military man. Momo didn't know which. The guy had short graying hair and piercing eyes that somehow increased Momo's sensation of guilt the longer he looked at the man.

"On vacation?" the official-looking guy asked.

"Yeah, man," Momo said. "Me and my man here is just takin' a bit of rest and relaxation."

"Oh, American," the man said, taking a cigar out of his shirt pocket. "Are you two married?"

Zann laughed out loud. Momo just cringed and said, "Get outta here, man. We ain't a couple. We's just friends. Straight friends." And then Momo added, "Sir."

"I'm sorry," the military guy said. "You just never know these days. I'm Colonel Travere. I head up the Gendarmerie Nationale here. We're one of the two police forces on the island. Actually we are part of the French military, but our duties here are law enforcement."

"Nice to meet you, Colonel," Momo said. "I'm Momo, this is Zann."

"You guys from Miami?" Colonel Travere asked.

"Yeah," Zann said, sounding surprised. "How you know that?"

"I thought so. You just strike me as Miami guys." The colonel took his funny French-looking hat that was tucked under his arm and placed it on his head. "Good day to you. Enjoy the rest of your vacation here." And then he stepped back onto the police boat, where he sat down and began to light up his cigar.

"He thought we was married," Zann said. "That ain't right."

"I wouldn't marry you if you was the last eligible bachelorette in the world, Zann," Momo said. "Although sometimes you be naggin' me like you *was* my wife."

Momo got his receipt for the gas and powered the Sea-Doo out of the marina, being careful to obey the posted speed limit. He waved to the two policemen on the way, then he opened the throttle and motored back toward the catamaran at its anchorage not far from that huge black and white yacht.

Momo made sure their route would make a wide sweeping arc past the long white pier on the overgrown ilet where Josue lived. Momo would make a quick drive-by, trying not to appear too suspicious.

"Keep your eyes peeled," Momo shouted to Zann. "Be on the lookout. We gonna swing by the spot where we seen Josue leavin' this morning. Look and see if you can spot him."

"Okay, Momo," Zann shouted back. "But I can't see much past you, 'cause you so big."

As the Sea-Doo drew up in sight of the pier, Momo spotted

a white and blue fishing boat at the dock, the same one they had seen hours earlier, when Josue had left the dock on a small black inflatable raft. But this time, Momo spotted Josue loading boxes into the bow of the docked fishing boat.

It was really him; the wretched traitor was right there in front of Momo, in full living color. Momo's mind raced to form the best plan possible. He knew that when he approached, Josue would recognize him and Zann within seconds. They would have to make their move quickly.

"There he is," Zann shouted from behind Momo's shoulder. "It's Josue!"

"Shhhhhhh!" Momo shushed back. "We gonna try to come up from behind him as best we can. I'm gonna ask if he have a first aid kit, 'cause my friend—you—cut himself pretty bad on some coral while skin diving. Dig?"

Zann nodded vigorously.

Momo motored the Sea-Doo toward the dock and cut the engine, hoping that by silencing the watercraft he might gain a couple more seconds of anonymity. Josue turned around to look at the Sea-Doo that was bearing down toward him.

Momo shouted in a soft, high-pitched voice, "Hello, friend. My brother here cut himself on some coral. Any chance you have a first aid kit in your boat?"

Josue turned his back to look down into a compartment in the stern of his fishing boat. Momo didn't waste a second. He stood up on the Sea-Doo, pulled the Taser out of his pants pocket, and aimed the weird-looking black and yellow "gun" at Josue.

Momo took his time. He lined up the sights and pulled the trigger. Two electrodes, connected to the non-lethal weapon by long thin copper wires, shot out of the Taser, riding a blast of compressed air, and striking Josue square in the middle of his back.

Josue Remy's back arched from the shock of having been

struck, his flesh pierced by the sharp barbed electrodes. Then he went rigid as the five-second charge of electricity coursed through his body, rendering him limp, facedown in the stern of his fishing boat.

"Take the Sea-Doo back to the cat, Zann," Momo ordered. He stepped onto the white dock. "I'm gonna drive over in Josue's boat."

Zann took off on the personal watercraft. Momo dropped from the dock into the Cobia center console boat and threw off the lines that secured it. He turned the keys to fire up each of the twin outboards, and then pushed the throttle handles forward. The boat quickened forward and Momo turned back to look at Josue.

The lithe Haitian stirred from his position on the stern deck. Momo stepped away from the helm and brought his fist down hard onto Josue's cheek.

"Oogh," Josue grunted as he fell back down to the deck.

"Think you can run away from me, thug?" Momo shouted. He hit the helpless man again, and then reached into his backpack. He grabbed out the black hood soaked in ether, and placed it over the defenseless man's head.

Then Momo grabbed out a thick zip tie from the bag and bound Josue's hands behind his back where he lay, facedown on the deck. The former Ti Flow member now lay slack and unmoving.

"Time you gonna pay for crossing Momo," Momo growled, as he returned to the helm of the fishing boat and grabbed the wheel. He looked back once more at Josue. "Time you gonna pay."

# Chapter 24

MAX WALKED OUT ONTO THE *Snowy Lady*'s swim platform, just above the mega yacht's three aluminumbronze alloy propellers, each as tall as him. He gazed west toward Ilet d'Ombres, the small island of shadows, which he called home. Josue should have finished loading the dozen cases of rum onto the Cobia and returned to Walsh's yacht by now.

Max felt uncomfortable wearing the clothes of a man savagely murdered in front of him only minutes earlier. But Everest Walsh had asked Max to go into Tito's stateroom, take a shower, and then put on some of the murdered thug's clean clothes. Then the cigar magnate called his yacht stewardess and ordered her to keep all staff members out of the cigar lounge on the upper deck until further notice, lest they walk in to see the aftermath of Marquise de Losa's bloodbath.

Max was careful to find something with long sleeves. He knew that revealing his bare arms would escalate things to a quick and violent resolution that Max just wasn't quite ready for. He tugged up Tito's cargo shorts; they were large enough that Max had to cinch them down with a black leather belt taken from the dead man's dresser.

As soon as Josue arrived with the boat, Max and Marquise de Losa would load up all of the blood-stained furniture and carpet. De Losa had cut the saturated rug with a sharp tanto knife, rolling it up like a morbid crepe, to be transfered to Ilet d'Ombres, where Max would burn it all on his sugarcane pile.

Max didn't mind doing it. Really, he didn't. It was a small price to pay to see Marquise de Losa turn like a dog on one of his own men. The extra hundred grand Walsh would pay him was just the icing.

Tito's body was wrapped tightly in sheets and weighted, and then dumped, likely settling right beside Chuy's on the sandy sea bed just below the massive yacht. *Everest Walsh is starting his very own undersea cemetery*, Max thought.

Max's cell phone vibrated to life in the pocket of his borrowed shorts. He slipped it out and looked at the name and photo of the caller. It was Isobel Greer.

Max didn't really care what she had to say right now. His dealings with Walsh and de Losa trumped any sort of germ of a relationship he might have had with the woman. Besides, he was pretty sure he had made it clear that things were over between them.

He tucked the phone back in his pocket. Marquise de Losa appeared at the black glass door that separated the yacht's swim platform from the passageway leading inside the lower deck of the great vessel.

"Who's calling you?" the suspicious killer asked. He no doubt worried Max might phone the authorities, and report Marquise for the vicious murder of Tito.

"A woman," Max said. "But I don't want to talk to her. Not now."

"May I see?" Marquise asked.

Max handed him the phone without protest. He wanted to prove he had nothing to hide. De Losa switched on the phone and saw Isobel Greer's name. A tone sounded that told Max she had left a voicemail.

De Losa handed the phone back to Max. "Women."

Max nodded, as de Losa walked back into the passageway. Max used the phone to call Josue. It rang and rang and then went to voicemail.

*Where the hell is he?* Max asked himself.

Max switched open the tracking app he and Josue used to keep track of each other; it used the GPS transponder inside each of their smartphones. He tapped Josue's phone on the app.

It took a moment, but a map of the area appeared on screen. According to the map, the young Haitian was located somewhere about halfway between Walsh's yacht and Ilet d'Ombres. He should be somewhere near Ilet Boisseau.

Max looked in that direction. All he could see there was the white power catamaran Josue had alerted Max to the day before.

As Max squinted to better see the looming vessel, he spotted something that made his guts quiver; his own Cobia fishing boat bobbed just beyond the catamaran's starboard hull.

Josue was on that boat. Whether he had gone there on purpose or taken by force, Max did not know. But Josue was so late, and Max couldn't raise him on the phone. Those facts gave Max a deep pang of concern.

Feeling panicked, Max burst through the door to the passageway that connected the swim platform to the inside of the *Snowy Lady*'s lower deck passageway. He opened the door to Walsh's private bar, and rushed inside.

"Hey, Max," Coyo said. "Everything okay overhead? I heard Mr. Walsh wanted the cigar lounge locked down. I wondered what might be going on."

Max ignored the suave bartender. He strode through the bar and climbed into Everest Walsh's heirloom Chris-Craft runabout.

"Hey," Coyo said, sounding surprised. "What are you doing?"

Max had paid careful attention to how Chuy had operated the buttons on the control panel beside the fancy yacht tender. He pressed a button to open the large doors on the side of the yacht, and then another to flood the chamber with water and lower the hydraulic hoist. The boat settled down into the water as the yacht garage flooded.

Max fired up the engine. The loud roar drowned out the shouts of Coyo, who had rushed over to try to stop Max from absconding with the boat. He watched the bartender pull out his cell phone. "Eric? Coyo. Max Craig is stealing Walsh's tender. You better get some guys down here."

Before anyone could stop him, Max backed the runabout out of the open doors, turned the boat around, and threw open the throttle.

Max's first instinct was to head directly for the catamaran. But he knew he would likely arrive there outgunned or otherwise underprepared. So he fought his instincts and drove the mahogany vessel wide open toward his dock on Ilet d'Ombres. Once there, he ran, full speed toward the villa, throwing open the door hard.

Max rushed into the spare room where he kept all of his skin diving gear well organized, and ready to go. He stripped down quickly and pulled on a black shorty wetsuit, reaching behind himself to tug on the long zipper pull to seal himself inside the neoprene shell.

Next Max spread open a large black Watershed dry bag, throwing in a Mares pneumatic speargun with half a dozen spare spears, some of which looked downright barbaric: a few featured barbed tips; one glinted with a shiny, silver, forked trident; and another sported a menacing-looking six-barbed spear tip, frequently used to skewer lionfish.

Max rushed to his gun room behind the bookcase in his accounting office. He swung the bookcase open and grabbed a twelve-gauge Mossberg Cruiser, knowing the short pistol-gripped shotgun would fit easily inside the bag. He also tossed in a belt bandolier filled with buckshot and slugs for the Cruiser.

Max also snatched his Sig Sauer MPX 9mm submachine gun, along with four spare magazines. His FNS pistol and his Smith & Wesson pistol were stuffed into holsters on a black tactical belt with spare magazines and other accessories.

He dropped the firearms and ammo into the dry bag and strapped an Aqua Lung titanium dive knife to his right leg. Max tossed his cell phone into the bag as well. He sealed up the dry bag, securing all of the dangerous contents inside.

Max picked up his diving buoyancy compensator with a single air tank, and slipped it on like a backpack, securing it across his chest. Then he grabbed the handle of his Sea-Doo Seascooter diver propulsion vehicle along with the sealed dry bag and he rushed to the rocky north side of the ilet.

Max tied a tether around his waist, securing the dry bag in place; it would drag behind him through the water. He placed the Sea-Doo in the water, allowing it to settle down below the surface. He placed the air tank regulator's mouthpiece in his mouth and tested its function. With his gear all good to go, Max settled down into the water and grabbed hold of the Sea-Doo DPV. He used the thumb controls to give the mini vehicle thrust, and he started forward through the water.

Max surged, only feet below the surface, gliding like a dolphin through the clear blue water of Le Robert Bay. He had to surface from time to time to get his bearings, but it only took about two minutes to reach the hulking twin hulls of the power catamaran anchored just off of Ilet Boisseau.

Max unstrapped his BCD and let it, the air tank, and regulator fall to the sea floor, maybe a dozen feet below the surface. He let the DPV go as well, and treaded water beside the stern of the catamaran, connected to the dry bag which floated just under the water's surface behind him.

Max found the luxury vessel's rear deck deserted. With caution, he climbed aboard and tugged on the tether to pull his dry bag up behind him. Max peeked over the granite-topped bar at the open rear wall of the galley area. That was when he spotted the body.

The dead man's eyes gaped open, staring blankly upward, his

tongue hanging limply out the side of his mouth. A long cord, apparently from a video game controller, had been wrapped around the victim's neck, trapping his fingers underneath as if in a defensive gesture. Judging by the bruises and scraped skin on his neck, Max figured the young man had been quickly and violently strangled to death by the cord. Probably a savage spur-of-the-moment killing.

*Kid must only be about seventeen or eighteen*, Max thought, taking in the disturbing sight of the bespectacled corpse that, strangely, was missing an eyebrow. *Shame, really.*

Max turned back and opened the dry bag. He wasn't sure if he should use the pistol-gripped twelve gauge or the Sig Sauer. He ultimately decided upon on the latter. The quarters would be incredibly tight onboard the catamaran. The buckshot might scatter too much, and rifled slugs would rip through everything in their path and continue on.

Max checked the magazine in the MPX. It was filled with 9mm NATO rounds Max had hand-loaded with Hornady 124 grain XTP hollow point bullets for maximum expansion; full metal jacket bullets would pass through anything they hit and just keep going. The submachine gun was equipped with a Vortex red dot sight, which Max could use to quickly acquire targets in the dangerous close-quarters environment.

He charged the weapon and stepped through the catamaran's galley, keeping his center of gravity low and the weapon at high ready. The galley and salon, which essentially occupied the same space, were cluttered with candy wrappers, empty cardboard food boxes, and empty Champagne bottles.

*What a mess*, Max thought; his eyes roamed intently from side to side.

And then he heard the first sounds of distress.

"Zann, grab me that piece of extension cord," a deep, threatening voice said. "See how you like me now, Josue." Then

Max heard a whipping sound that made him cringe. They were beating Josue with an electrical cord. *Bastards.* But at least he was alive.

Max passed two open doors, on opposite sides of the salon, each one leading a few steps down into a stateroom. Max quickly crept down the steps to clear the port side stateroom, finding the room cluttered with traces of weed and a crack pipe on the dresser. Then Max stepped quickly and quietly to the starboard side, clearing that side's stateroom and head, finding more empty Champagne bottles and a few vials of coke and a rolled-up hundred, U.S. currency.

As Max moved further forward, it became clear the grunts and groans were coming from near the bow of the cat. Max approached a companionway door, partially ajar. As he reached forward to carefully open the door, Max heard the deep, menacing voice from before say, "You seem thirsty, Josue. Tiny Deege, grab me that bottle of Drano. Get me the funnel."

And then, a familiar female voice said, "Don't do it, Momo. Just get it over with. You've hurt him enough."

"I ain't gonna 'get it over with' until I had as much fun with this traitor as I wanna have, Isobel," the one called Momo said. "I got a blow torch, a nail gun, and a ball peen hammer, and I ain't gonna be done 'til I used 'em all."

Max slid the door open just in time to take in a horrific scene: a good-sized stateroom had its queen bed unbolted from the floor and leaned up against the wall to create more space, with the floor completely lined in plastic sheeting. Max figured he knew what it was for.

Josue sat in the middle of the room, bound to a dining chair, with about a dozen wrappings of white and blue nylon rope restraining him tightly. Four people occupied the room besides Josue. One was a huge black guy standing beside the chair, so tall his head scraped the roof of the stateroom. Two more black guys stood on either side of the room, one really short and thin, almost a midget, and the other a bit taller, with a big tuft of orange afro and a mouthful of shiny silver.

The fifth occupant of the room was Isobel Greer. Her bright blue-green eyes glistened with tears that sparkled on her cheeks as she stood behind Josue, watching these barbarians torture him.

In an instant, Max wondered if these men had gathered everyone in the world Max cared about, to hurt them, in turn hurting him. But it didn't make sense. Who would know about both Josue and Isobel? As much as he had grown to like her, Max had barely gotten to know the Scottish substitute teacher.

As Max readied himself to step into the room and confront the three men who threatened his friends, he froze as Isobel Greer reached deep down into the bottom of her ridiculous oversized handbag. She searched for a few seconds, digging her hand around at the bottom. From the depths, she produced a Glock subcompact pistol with a suppressor, and she placed the muzzle against Josue's head. Isobel Greer pulled the trigger.

Blood splattered across the room toward Max. His best friend in the world—his only friend—slumped forward in the chair, dead.

# CHAPTER 25

"**N**o!" MAX SHOUTED. WATCHING HIS best friend die in the blink of an eye right before him felt like a cold blade being thrust into his abdomen.

"Max?" Isobel shrieked. "Oh, Max!"

Max wasn't sure whom to hold the Sig's red dot sight over: Isobel, or one of the gang members: Momo, Tiny Deege, or Zann. In less than a second, Max's brain processed the reality that he should shoot the only person in the room holding a deadly weapon—Isobel Greer.

Max rejected the instinct, and instead turned the barrel of the submachine gun toward the hulking thug who had seconds earlier been torturing Josue. But the one called Momo was quick. He pulled a pistol, a big pistol, from his waistband and opened fire.

Max let his body fall back away from the companionway door, landing on his back in the middle of the salon floor. Bullets ripped through the companionway. They whizzed past his head in a violent flurry, tearing up the furniture of the salon and galley, and shattering the windows.

Momo's gun looked like a Desert Eagle. The sound of the pistol's report suggested a big caliber, .50 AE, or maybe .44 Magnum. But the gunman fought like a gangbanger, slinging bullets without regard.

Max reacted by firing back just as he and Josue had trained for years; by the book. Max calmed himself, quickly picked himself up to his knees, and then he brought the Sig up to his line of sight as he peered through the open companionway.

Almost instantly, Max placed the red dot on the bridge of Momo's nose, directly between his eyes. Max squeezed the trigger twice, hitting the large gangster in the face and the throat. The burly thug dropped to the ground in a loud, heavy heap.

"Oh, man! Momo dead," one of the other men in the room shouted. "He killed Momo!"

Max stood up and walked as far to the starboard side as he could, holding the Sig at the ready, hoping to get a good sight picture on one of the other guys.

Sure enough, just as Max leaned over a sofa under the starboard windows, the man with the orange afro came into view. The guy spotted Max. He raised a shiny nickel-plated pistol.

Max put three 9mm bullets in his chest, dropping him like a stone.

"Ahhhhhh!" a loud high-pitched shriek erupted from inside the forward stateroom. At first, Max thought it was Isobel's voice. But then he realized it was more likely the one they had called Tiny Deege. The young gangster was probably completely freaked-out at the sight of his buddies' sudden deaths.

An arm reached out of the companionway, throwing bullets randomly from a small, shiny, semi-automatic pistol. Bullets ripped all around the spot where Max was standing.

Max backed up and scrambled to find some cover. He ended up climbing over the bar at the rear of the galley. He crouched on the rear deck, looking through the sight toward the arm that poked through the open doorway, indiscriminately slinging bullets.

Max wanted to start putting bullets through the wall, right where Tiny Deege would have been standing. But Max and Josue had always trained to only fire upon a target that could be fully identified. *What's the worst that could happen*, Max asked himself, *you might hit Isobel? She just killed Josue.*

Suddenly the firing stopped. Max squinted into the cloud of smoke produced by all of the guns shooting inside such a confined space. Max made out the wiggling shape of a small body struggling to writhe through a small vent hatch in the ceiling of the forward stateroom. *Tiny Deege must think he can get away,* Max thought.

He considered shooting the man's wiggling lower half with the Sig. Max ultimately decided such an act to be unnecessarily violent and cold-blooded. He bolted back through the salon and galley, reaching the steep steps to the vessel's flybridge overhead.

A cluster of white-cushioned marine seats surrounded Max as he reached the top deck, all shaded by a fiberglass roof. Max stepped quickly around a counter with a BBQ grilltop and an undercounter fridge, and then slipped past the helm to reach the steps leading down to the catamaran's expansive forward deck.

Max reached the top step just as Tiny Deege had managed to pull his body through the vent, and stand up to his full diminutive height.

He looked like a child on the wide bow deck, clutching his nickel-plated pistol, which appeared to be a Beretta Cheetah. The compact pistol looked huge in the little guy's hand.

The petite gangster spotted Max, and he fired twice before Max could raise his own weapon. One of the thug's bullets struck the ejection port of Max's Sig Sauer submachine gun, jamming it.

Max slipped the titanium dive knife out of its sheath and took great care in throwing it at the miniature gunman. The knife missed its mark of center mass, near the heart, but it lodged a few inches into the gang member's right shoulder.

Tiny Deege dropped his pistol on the deck and started screaming, as he looked down at the knife.

Max bounded down and grabbed the knife handle. He snatched the blade out of the little man's flesh and slipped behind him, holding the knife to his throat. "You have five seconds to make your case for me not cutting your head clean off," Max said icily.

"Oh, man," Tiny Deege said, as he burst out into uncontrollable sobs. "I didn't even want to come on this trip. Zann made me come. Zann!" Deege cried out like a wailing widow. "Zann! Why, Zann?"

"What the hell happened to the kid?" Max asked, still holding the blade at the man's throat, more willing himself not to use it than anything.

"Reggie pissed off Momo for the last time," Tiny Deege said, wiping his nose with his sleeve. "Told Momo that Mama Dorah wouldn't like that we stole Josue's boat from the dock. Momo wen' nuts. Grabbed the Xbox controller out of Reggie's hands and killed him with it."

Max's mind swirled in disorienting waves of sadness, anxiety, and horror. "You guys the ones I saved Josue from? Six years ago? Ti Flow?"

Tiny Deege nodded as tears streamed down his face.

"Honestly didn't think you guys would be smart enough to ever find Josue," Max said woefully.

"I can't go back to Miami now," the little man said. "Mama Dorah sees me, knowing I let Reggie get killed, and she'll see me gutted out like that dead cat."

"Reckon you'll rot in an island prison before you get the chance," Max said, digging his hand into the man's shorts pocket. First thing he grabbed was a glass crack pipe. Max tossed it aside and checked the other pocket. Finding Tiny Deege's cell phone, Max dialed 17 and dropped the phone into the hatch near their feet.

"Who you call, the 5-0?" Tiny Deege asked. "You know how much them roaming minutes gonna cost?"

Max marched the bleeding man back up the steps to the flybridge and set him down on a cushioned seat under the flybridge's roof. He zip-tied the man's wrists together, then zip-tied them to a powder-coated bar supporting the fiberglass roof.

"Ahhhh!" Tiny Deege screamed as the extension of his arms aggrieved the wound in his shoulder. "Man, I'm gonna lose circulation you keep me like this."

"Cops should be here in about fifteen minutes," Max said. "Hang out 'til then." Just for good measure, Max punched Tiny Deege square in the face, knocking him into delirium. The little guy moaned as his head bobbed around in a slow circle.

Max climbed the steps down to the rear deck. He moved gingerly toward the forward stateroom near the bow, knowing Isobel Greer was still inside. Max stepped into the room, finding the two dead thugs lying in sickening, bleeding heaps next to the chair where Josue slumped over, lifeless.

"Why, Isobel?" Max asked. "Why did you kill him?"

Isobel's face lay on Josue's lap, her body wracked with violent sobs. She hyperventilated for a moment, and then took a deep breath, letting it out slowly. "I tried to warn you, Max," Isobel said, her voice scratchy and hollow, like a desperate whisper. "I told you they were coming for Josue."

Max remembered the voicemail Isobel had left on his phone. He stepped to the rear deck and dug his cell phone out of his dry bag, and tapped the screen until Isobel's message played.

"Max, it's Isobel. I'm sorry I didn't tell you in person, but my boyfriend, a dangerous gang member from Miami, has come to Martinique to kill Josue. They are going to grab him now. Please get Josue to safety if you can. Please. They'll torture him. They'll kill him."

Max dropped the phone. "You brought them here? You told them where to find Josue?"

"Yes," Isobel said, her bright eyes now appearing blank and desolate. "I was afraid of that monster. I knew I'd be killed too if I didn't do what Momo told me."

"You were playing me," Max said. "The whole time. I let you play me."

"No," she whispered. "That was real. We met by chance, Max. My feelings for you were real, Max... *are* real."

"Why didn't you tell me sooner, Isobel?" Max said, sounding irritated. His hands clenched into fists by his sides. "I could have helped you, could have made you safe. I could have saved Josue!"

"I wanted to," Isobel said, wringing her hands together tightly. "I tried a couple of times. I thought I could warn you before they got here. I didn't want you to know I was involved with Momo, and I didn't want you to go after him; I was afraid he would kill you. And then, it was just too late."

"But why did you kill him?" Max asked, looking down at his friend's lifeless body. His teeth clenched. "I was about to save him."

"I didn't know you were coming," Isobel said. "I knew that after they finished torturing him they were going to kill him. I just couldn't stand to let him endure any more pain. So I did it myself, so it would be quick. I'm so sorry, Max."

Max turned his back. "I can't ever look at you again, Isobel."

He began to walk away. Then he stopped.

Max turned around. He flicked open a spring-assisted folding knife that had been clipped to his wetsuit, and slashed the ropes binding his best friend's body to the chair. Max dropped the knife and leaned down to scoop up Josue's remains.

He struggled against the younger man's long, gangly, and now limp limbs, but at last Max hoisted up the man's lifeless form from the chair. Max strained and heaved to lift Josue's body over his shoulder. Then he carried his friend to the Cobia, lowering Josue's body onto the stern deck beside several cases of broken Fleur de Lis rum bottles.

Max grabbed his dry bag of weapons. He tossed his cell phone back inside, along with the Sig Sauer MPX, still hot from shooting, and threw it all into the boat.

Max used his bloody diving knife to cut loose the ropes that secured the fishing boat to the catamaran. And then he drove the boat back to the dock at Ilet d'Ombres. It only took about a minute, but Max felt the seconds drag on like miniature eternities that never seemed to end. At last he reached the dock.

Max tied off the boat and carried Josue's body to the grassy area behind the villa. He laid him out, carefully placing his hands across his chest. Then Max leaned over the young Haitian's remains and tried to contain his tears as his stomach twisted in knots.

"Max?" a voice called from the side of the villa.

Max looked up blankly and spotted Vivienne Monet, the lovely Martinican private detective, stepping through the grass toward him. He couldn't speak. He tried, but no words came out.

"It's just me, Max," Vivienne said, stowing a shiny stainless steel Walther PPK into a purse she carried on her shoulder. She wore a short white sundress and wedge sandals. "Oh no," she said, clutching her hand to her mouth. "Is that Josue?" Tears instantly filled Vivienne's stunning brown eyes.

Max felt his chest tighten. He didn't know if it was anxiety, or if he was being gripped by a heart attack. He stood up from Josue's body, but stumbled and stooped over as if he was going to throw up. "Can't breathe."

Vivienne hurriedly stepped over to Max and put her hand on his back. "You are not alone, Max," Vivienne said in a soothing voice. She began rubbing his back in soothing circles.

Max began to hyperventilate. "Can't breathe."

"You've got to try. Slow it down, Max. Just try to take long, deep breaths. Okay? That's it." Vivienne took Max's hand and held it between both of hers. "It's going to be okay, Max."

Max clenched his eyelids closed so tightly he thought his face might be crushed. He tried so hard to internalize his pain. He ached to bottle it up and lock it all away inside.

And then Max sobbed, uncontrollably. Tears flooded Max's cheeks, and there was nothing he could do about it. He cried as he hadn't cried since he had lost his children, his wife.

Vivienne Monet put her arms around Max and hugged him tightly. "That's it, Max," she whispered soothingly into his ear. "Let it out. It'll help."

Max felt like a little kid. It was embarrassing. But Vivienne didn't let him go. She held onto him until his breathing was normal and the sobbing had ceased.

"It's okay, Max."

"What made you come here?" Max asked, when he finally felt as if he had some measure of composure.

"I like to listen to a police scanner," Vivienne said with a hint of a smile. "Old habit from my gendarme days. It's soothing to me. I heard someone made a distress call from somewhere near Ilet Boisseau and I thought of you. Had to come and make sure you were okay. Max, I'm so sorry about Josue. Who did this?"

"I'll tell you, Vivienne," Max said. "But could you do me a favor first? Could you run up to my master bedroom on the second floor and grab my bottle of Percocet?"

"Of course, Max," Vivienne said. She disappeared inside the kitchen door of the villa.

With Vivienne heading upstairs, looking for a prescription bottle that wasn't there, Max stepped into his gear room and grabbed a fresh black shirt and trotted out the villa's front door. He rushed down to the dock and opened the dry bag he'd left in the stern of the Cobia.

Max strapped on his tactical utility belt and checked that everything was there: his holstered FNS .40 caliber pistol; two extra magazines; a second holster with the Smith & Wesson 6906 with three hollow points; a KA-BAR knife with a seven-inch blade; and a small, folding pocketknife made by Cold Steel. Max checked that both pistols had chambered rounds, were cocked, and ready to fire. He grabbed his cell phone from the bag and snapped it into a smartphone holder on his belt. Still in his wetsuit, Max pulled on the Columbia Bahama shirt as he fired up Everest Walsh's elegant wooden runabout. For the first time in years, Max rolled up his sleeves.

Max threw the throttle lever forward and immediately felt the wind whipping through his hair. He pointed the boat toward Everest Walsh's mega yacht.

By the time Vivienne stepped out onto the porch, wondering what Max was up to, he was gone.

# CHAPTER 26

A S MAX DROVE EVEREST WALSH'S Chris-Craft runabout toward the rich mogul's mega yacht, he unlocked his smartphone and speedily flipped through his photo albums, eventually finding a photo he had snapped of Colonel Travere's business card. Max dialed the number and told the head of the Gendarmerie Nationale on Martinique everything that had transpired on Momo's catamaran.

"You killed two men?" Colonel Travere said. He sounded incredulous. "You're sure they're all dead?"

"Josue is dead too," Max said.

"Maxwell, I am sorry. But I don't know what to say about what has happened. I will have to bring you in, Max. Maybe arrest you. I need to interview you and sort things out."

"I know," Max said. He told Travere where he could find the catamaran with three bodies, a bound Tiny Deege, and Isobel Greer, if she was still there.

"A woman killed Josue?" Colonel Travere asked. "Was it that woman you were sitting with the day we first met, Max? She was setting you up?"

"It's the same woman," Max said woefully. "But I don't know. I believe that she killed Josue out of mercy. She knew these guys were going to kill him, but they wanted to torture him first. She couldn't let them."

"All right," Colonel Travere said, sounding out of breath. Max figured the lawman was already halfway to his helicopter.

"I've dispatched a team. We'll be there soon. Stay where you are, Max. Okay?"

"Hey, Max," Travere continued, sounding as if a light bulb had just popped to life over his head, "were these the fellows that killed your family in Florida? Did you go gunning for them? Did you murder these guys?"

"No, Edgar," Max said, sounding cold and dangerous. "It wasn't those guys. But I'm going to square up with *them* right now."

Max hung up the phone.

# CHAPTER 27

MAX AIMED THE CHRIS-CRAFT'S POINTED hull directly at the rear swim platform of the *Snowy Lady*. As many times as he had approached the imposing vessel, it surprised him each time how enormous the hulking white and black craft appeared when he got really close to it.

Max knew his revenge plot against Marquise de Losa was out the window. Josue's death changed everything. Max would not be bothering with the ricin. He now planned to confront de Losa directly. Today, Max would avenge his family. Justice would be served, swiftly and violently.

The vintage runabout neared the teak swim platform at the stern of the mega yacht, and Max throttled down. He climbed up onto the bow and balanced himself, poised to jump. The second before the runabout's hull crashed into the yacht's swim platform, Max sprang down, rolling his body across the hardwood surface.

Eric Pepperdine stepped out of the tinted glass door to the lower deck passageway. Perhaps he had been standing watch at the stern. But when the yacht's first mate saw what Max had done, he did not look happy.

"Max?" he shrieked, taking in the sight of the crashed yacht tender. The boat's hull had caved in where it had impacted with the swim platform. "What the hell?" He pulled a Glock 26 from an inside waistband holster and moved to aim it at Max.

Max didn't know if the *Snowy Lady*'s first mate meant to shoot him, or just cover him until he could be detained by the authorities. Max caught the crewman's wrist and easily stripped the pistol from his hand, allowing it to splash into the ocean behind him. He and Josue had been running disarming drills for years.

With Eric Pepperdine's wrist in his grasp, Max twisted the man's arm behind his back until a loud, demoralizing "pop" erupted from the crewman's shoulder as it separated from its socket.

"Ahhh!" the first mate shouted in horror and pain. Max shoved him off the deck into the Atlantic Ocean, and opened the door to the passageway as if nothing out of the ordinary had transpired.

Max walked past the open door to Walsh's bar, *Rum Lord's Reef*.

Coyo caught sight of Max. "Max?" he shouted. "What's up? Wanna drink?"

Max flipped him off and continued, undeterred, down the passageway. Then Max rushed up the spiral staircase, all the way to the elegant cigar lounge on the upper deck. He wondered if he should draw his Smith & Wesson pistol, but decided to see how things would unfold first.

Max was startled to find Everest Walsh standing in the middle of the room, with Marquise de Losa stooped over nearby, arranging the sofas, trying to get them lined up just right. Remarkably, the room looked brand new: fresh carpet, replaced furniture, even the walls had been painted a fresh off white color.

"And just where in the hell have *you* been, Maxwell?" Everest Walsh asked. His face reddened as Max approached. "You take off with my boat, you tell me you're gonna haul all the bloody furniture to your island, and then you disappear—with my boat! What is the deal?"

Max stepped forward and pounded his fist into Everest Walsh's face. Walsh's head bounced backward off Max's fist, and then sprang forward, like a punching bag. The rich drug trafficker stooped over, hands grasping his nose.

Marquise de Losa stood quickly. He reached for the submachine gun under his olive green coat.

"I wouldn't," Max said, producing a Cold Steel folding knife with a tanto blade from his belt. He flipped open the blade and pressed the razor-sharp tip lightly into Walsh's jugular.

"Let it go, Marquise," Everest Walsh shouted at his right hand man. Blood dripped from the cigar magnate's nose onto the fresh white carpet. "He'll bleed me out."

De Losa's hand dropped to his side. He squinted his eyes at Max.

"I've been waiting so long, I was starting to wonder if this day would even come," Max said. He pulled the knife away from Walsh's neck and twisted his forearm so that Marquise de Losa could see the black tattoo that stretched from his wrist, to the crook of his elbow. The indelible mark depicted a long barbed trident that stretched the length of his forearm with a maddened-looking octopus wrapping the shaft of the long spear-like weapon.

"That's the same tat Marquise has got," Walsh said, his eyes huge with confusion.

"Why?" the vicious murderer de Losa asked. He looked just as confused as Everest Walsh.

"I had this inked into my skin to ensure I would never forget the man who killed my family, Marquise," Max said. "After you killed my wife, my daughter, and my son in cold blood—simply because we happened to stumble upon your drug transaction in Islamorada—I had this done to remember you. Every day when I wake my first thoughts are of revenge, and every night before I go to sleep I pause to remember your hideous face."

De Losa's hand reached slowly for his 9mm Heckler & Koch.

"Do it," Max said, dropping his folding knife and placing his hand on his Smith & Wesson 9mm pistol. "Let's do this."

Marquise de Losa desisted.

"Oww!" Everest Walsh shrieked. The tanto-tipped lock blade

had dropped onto his foot, sticking through his suede slipper, standing on end, lodged into his flesh. He bent over and yanked it out with a lady-like scream.

"I picked up a partial magazine you dropped at the murder scene, Marquise," Max said, speaking the words he had spoken in his head a hundred times before. "Three hollow points left. I managed to keep the police from bagging the magazine as evidence by hiding it in a storage compartment on our rented boat. Even though I was shot and bleeding, I crawled to hide the bullets. I knew someday I'd get the chance to use your own bullets against you. Now they're in here," Max said, beaming as he drew the Smith & Wesson pistol from its holster.

Marquise looked legitimately terrified.

"You know, Everest," Max said, turning his attention toward the cigar magnate, "I only started making rum after I learned of your lust for small batch boutique rum. That article I read about you in GQ revealed your particular penchant for bootleg rhum agricole, and it was clear what I had to do. I moved to Martinique to make the best damn rhum agricole in the world. I believed with every fiber inside me that someday my reputation would reach you, and you'd come looking for me. I didn't know you would have my friends Jacques and Susan killed. And for a few cases of *my* rum!"

"So you're saying you only made the rum to get even with me and Marquise?" Walsh asked. He looked as if everything he had known to be true in life was now upside-down. "But your rum, it really *is* the best in the Caribbean. You can't tell me you don't have a passion for making it."

"You know that old adage, Walsh?" Max said seriously. "Someone bakes a cake or something, and they say they have a secret ingredient. They say the secret ingredient is love."

Walsh nodded and looked intensely at Max. His reddened face dripped with perspiration. He looked like he might have a stroke.

"Every moment I spent distilling every batch of my rum I thought about you and de Losa," Max said viciously. "I craved this day. The day I would finally get even with both of you. Each time I distilled the Fleur de Lis rum, Everest, I didn't do it with love. *My* secret ingredient was revenge."

Walsh's mouth hung open. It was clear he didn't know what to do or say.

"Josue put the cocaine in Chuy's handbag," Max said. "That big lump wasn't stealing from you. We set him up and you shot him. You shot your own guy for no reason," Max said. He wished he was relishing every second of his revenge. Now that it was here, Max felt hollow and empty. It just brought back the sick feelings he'd had in the aftermath of his family's murders.

"Tito?" de Losa asked.

"I put your whore's cell phone in his jacket pocket," Max said. "You killed Tito for nothing. Nothing, Marquise."

"Son of a—" de Losa started to say, but never finished.

Max raised the Smith & Wesson and shot Marquise de Losa twice in the heart.

Everest Walsh gasped.

"That just leaves you, Walsh," Max said, coldly.

"What do you want?" Everest Walsh said in a pleading tone. "Anything."

"Where's my money?" Max asked.

"What money? Oh, the rum money. It's in a bag up on the sundeck. We thought you'd be right back. But you took off with my granddaddy's boat. Almost thought I'd have to deduct *that* from the total." Walsh forced a laugh. He was obviously doing his best to get out of the situation with his life.

"What's all that about?" Walsh stared out the huge panes of glass on the yacht's port side bulkhead. His gaze pointed toward the suspicious catamaran anchored near the shore of Ilet Boisseau. A helicopter hovered over the cat, causing expanding concentric circles in the water around the vessel; two police boats converged on the scene, moving swiftly, lights flashing.

"Four gang members captured Josue," Max said, matter-of-factly. "They tortured him before they killed him. But I killed them."

Everest Walsh swallowed hard. "Now, Max," he began, but Max's eye caught unexpected movement reflected in the starboard glass windows. It was Marquise de Losa getting to his feet behind Max. *Bastard must have been wearing a vest.*

Max turned to face the menacing killer as he raised the submachine gun out of his coat. Marquise de Losa opened fire.

In a blur of motion, Max slipped behind Everest Walsh just as the bullets started ripping into the large man's body. Max grabbed hold of Walsh's bright orange Hawaiian shirt. He struggled with all of the strength in his grip and his arms to hold the unfortunate meat shield upright. If Everest Walsh hit the ground, Max would lose his cover.

Marquise de Losa was foolish enough to unload his entire magazine on Walsh. The Cuban thug dropped his empty mag at the same time Max dropped Everest Walsh.

Before de Losa could slam another magazine home, Max holstered the Smith & Wesson and drew his FNS compact pistol and fired twice, shattering the glass behind the murderer. Then Max rushed him, grabbing hold of his throat and forcing him through the shattered glass, and over the railing.

Marquise de Losa landed in a heap on the main deck near the railing. But not as hard as Max had anticipated. Max had wanted to hurt him, to break his bones. But de Losa scampered to his feet and limped away toward the stern of the *Snowy Lady.*

"No, no, no," Max said rapidly, desperate to keep the murderer from getting away. *Why didn't I just shoot him?*

Max couldn't let the cold-blooded hitman get away, not after all the vicious man had done; all that he had taken from Max.

And not after all of Max's efforts to make the rum that would draw Everest Walsh to him, and all of the years of combat training and other preparations he and Josue had made in anticipation of this day.

Max turned around and looked at Everest Walsh's body. The wealthy cigar plantation owner and drug trafficker had been reduced to hamburger by de Losa's 9mm bullets. Blood pooled around him, staining his brand new off-white carpet.

Max felt an irritating sting in his left hip. He lifted his shirt to see a half-inch deep gash just above his hip; a good graze by one of de Losa's bullets. *No time to worry about that now.*

And then Max heard the sound of gunfire down below. He leaned far out of the shattered window opening in the cigar lounge to see a cloud of black smoke from somewhere down below, just out of sight, at the end of the main deck near the stern. Max spotted Marquise de Losa limping back toward the bow just below him. Someone was chasing him.

"Vivienne!" Max shouted. "What the hell are *you* doing here?"

"Tell you later," she shouted up to Max through the fractured window.

Max ran pell-mell toward the spiral staircase, virtually floating down the steps to the main deck. He practically knocked down Vivienne as she bolted through an outer door to the inside passageway.

"Where'd he go?" Vivienne asked, slightly out of breath. She clutched her Mossberg twelve gauge; seeing her holding the weapon a second time, it struck Max how comfortable it looked in her hands.

"I've studied the blueprints of this ship for years," Max said frantically. "There's another staircase near the bow, for the staff."

"Vivienne. This guy de Losa killed my wife, kids. I can't let him get away."

Vivienne nodded with a look of both tenderness and pity.

"Search the main deck for me, will you?" Max asked. "Just in case he doubled back, and then the lower deck. I'll head up to the upper deck, clear it, and then check the sundeck."

"Right," Vivienne said. "Don't worry, Max. He won't get away."

Max rushed up the spiral staircase. Vivienne peeled off and started checking doors on the main deck. Max continued on toward the upper deck. He caught a blur of green fabric near the far end of the cigar lounge where Everest Walsh lay in a heap. The fleeing thug dashed toward a door near the bow, leading to the bridge.

"De Losa!" Max shouted. "Stop running, coward!"

But Marquise de Losa disappeared through the door. Max sprinted after him, kicking the door open. As Max burst through, he came face to face with the butt of Marquise's submachine gun.

"Hey! What's the deal?" the *Snowy Lady*'s captain said. He appeared aghast at the tussle taking place in the yacht's handsome control room, which was fitted with hardwood flooring and wall panels, and polished brass accents.

Max hit the ground hard. He lay flat on his back, the wind knocked out of his lungs. Marquise turned his weapon to fire. Max pulled his FNS, firing several times at the murderer, hitting him square in the chest.

"Aghh!" De Losa grunted, letting go of his Heckler & Koch, as the Ruger 107 grain bullets ripped into the man's bulletproof vest. The criminal wheeled back, then dropped to a knee, gasping for air, but not before knocking the .40 caliber pistol out of Max's hands.

Max guessed at least one of the ARX copper-polymer hybrid bullets might have gone through the vest, likely made of Kevlar, lodging at least a short distance into the man's chest. But as he regained his breath and moved to get to his feet, Marquise de Losa dove forward and grabbed onto Max's throat.

As they struggled, Max slipped a KA-BAR Becker Combat

knife from its sheath on his belt, and stabbed it into de Losa's back. The knife bounced off de Losa's vest, doing no damage. Max raised it for another thrust, but Marquise wrestled the knife away, sticking it into the floor during the struggle.

Max grasped for de Losa's submachine gun, still slung around the killer's body. The two men rolled across the ground, each one desperate to gain control of the weapon. Suddenly it burst to life, spraying 9mm rounds all around the bridge until it was empty.

The yacht's captain cowered in the corner, hugging himself into a ball to avoid the flying bullets that were ripping apart the yacht's control room.

Max grabbed the knife out of the floor and slashed the sling on de Losa's submachine gun. The weapon tumbled free to the floor, and Max sprang to his feet, slipping the KA-BAR back into its sheath.

Marquise de Losa bolted, scrambling up a service ladder to a hatch on the sundeck. Max chased closely behind. He felt a tug on his leg and realized the *Snowy Lady*'s captain had emboldened himself enough to grab onto Max's leg. He was trying to pull him off the ladder.

Max kicked the well-built captain in the chin. The yacht's skipper stumbled back away from the ladder. He reached for something behind his back, and Max pounced off the ladder, taking the captain down hard on the floor of the bridge. A Glock subcompact pistol, just like the one Eric Pepperdine had carried, slid across the polished cherry wood floor.

Max brought his fist down hard again and again into the captain's face until blood had splattered from both nostrils and he had clearly lost consciousness. Max turned to the ladder and climbed, exercising extreme caution at the open hatch, lest Marquise de Losa lay in wait.

He poked his head up like a prairie dog on the sundeck. De Losa stood nearby, waiting, his unsheathed machete clutched in his grip. "You made me use this on my friend, Tito," he said, sounding strangely forlorn for as hard of a man as he clearly was. "Now I am going to use it to cut out your heart."

Max slipped out his KA-BAR from its sheath, holding the blade in a defensive position. As far as weapons go, De Losa had the size advantage with the machete, but Max doubted he had as much skill at blade-fighting.

Marquise de Losa lurched toward Max, swinging the machete like an axe. Max immediately lowered his center of gravity and moved to the left, stepping lightly, just as he and Josue had trained in *tire machet* for years. De Losa's machete clanged against Max's knife and glanced off.

Max blocked another of de Losa's blows. Sometimes he would deflect them with his knife, sometimes he would knock the criminal's arm out of the way. Other times he would slip out of the way altogether, as de Losa's machete swished through empty air.

Then Max went on the offensive, stabbing the KA-BAR again and again toward the retreating thug's face. De Losa did his best to defend himself, using his machete to deflect Max's knife, all the while stepping backward, closer and closer to Walsh's outlandish waterfall-surrounded hot tub.

Marquise de Losa, realizing he was outmatched, spoke, likely hoping to halt Max's onslaught. "I remember your family, Max," he said, his yellowing teeth stained red with blood.

Max knew what de Losa was trying to do. But Max was determined not to let the murderer get inside his head. He said nothing.

"I usually don't. I kill so many people, they sort of all blend together. Each gruesome face dissolving, one into another." Marquise de Losa coughed and placed his hand over his chest, no doubt still feeling the sting of Max's bullets. "But those kids of yours went down so easy. Didn't they? You saw it."

"For me, it was fun," Marquise de Losa goaded. "Like shooting a pair of sick dogs."

Max clenched his jaw and considered when he would lunge with the knife.

"But it was your wife who must have gotten the worst," de Losa said, continuing his taunting. "Did she even die? If she did it must have taken awhile, because my bullets ripped her guts apart."

Max tried not to think about Marquise de Losa's words. He just waited for the other man to strike. He would deflect the other man's blade, then he would bring his knife up to the man's throat, cutting it, and watch the man who killed his family bleed out before him.

"It must hurt to know they all suffered so much, but you lived," Marquise de Losa said. "You must struggle with it. The guilt, I mean," he spat.

Marquise de Losa reached back with the machete. In a flash of fluid motion, he swung it down ferociously toward Max's neck. It was the same blow he had used to kill Tito. Max had known he would use it.

Max ducked down and deflected de Losa's arm with his own. De Losa's carbon steel blade swished over Max's head. Max reached in and grabbed the front of de Losa's shirt, pulling him and his nemesis together tightly, locked face to face.

Max brought the seven-inch blade up to de Losa's neck, and then—

The left side of Marquise de Losa's head erupted into a repugnant shower of blood, skull fragments, and brain matter. The remorseless killer slipped out of Max's grasp, falling backwards into a bleeding heap in Everest Walsh's hot tub.

Vivienne Monet poked her head out of the trapdoor leading up from the yacht's control room. She spotted Max on the sundeck, and she lay her shotgun down on the deck before climbing up to reach the sundeck.

"What happened?" Max gasped, his eyes bulging. "Who?"

Max looked over the sundeck's railing toward the lapping Atlantic Ocean water below. Colonel Travere stood on the deck of a Zodiac police boat, braced against the boat's control console, an FN P90 in his hands. The Gendarmerie Nationale commander had picked off Marquise de Losa from the moving boat with the bullpup-style personal defense weapon. And he stood by, ready with a follow-up shot, if necessary.

Max turned away from the rail and looked at Marquise de Losa's floating body. His blood had tainted the water that circulated between the waterfall and the hot tub. The steaming water that trickled over the grey stones on either side of the tub now flowed in a disquieting pink color.

Max pulled his Smith & Wesson pistol from its holster and let it dangle by his side. "You know, Vivienne," Max said in a sad, monotone voice, "I've carried around three bullets that Marquise de Losa dropped at the murder scene where he killed my wife and kids. I always intended to use one or all three of these to kill the man who took their lives. Now that's been taken away from me. He's dead, and I didn't do it."

Max chuckled. "You know, I also considered how, even though I wasn't killed alongside my family, maybe one of these bullets might still be destined for me. And now, I only have one left."

Vivienne Monet stood nearby with her shotgun slung over her shoulder by its leather sling. The wind played with the thin fabric of her white dress. She looked like a picture out of a magazine. "Max?" she asked, deep concern apparent in her voice. "What are you doing with that gun?"

# CHAPTER 28

MAX CLUTCHED THE GUN BY his side in a way that frightened Vivienne. She was not afraid for her own safety, but she had been around suicidal people before. "Why don't you just put it away," she said.

Max paced the deck like a wounded animal. He swung his gun hand up and down as he stepped. Vivienne could not take her eyes off the semi-automatic pistol. She wondered if she should intervene by force.

"Max, you don't want to harm yourself," Vivienne said.

Max turned toward her with a vacant expression. "I honestly never knew what would come next."

"You mean, after you took revenge against your family's killer?"

Max nodded. "I suppose I just thought I would keep moving forward. But now Josue is gone as well. Everyone in the world I've ever cared about has been taken from me. Do you know what that's like?" Max turned to Vivienne. At first she had thought it was a rhetorical question, but it seemed like he was really asking.

Vivienne stepped forward and placed a hand on Max's shoulder. "I do. I mean, not exactly like you, Max. But my mother was taken from me when I was very young. And my father died just after I moved to Paris when I was only seventeen. I was going to be a model, you know?" Vivienne flashed a smile at Max.

"The small plane my father was piloting crashed off the coast of St. Croix. It was a seaplane, and he was at two thousand feet when the engine failed. My father lost control. He died."

"I'm sorry," Max said. "I didn't know."

"Of course you didn't," Vivienne said. "I came back to the island to raise my siblings—my brother and two sisters—the way I knew my father would have wanted them to grow up. In a stable home, as normal as possible.

"Sure, I wasn't alone," Vivienne said, her eyes welling with tears. "But there were a great many times when I felt alone."

"What difference would it make if I wasn't here anymore, Vivienne?" Max said somberly. "There's nothing left. There's no one left for me. Just a deep, aching, heart-sick pain."

"*I* care about you, Max," Vivienne said. She put her arms around him and held him. She chuckled a little bit. "I've only known you a few days, Max. But it's been more than enough time to know that you are one of the great friends of my life. And Colonel Travere cares about you, Max."

"Travere?" Max said with a smirk. "He's probably itching to put me behind bars."

"I ran into the Colonel the other day at a grocery store in Sainte-Marie," Vivienne said. "I had never met him before, but he knew who I was. He introduced himself to me. He would not shut up about you; must have gone on and on about how great you and your rum were for like fifteen minutes or something. He really admires you, Max. Don't sell him short just because he's on the other side of the line from where you've been walking."

"What if I'm going to prison for the rest of my life?" Max said, sounding as if his mind was racing a thousand miles a second. "Wouldn't I be better off checking out now?"

"You know what my priest tells me all the time, Max?" Vivienne said, still holding her arms around the vulnerable man. "He says the purpose of life isn't to be happy. It's to be useful, honorable, compassionate, to have it make some difference that you have lived and lived well." She looked at Max thoughtfully. Maybe she was trying to let the words sink in.

"I don't know why he quotes Ralph Waldo Emerson," she added with a tender smile, "and not Scripture, and I'm sure I botched the quote. But I believe it, Max. Maybe the rest of your life won't be as happy as you want, but it can still have meaning to those who are still left around you. Even if you *are* thrown in prison for the rest of your life, I believe that God will redeem your life, and make something good out of it."

"Priest?" Max asked.

"Don't be so surprised. Almost everyone on the island is Roman Catholic. I am no exception." Vivienne let go of Max and looked him in the eyes. "It's all going to be okay. Really. Even if you get locked away forever. *I* won't leave you behind. Not ever."

Max's eyes glistened. She hoped she had said enough, and that she had said the right things to convince him not to take his life. It did seem absurd that she had come to like a man so much in such a short time. Especially one who treaded on the fringes of the law, when her life's purpose seemed to be about following the rules, and standing up for justice. But she could tell that deep inside, Max was a good man.

"Let it go, Max," Vivienne said, rubbing his back.

"I would have liked to have seen you in that Catholic schoolgirl uniform," Max quipped.

"Don't get any ideas, Mister."

Max's phone rang. He reached his hand into his pocket, Vivienne guessed, to silence it, because he pulled his hand right back out without the phone. "Hello?" Max's pants said in a robust, masculine voice. It reminded Vivienne a bit of James Earl Jones. "Hello, Max? Have you finally picked up the phone after all this time?"

Max absent-mindedly reached into his pocket and took out his phone. He put it close to his face, even though it was obviously on speakerphone. "Hello, Terry?"

"Ahhhh, Max," the other man said. "I've been trying to

reach you for, well, forever now. I am so pleased to have finally connected with you."

"I'm sorry," Max said. He looked embarrassed. "I'm sorry I haven't been taking your calls."

Vivienne wondered if it was the same guy who always called Max, though he never answered. He must be a significant person in Max's life; or at least he had been at one time.

"I kept calling, Max, because I knew you would pick up the phone when you were ready to talk," Terry said. "How is everything going in your life? Anything new happening?"

"A bunch of gangbangers tortured and killed my best friend, Josue. I set up a ruthless drug-dealing hitman to kill two of his men. I watched the same man kill a millionaire cigar magnate and drug trafficker, and then I fought my nemesis—the man who killed Lovelle, Lucy, and Lionel—to the death; but I didn't kill him. Someone else did before I got the chance. I would have done it, though. I was about to."

There was silence on the other end of the phone for a long time. And then, "If all of these things have been going on in your life, Max, I wish you would have contacted me. At least to talk about some of these things. You shouldn't go through them alone."

"I might have called you, Terry," Max said, "but most of those things happened today."

Again there was a long period of silence before Terry said, "Well, I've got you now, and I just felt like telling you today, Max, that you are not alone. I'm here for you, and I care about you. Somehow I felt like I needed to tell you that."

Vivienne saw Max's eyes water and his chin quiver against his will. And then Max raised his pistol and pulled the trigger.

"What?" Terry shouted into the phone. "What was that? Is everything okay, Max?"

"Everything is wonderful," Vivienne said, taking the phone

out of Max's hand. She looked at the smoking pistol in Max's hand, and she smiled.

The fateful bullet Max had carried around with him for years, the one he had believed was either meant for the man who killed his family, or else was meant for him, sailed harmlessly toward the open Atlantic Ocean. Max had fired the bullet into the air to get rid of it.

Then Max tossed the Smith & Wesson pistol over the side of Everest Walsh's yacht.

"I am Max's friend, Vivienne Monet, sir. And something tells me that your message for Max was just what he needed to hear today."

"She sounds pretty," Terry said. "Are you and Miss Monet dating, Max?"

Max smiled, and Vivienne could see the genuineness of the gesture. He really was okay.

"What was that shot?" Colonel Travere asked. He trotted up to stand between Max and Vivienne. "Are you two okay? Are there any more hostiles on board?"

"Just the crew," Max said to the colonel, "and I think they're pretty harmless without Walsh and de Losa around, although they are strapped."

"I'm going to go now, Terry," Max said into the phone. "Maybe for a long time. But I promise to call you later tonight, and we'll finish our conversation. I promise to tell you everything. I do get at least one phone call, right?" Max said, looking at Travere.

Colonel Travere nodded.

Max hung up the phone.

"I'm ready," Max said. He placed his hands behind his back, and looked over his shoulder at Colonel Travere.

"What are you doing?" Travere said, running his fingers through his graying hair, his P90 dangling in front of him from a one-point sling.

"Aren't you going to cuff me?" Max asked, as he unbuckled his tactical belt and handed it to the colonel.

"You watch a lot of police movies, don't you? I would like you to come to the station for questioning, Max. You are not under arrest at this time. These men killed your family, and now they are dead. You are going to walk off of this boat as the man that you are." Travere nodded his head at Max. "After you."

# Chapter 29

MAX WOKE UP ON THE uncomfortable cot in a tiny room inside the Gendarmerie de Martinique building in Fort de France. He wasn't certain, but it didn't seem much like a holding cell. The room, approximately eight feet by eight feet, held the cot, a rack of gendarme uniforms, and boxes and boxes of copy paper and toner cartridges. It struck Max as a supply closet, or maybe a room where a gendarme who's been on shift too long can sneak away and catch a nap. But for the past twelve hours, it had been Max's prison. Other than a couple of requested bathroom breaks, and the one time when a young cadet had brought him a box of takeout Chinese food, he had been secured inside.

Max recalled how earlier, before he and Colonel Travere had left the *Snowy Lady*, Max had whispered to Vivienne about the bag of cash he had gotten from Everest Walsh. He had asked her to find it, and take it off the boat discreetly. He knew that if she hadn't, all of the money from the sale of his rum would be seized by the French government, and he would never see a dime. He wondered if she had succeeded, not that he cared a great deal about it.

Max got it, though; there was a lot to sort through. Multiple crime scenes. The catamaran, Walsh's cigar lounge, Tito's room, Chuy's room, the ocean floor beneath the yacht. Max had told Colonel Travere everything he knew about everything that had happened, holding nothing back, including his own involvement.

The colonel had videotaped the entire conversation, and made copious notes on a fresh legal pad, before finally locking Max away in the room.

It was a strange kind of solitary confinement. Max considered putting on one of the Gendarmerie Nationale uniforms from the coat rack, just to freak out whoever walked in next. Instead, he sat on the cot, whistling, and it was only a half-hour longer before the door opened, and Max saw Edgar Travere's face looking down on him.

The colonel was accompanied by another guy. Dark-skinned, gray-haired, brown suit, he was likely a prosecutor or lawyer, and very likely an island native.

"If you would come with me, Max," Colonel Travere said, "there are just a few more things to go over with you before we proceed to the next step in processing you."

Max stood up from the cot. He wore a fresh black Columbia shirt and coordinating nylon pants that Colonel Travere had brought him from his villa. A paramedic had treated the bullet graze above Max's hip, irrigating it with an antiseptic and closing it up with butterfly bandages and a gauze pad. As he stood, the closed wound pulled a little, giving him a stab of pain in his side that made him wince.

But he followed the head of the Gendarmerie to a well-lit interview room, and took a seat across from Travere and the other man. Max noticed that this time, Colonel Travere did not bother to turn on the video camera, which sat on a tripod behind the colonel's chair.

"This is Roger Devilleneuve," Travere said, and Max noted that he used the French pronunciation, Roh-jay. "Monsieur Devilleneuve is the chief prosecutor on Martinique. He and I have been reviewing the details of what events have transpired recently on the rented catamaran off the coast of Le Robert, as well as those onboard the yacht of Everest Walsh."

"Bonjour, Monsieur Craig," the prosecutor said. He smiled a friendly smile and put on a pair of reading glasses. He seemed like a nice enough fellow.

"Hello," Max said. He was too tired to keep up with the French affectations.

"After reviewing all of the evidence, Max," Colonel Travere said with deep gravity in his tone, "I am afraid that we are going to have to charge you with the distribution of unregulated rum and the possession of several unregistered firearms."

Travere pulled a stapled document out of his briefcase, several pages thick. "This is a plea deal from the chief prosecutor," Travere said. "He and I are very much on the same page in our approach to law enforcement. If you sign the agreement, you will plead guilty to having operated an illegal still, and being in the possession of a couple of unregistered semi-automatic firearms which were found on your property. As part of the agreement, your sentence will be reduced to time already served. Oh, you will also be required to turn over any evidence in your possession of the criminal activities of Everest Walsh and his associates."

"That's it?" Max asked. He was dumbfounded.

"Monsieur Craig," Roger Devilleneuve said, "these are some serious crimes which you have been charged with. I would advise you to not take them lightly."

"Monsieur Devilleneuve has consulted with me at length before preparing this plea deal which, if you sign, will allow you to go free with time already served. You will not be allowed to continue to produce unregulated rhum agricole, and your unlicensed weapons shall be seized by the Gendarmerie Nationale."

"But I only spent twelve hours in jail," Max said. "I killed people. Shouldn't I be held a little more accountable for that?"

"You're not making a very good case in defense of yourself, Max," Travere said, scratching his fingers through his short hair. "It is fairly common for individuals in your shoes to argue with us for lesser charges." Colonel Travere shared a smirk with prosecutor Devilleneuve.

Travere pushed the papers toward Max. He gave the haggard rum runner a big-brotherly look that told him, "This is the only chance you are going to get."

Max quickly flipped through the pages, his eyes quickly browsing the copy. "Pen?" he said, holding out his hand.

Devilleneuve reached into his coat pocket and handed Max a very fine-looking Parker fountain pen. Max signed the plea.

"Monsieur Devilleneuve," Travere said. "I believe we have everything taken care of as far as Maxwell is concerned. Thank you very much for all of your guidance and willingness to consult with me at such ungodly hours of the morning. I believe you are free to enjoy the rest of your day."

The prosecutor stuffed the signed agreement into his briefcase and shook hands with Colonel Travere. He left the interview room, closing the door behind him. Travere looked Max squarely in the eye.

"Let me ask you this." he said. "When you tried to save Josue, did you engage the individuals on the catamaran with your firearm first? Or did they first fire upon you?"

"Soon as they saw me they started slinging bullets," Max said. "But I killed 'em. All of 'em. Except for that little guy, Deege, or something. And I didn't kill that kid with the Xbox controller. But shouldn't I at least get manslaughter or something for that?"

"That little guy, 'Tiny Deege,' is actually named Derek Jerome Labat," Travere said. "From Miami. Despite the fact that you stabbed him with a throwing knife and hog-tied him with zip-ties, his account actually corroborated the fact that you acted in self-defense. He'll be facing prosecution as an accessory to the torture and murder of Josue Remy. I hope that gives you a tiny measure of comfort."

Max stared off into the corner, where two walls met the

ceiling. It was hard to believe that Josue was gone. The gentle soul had been like a brother... or a son to Max. It broke his heart that he would never see that bright smile with the pearl white teeth ever again.

"Did you kill Chuy Mendoza?" Colonel Travere asked.

"Um, no," Max said, considering for the first time how Chuy's death might have a bearing on his legal culpability. "But I did plant two kilos of coke in the guy's gym bag. Everest Walsh found it, thought Chuy stole it from him, and capped him twice. Dumped his body with weights directly below the *Snowy Lady*. I believe I've got some video from my security cameras I can turn over. Maybe not the best video, but you can see the two flashes of light when Walsh fires his gun in the guy's stateroom."

"And Tito Fuente?" Travere asked.

"Josue stole, I mean, I stole a cell phone from the mistress of Marquise de Losa," Max said, not wanting to implicate Josue in anything, despite the fact that he was dead and couldn't possibly face any charges. Now that Josue was gone, Max could only protect the deceased young man's reputation.

"I planted the phone in Tito's pocket. De Losa tried to call his mistress, heard the very specific ringtone belonging to his girlfriend's phone singing from inside Tito's pocket, and he went nuts with his machete."

"So you are guilty of moving Everest Walsh's cocaine from one room on his yacht to another, and stealing a cell phone," Travere said, his left eyebrow raised. "Maybe we *should* lock you up and throw away the key." An obvious facetiousness spread across the lawman's visage.

"I shot de Losa in the chest twice, trying to kill him. His bulletproof vest stopped the bullets. Then I grappled with him, tried to stab him, I was about to cut his throat before you took away my chance for revenge. What the hell were you thinking, Edgar?" Max asked, genuinely dismayed by the gendarme's actions. "You knew de Losa's life was mine to take, and you took it anyway."

"Marquise de Losa's life was no one's to take, Maxwell," Travere said seriously. "I arrived at a moment when he was trying to kill you, and when my shot became clear, I took it. I wasn't trying to keep you from getting revenge. I wasn't trying to save you from the burden of having taken the man's life, something you would have to live with for the rest of your days. I saw the shot, and I took it. I did my job."

"*I* was trying to kill de Losa when you took the shot," Max stated flatly. "How come the shot didn't kill *me*?"

"I made a call, Max," Travere said, leaning back in his chair. He folded his hands together behind his head.

"Can I get something to smoke?" Max asked.

"Some cigarettes? Certainly."

"No, I mean a halfway decent cigar, maybe," Max said. "I've been smoking Everest Walsh's rolled-up newspapers for the better part of a week. I think I might already have developed emphysema."

Travere smiled. He pulled a leather cigar sleeve from his briefcase. He handed Max a Fuente Fuente Opus X. He slid a cutter and torch lighter across the table.

"Are you sure?" Max asked.

Travere nodded. "I would say you've earned it, Max."

"How's that?" Max asked, blazing the Opus X to life.

"A lot of my fellow law enforcement professionals have changed with the times, you see. They value sensitivity and rule-following in order to keep themselves from getting in trouble or ever offending anyone. Whereas I prefer to take a much more practical approach to crime-fighting. I value a results-based technique much more highly than a by-the-book one."

"Yes?" Max asked, intrigued.

"Do you know who those men were that you killed on that rented catamaran?" Travere asked.

"I figured they were part of Ti Flow," Max said, taking a long draw on the very expensive and exquisite Dominican cigar. "I helped rescue Josue out of his life as part of a violent Haitian gang about six years ago, right after my family was killed. It was all an accident, of course. I was drunk as hell, on a self-destructive bender, and I stumbled upon these guys about to execute Josue right in the middle of Lemon Street in Little Haiti. Now that I think of it, it might have been that first guy I dropped—Momo—who was about to execute Josue when I intervened."

"Momo was about to take over the leadership of the ultra-violent Miami gang," Travere explained. "After speaking with some colleagues in the Miami-Dade Police Department, we believe he was coming to Martinique to finish the job he began six years ago, to execute Josue Remy. By killing Momo and these others, Max, you may have single-handedly disbanded Ti Flow. A power void has been created, sure. And someone will move in to fill it, but for now, your actions may have potentially saved lives and reduced at least some measure of crime in that community."

"That's a rather gray way of looking at things," Max said. "You're the head of the Gendarmerie here. Things are supposed to be black and white."

"Are they?" Travere asked. "Were they black and white when you took out that rapist on that beach near Château Dubuc?"

Max looked at the floor and started laughing.

"What is so funny, Max?" Travere asked.

"Sometimes all you have to do to make the world believe you are dangerous, is nothing," Max said. "You see an opportunity to do that, you'd be a fool not to take it."

Colonel Travere nodded. "I can see that, but how do you mean. Specifically."

"Just because I never confirmed or denied the rumors about that bastard, folks believe what they want to believe. *I killed him. I dumped his body.* Truth is, if you looked hard enough, I suppose you'd find him eventually. Probably set up shop, casting his nets somewhere else, like Guadeloupe or Dominica. Possibly messing with the young ladies there, but hopefully not."

"But you ran him off of the island, Max," Travere said. "And my hat's off to you for that."

The colonel pulled a second Opus X out of his cigar sleeve. "The aroma of yours has tempted me too much, I'm afraid." The Gendarmerie colonel clipped off the end of his cigar and roasted the tip until he could draw smoke through it.

"Everest Walsh and all of his thugs are dead, Max," Travere continued, his eyes wandering over his notes on the legal pad. "Walsh was moving an insane amount of product between Bogota, the Keys, the Bahamas, and a bunch of other locales in the West Indies. Rather brazen in his approach, he was. I mean, his boat was called the *Snowy Lady,* for pity's sake.

"Because of your actions, his yacht has become a major crime scene. It has produced enough evidence for us to seize his entire cigar plantation and investigate any business he might have been associated with. Once again, Max, your actions will have an unintended, but positive, effect on the world. You've interrupted a large supplier of coke to the states. There will be crack addicts who can't get rocks because of you. There will almost certainly be folks who will not overdose and die because of you. Maybe you have only saved one. Maybe you've unknowingly saved a thousand," Travere said with a coy smile. "We'll never know, will we?"

"So what now?" Max asked. He didn't much care what happened to him now that everyone he cared about was no longer around.

"You will no longer be allowed to produce illicit, unregulated rum on Martinique," Travere said. "All of your distillery equipment will be seized and sold at auction."

Max nodded.

"A very quiet and poorly-attended auction," Travere said with a wink.

Max frowned. He wasn't sure what was happening.

"I never really cared about the rum, Edgar," Max said. "Just getting even with de Losa."

"But there *was* passion that you put into that product, Max," Travere said. "Fleur de Lis rum would not be possible without a deep fervor inside the man making it. It is truly special."

"Like I told de Losa," Max told the colonel. "My secret ingredient was far from love—it was revenge."

"No," Travere said. "It was much more than that. There are thoughts and feelings that you put into your work without even knowing you were doing it. The care in separating the hearts and heads, and mixing them back together. The careful aging process. Even the fact that you cut the sugarcane yourself, by hand, Max, shows how deeply you cared about the process. What did the fleur de lis mean to you, Max?"

Max was quiet for about thirty seconds. He fought against the lump that had formed in his throat before he spoke. "My wife had a tattoo of a fleur de lis on her wrist. She thought they were beautiful; it was her favorite symbol."

"That isn't just revenge, Max," Travere said with a warm smile. "You honored her with every batch of rum that you made."

"I don't know if I'll ever make rum again," Max said.

"A shame to hear," Travere said. "I have been thinking about starting my own legitimate rhum agricole operation on my family land. But I would need a master distiller to help me. Someone who has a lot of experience making rhum agricole, very good rhum agricole, and understands every aspect of the business."

"Are you offering me a job?" Max asked, dumbfounded.

"Not today," Travere said, his lips curled into a furtive grin. "But ask me again tomorrow. Maybe."

It suddenly became clear to Max why the colonel would stick

his neck out for him, to cut such a ridiculous plea deal with the prosecutor. "It's because you want me to work for you that you dealt on my behalf, isn't it? I suppose if I don't take the job, the deal goes away."

"It's not like that, Max. The plea that I worked for you isn't about a job. If you don't want to work with me, I respect that. The plea is about something more."

"What?" Max asked.

"I suppose it is about the hope that I have for you," Travere said. "You are a good man, Maxwell. And I believe under the right conditions you will thrive, and become a great man."

Max looked down at the table. He was stone-faced. He knew he was being offered much more than he deserved. It was a powerful display of mercy.

Max extended his hand across the table to Colonel Travere. "Thank you, sir. For everything."

"It is my pleasure, Max," Travere said, shaking Max's hand. "Now, my friend, you are free to go." The colonel stood up and opened the door to the interview room. Travere slapped Max on the back as he stepped through the door.

A lot of eyes watched Max as he walked through the office, past desks occupied by gendarmes on the phone, or looking up from the reports they were typing at their computers, or otherwise just standing in the room, staring at the rum runner who had killed the men who had murdered his family, and those that had tortured and killed his best friend.

At the far end of the room near the corner, sitting at a desk next to a very muscular, dark-skinned corporal, was Isobel Greer. Max hadn't been ready for it, and as their eyes met, he felt as if someone had just plunged an ice pick into his heart. Tears streamed down the diminishing sunburn of Isobel's cheeks as Max walked toward the door.

Max felt the colonel's fingers grasp onto his neck in a

comforting rub. "Right this way, Max," he said, knowing it would be best to separate Max from Isobel Greer as quickly as possible.

Max stepped through the front door, and was nearly knocked down by the bright, late morning sun that seared down on him. It took a few seconds for his eyes to adjust enough that he could see, and when they finally did, Max spotted the unmistakable form of Vivienne Monet standing in front of the building, as if she had been waiting for him.

"Hello, Max," Vivienne said, giving him a hug as he stepped out of the building. She reached her hand into a white shopping bag. "I saw this and I thought of you."

Max squinted his eyes and saw that she held a brand new Columbia Bahama shirt. "Thanks, Viv, but I don't wear pink shirts," he said.

"It's called Bright Peach," Vivienne said, stuffing the shirt back in the bag and handing it to Max. "It's about time you added a splash of color to your life. Don't you think?"

"I like black," Max said unapologetically.

"You need not mourn forever, my friend," Vivienne said, flashing her million-dollar smile. It had a way of winning a man over. "Besides, you're not Johnny Cash."

"How do *you* know about Johnny Cash?" Max asked.

Vivienne looked at Max as if he had just run over her pet Chihuahua. "I'm from Martinique, Max, not Uranus."

Max laughed. So much of life *was* out of his hands; he certainly wouldn't have chosen so much pain for himself. But there *were* little bits of joy to be found here and there, if he just opened his eyes to see them.

Max knew he did not have the same feelings toward Vivenne Monet as those that had just started to develop between him and Isobel Greer. But he loved Vivienne's joviality in spite of the tough work she did. It was an inspiration. And, like Edgar Travere, she had shown him so much kindness that he didn't deserve. Max knew he wanted the would-be model, turned cop, turned private investigator in his corner.

"Come on, Maxwell Craig," Vivienne said, throwing her arm around his neck. Her cork wedge heels made her a good three inches taller than his six feet. "I'll take you to see the lady who grills the tastiest poulet boucané in Fort de France, maybe in all of Martinique."

Max recalled eating the smoky island specialty of buccaneer chicken a couple of times before. But today, he couldn't help but think it would taste even better because of the company he would keep.

"By the way, Max," Vivienne said, unable to contain a sort of giddiness, "I have the bag you left on Walsh's yacht in the trunk of my car. It is safe and sound, and complete."

Vivienne had secured Max's money. Now that he was free, he would have something he could use to start over on what would come next, whatever that might be.

"Wait, Maxwell!" a voice shouted from the front door of the Gendarmerie building. Max wasn't sure if he should run, or maybe just put up his hands. "Hold up. Max!"

Colonel Travere trotted toward him, placing his white and black kepi on his head. The very French-looking military hats always suggested to Max a cartoon character of some sort. Travere rushed up to meet Max and Vivienne.

"I just wanted to offer to take you out for lunch, Maxwell," Colonel Travere said with a likeable half-smile. "I'd like to talk to you a bit more about my future plans for my family land near Sainte-Marie; if you are not previously engaged, that is."

"I was just going to take Max to Madame Sabine's shack for a bite," Vivienne said. "Would you join us?"

"Oooh," Colonel Travere said, wiping his mouth as if it were covered in drool. "The poulet boucané here has spoiled me against my wife's cooking. Don't tell her! If it is all right with Maxwell, I would love to join the two of you. But I don't want to intrude."

Max just nodded. He wasn't sure how he had come to such a place in such a short period of time. The memory of his murdered family lingered in his mind, even now. And the sting of having lost his best friend burned inside of him, even more freshly. But his enemies were now all dead, gone from this earth. It left him with a mixed sort of satisfaction: he was glad that justice had finally met them, but their passing also left him hollow and empty, as if getting revenge against them had cost him a piece of his soul.

But the most unexpected result of recent days, to Max, was that despite his solitary nature, despite that stiff arm he always put forward to keep people away, he now had some unlikely friends. And he felt something inside him he hadn't felt in a great many years. Somehow, some way, Maxwell Craig's anger had changed into something. It felt like some semblance of hope just flickering inside him.

Maybe Vivienne was right. Maybe his life still mattered and could be useful, and honorable, and could make some difference that he had lived and lived well.

THE END

# ABOUT THE AUTHOR

Growing up in sunny south Florida, Dannal fished, snorkeled, and dodged jellyfish washed up on the beach. His frequent exploration of Florida's A1A Scenic & Historic Coastal Byway on his bike without permission resulted in numerous groundings. Dannal eventually moved out west, settling in southern Oregon, where he currently resides with his wife and two kids.

In addition to the Maxwell Craig series of thrillers, Dannal is also the author of a quirky series of short reads for younger readers, called *The Trying Tales of Chumbles & Grim*.

Catch up with Dannal at his website Dannal.com, or go to

www.facebook.com/dannaljnewman

Twitter@thedannal

Instagram@thedannal

CPSIA information can be obtained
at www.ICGtesting.com
Printed in the USA
LVOW12s1730290318
571634LV00003B/775/P